Table of Contents

Take Chances, Make Mistakes, Get Messy

The title of this introduction is Ms. Frizzle's mantra from *The Magic School Bus*, a wonderful book and television series that introduced a number of kids to science. My education is in physics and my "day" job is operating telescopes at Kitt Peak National Observatory. I routinely see science in action. Over the years, I've known many people who believe scientific theory and observation are a kind of dogma—that the statements of scientists are, in themselves, Truth. In fact, science is a process. A scientist observes the natural world, does their best to form a theory that fits the results, then tests that theory with more observations. The very process is one of taking chances, making mistakes, learning more, and moving forward.

In the publishing world, it's common for reviewers, editors, and writers to speak in absolute terms. They tell you how a piece of writing is terrible or another piece of writing is wonderful. Most of the time, these absolute opinions are rubbish and only reflect how well a piece of writing resonated with a particular reader. A writer observes the world around them and tries to capture that honestly, completely and succinctly in a poem, short story, or novel. A writer succeeds if they have made their best attempt to do that. The only writers I know to have failed are the ones who don't see it as a process—who stop improving, or stop writing altogether.

In my opinion, the most enjoyable stories are the ones about people who take chances, make mistakes, and get messy. You'll find plenty of that in this issue of *Tales of the Talisman*. In Robert Redwine's "Missing Mittens," a warrior makes the mistake of vowing to take the next quest she's offered. In David B. Riley's "Where'd That Come From," Sarah Meadows takes a chance and lands aboard a mysterious space station that has been missing for twenty years. In Simon Bleaken's "Thornway Hollow," investigators get messy investigating ghosts in an abandoned nursing home.

Science is not dogma, it's merely a process for observing the natural world. In much the same way, there's no mystery to good writing. It's just another way of observing and predicting the way people will react to a set of circumstances. Turn the page and have fun with these characters who take chances, make mistakes, and get messy!

— David Lee Summers
Las Cruces, New Mexico

Tales of the
Talisman

Volume 9   Issue 3

ISBN: 1-885093-73-X

William Grother
Publisher

David Lee Summers
Editor

Laura Givens
Art Director

Kumie Wise
Assistant Editor

Tales of the Talisman
(ISSN 1558-0377)
is published quarterly by
Hadrosaur Productions
P.O. Box 2194
Mesilla Park, NM 88047-2194
www.hadrosaur.com

Subscriptions: $24.00 per year
$48.00 per two years
Subscriptions available at:
www.talesofthetalisman.com

Missing Mittens

Story by Robert Redwine
Illustration by Tom Kelly

"By the gods assembled, I will take the next job offered and succeed or die!" Ino shouted at the sky. Well, the roof of the inn, anyway.

Nothing happened.

She sat down at her table in disgust and waved to the barboy to bring more ale. She glared down the other patrons who had looked up at her outburst. She shook out her long red hair, wild and untamed. As she waited, she stretched her five-and-a-half-foot frame and adjusted her sword. Sight of her sword turned the rest away; she had earned a reputation of skill and quick use of that blade.

The ale arrived and she drank deep. Ino of Labdacos, a tributary of one of the great cities of Maz, was bored. The rich job prospects that had brought her to Remingtown had turned out to be little more than rumor. Now she sat in the Wounded Strumpet, an inn that catered to adventurers such as her with good food, and more importantly, cheap rates.

Her cloak shifted, tugging at her shoulder. A small human girl with wide, terrified eyes looked up at Ino.

"Are you an adventurer?" asked the girl in a high, piping voice.

Ino gave what she hoped was a reassuring smile. "Yes I am. Though there seems to be no adventures to be had here."

"Can you find my Mittens? I have three coppers."

Ino froze. She wanted to bang her head on the table in frustration. She wanted to run. She *really* wanted to say no. But an Oath was an Oath.

"Where did you last see your mittens?"

"I went to bed with Mittens on my pillow next to me. In the morning she was gone! I only had her a tenday." The little girl fought down tears. She wore a pretty blue dress and leather slippers. Her brown hair was braided down her back. Ino guessed Mittens was actually a pet.

"Tell me everything about your Mittens," sighed Ino. "You may as well have a seat."

The girl, Ella by name, had received a kitten, black and brown with white paws—hence the name—for her birthday. Like all kittens, Mittens was cute, affectionate, and curious. She slept on Ella's bed and, until this morning, followed the girl everywhere. Ella's mother, a fruitseller, said the kitten was only hiding, but the child knew that Mittens was gone.

"On my honor and my life, I will reunite you with Mittens or die trying." The words escaped Ino's lips before she could stop them. How could she say such a thing?

The little girl's smile almost made it worth it. Ino drained her mug, stood, looked up, and murmured, "At least I know two things. You do listen and you have a sense of humor."

"'Who are you talking to?" said Ella.

"The gods."

"Mother says that is dangerous."

"Your mother is a wise woman," sighed Ino. "Take me to your home so I can start my search."

Ino followed the child through crowded streets until they reached a residential quarter. The home itself was mostly stone, with a slate roof, whitewashed against the mountain weather. A stout woman fretted at the doorway, older, wearing a stained apron.

"Ella!" she shrieked and ran to gather up the child. "Where have you been? I have been worried sick," and other such outbursts came as she bundled Ella toward the house.

Ino followed. At the threshold, the older woman realized it.

"Thank you for bringing Ella home. If you return this evening, I am certain the mistress will reward you."

"But Nana, Ino is going to find Mittens! I hired her for three coppers."

The older woman froze and looked over Ino anew. She obviously did not like what she saw.

"And I suppose she wants to see the inside of the house. No doubt to look for valuables. I mean Mittens." Her tone was unmistakable.

"I was hired by Ella. And will complete my charge." Ino laid her hand upon her sword. "And that is all I shall do." She let her gaze harden into the same steely glare she used to face down giants.

"See that you do," said Nana briskly. "I will be watching."

"Bargained well and done." Ino released her sword and followed the pair inside. It was never good to kill a relative of one's employer.

Clean and modest best explained the house. Rugs kept the floors warm and the table and chairs in the main room were well-scrubbed. Nothing seemed extravagant, but every item Ino saw was well made and built to last. Every cabinet, door, and wardrobe could be a cycle old, a decade, or much more.

Ella's room lay on the third floor, this one made of wood. It was smaller than Ino's room at the inn. An assortment of dolls and stuffed animals lay about or sat on the shelves. An open wardrobe stood in one corner. A small box of sand lay by the chamberpot.

Ino prowled around the room. She checked all the places a kitten could hide. No kitten. She did find some shed fur. She would have to resort to magic.

From a pouch, she pulled out a small diamond on a necklace. She did not normally wear it; displaying wealth around strangers was never a good idea. Especially wealth with magic upon it. She used it to help focus what little magic she had to sharpen her senses. It also carried a Mark of Ownership. The same Mark dragons used for their property. Her Mark.

Ino was, in actuality, Inoth, a dragon with scales of sky blue and fire as her weapon. Ino the Swordswoman was the face she had worn for most of her thirty-five cycles. Compared to most dragons her age, her magic was meager; but with her focus, it was enough.

She breathed and reached for the flame, buried deep within her human form. She followed the kitten's path from the pillow and out into the hall. Nana trailed her as she tracked the faint kitten traces. The going got harder in the kitchen and front room, recently cleaned. She lost the trail for a few minutes, and then picked it up again, going out the front door.

"Who let Mittens out?" Ino asked as she followed the trace out the door. The tracks went four more kitten-steps, and then vanished.

"No one let out the kitten. We all loved her," said Nana.

"The tracks lead out the door and vanish. Mittens did not walk through the door, nor did she open it herself." She held up her hand to stop an answer. She expanded her senses almost to where they would be in dragon form. She smelled the faint trace of another dragon, older than her, and male.

"What is it, Ino?" asked Ella.

Her concentration broke and she lost the trace. She quickly put the diamond necklace away.

"Looks like I will have more excitement than I expected. A dragon has your Mittens." She held up her hand again. "Remember my Oath. You need not pay me until you have Mittens in your hands."

"Why would a dragon take my Mittens?"

"I do not know. I will return when I do."

Ino left Nana and Ella and started wandering around Remingtown, looking for any clue, some lead to give her a path. She also checked at various farms and warehouses around the town. She could not find or buy a kitten with similar markings. Indeed, there were far fewer kittens around than the cat population would explain.

"The cute little critters just vanish," said one farmer. "Over half the kittens of each of Mama Cat's litters disappear after weaning. Been happening for cycles."

The story was similar all over Remingtown. She heard many wild theories, though none involved dragons. Kittens just vanished. Why would a dragon be involved?

Ino, lacking any other ideas, went from sage to wizard to temple, looking for information on local dragons. Information was cheaper than magic. Adventurers and sages reported at least six dragons of seven letter names—over twice Inoth's thirty-five cycles of age and thirty feet long to her fifteen—or more. Of those, four were male.

The reports of their sizes, names, lairs and treasures were sketchy at best. Most rumors consisted of, 'Adventuring band of _____ went looking here for a dragon and never returned.' Only a few were accounts of survivors. Fights between adventurers and dragons tend to leave either all the adventurers dead or the dragon.

She broke down and paid a magus to trace Mittens through the shed fur.

"I cannot scry the kitten itself, but I can tell you she is to the north," said the seer, an older human male.

"That will have to do," sighed Ino.

She returned to the Wounded Strumpet that evening armed with little more than a direction and rumors.

"So!" she announced to the room at large. "Who in here is up for a dragon hunt?"

"What do you know about it?" asked a grizzled hunter.

"What kind of treasure does it have?" asked an elf.

"Does it hold any captives?" asked a knight in shining armor.

"How many people are you recruiting?" asked the barkeep.

Ino waved her hands for silence. With all eyes upon her, she got a mug of ale from the barkeep and found a large table. Many joined her. "I seek to recover a specific treasure from a dragon to the north for my employer. I know it is male and I suspect a name of seven letters or more." A few people left the table. As she talked, more drifted away. "It lairs within a hundred miles of Remingtown. The terrain is mountainous and treacherous; unless a mount can climb or fly, it will be footwork all the way there and back. According to rumor, a flame-wielding dragon lives in that area, so potions or magical protection from fire is recommended. As to the hoard, any settled dragon of that size should have plenty for everyone. Equal shares for all once my employer's property is secured."

"What be this property?" asked a dwarf clad in mail and bearing the symbol of Grim the Battle-lord.

"Mittens, stolen by the dragon."

Silence fell. The men, women and non-humans at the table stared at her. Ino forced her cheeks not to redden.

"Shall we draw up a contract concerning the expedition, the disposition of the treasure, and the exclusion of the mittens?" intoned the knight in shining armor.

Eventually, six other names joined Ino of Labdacos on the contract. Sir Kit, a knight of Libra the Lawgiver, complete with shining armor and tabard bearing the Scales. Sergeant Erik of Thorvaldin, a priest of Grim the Battle-lord, an older dwarf of many battles. Lonsita, a sorceress of the winged folk, delicate and pretty as an elf. Gillos, sky magus, an ugly human male who played with lightning between his fingers. Jenkin the Quick, an elven 'finder of lost things,' who seemed more interested in the women than the mission. Lastly was Sarchos the Hunter, an older human with a face like leather, a sense of humor, vast experience, and a faded Mark of the Gods on his forehead.

"I would suggest protections against other elements as well," offered Sarchos. "A smart dragon would spread rumors that he uses a weapon other than his own for surprise value."

"Smart thinkin'," said Sergeant Erik.

"How soon do we leave?" asked Sir Kit.

"In the morning. An hour past dawn," said Ino. "Gives plenty of time to visit the alchemist or temple."

The meeting broke up.

* * *

In the morning, outside the Wounded Strumpet, they assembled. Ino blinked at the mounts. Sir Kit stood next to a spider the size of a warhorse, a jumping spider at that. Sergeant Erik sat astride a lightning worm; a strange cross between a caterpillar and lizard, that could electrify itself and spit lightning. Jenkin and Sarchos would, like Ino, go afoot. Lonsita and Gillos would fly; indeed, both preferred the air to ground.

Not four miles into the trek, Sir Kit's spider proved invaluable. Though every member could climb or fly, the spider's silk made ascending nearly sheer rock walls easier than climbing a ladder. Thanks to Sarchos, they held a course due north no matter what the obstacle.

The first day, they made over ten miles. Evening brought stories, weapons practice, and armor maintenance. Everyone remarked at the beautiful blue dragonscale armor Ino wore. She told a fanciful story of how she won it, rather than reveal that it was made from her last shedding.

Little disturbed their journey. Sarchos had no trouble hunting game to provide fresh meat. Gillos and Lonsita advised of upcoming obstacles and possibly dangerous monsters. Seven days out of Remingtown, their aerial scouts spotted a soaring dragon. Using their own magic for concealment, they followed at a distance. That evening, they reported the area where they suspected the dragon to lair.

Another day of climbing, sliding, and now hiding, brought them close enough for Sarchos to start his tracking. He pointed out signs of many wolves; the wolf pack had fed well, it seemed. He also found signs of wolves being eaten by a dragon, one that used frost as a weapon. A *very* large dragon.

That night they made cold camp. Ino spotted boundary stones carrying the dragon-Mark, though she said nothing. She would not reveal herself to these people.

A cry awakened Ino and the others. Jenkin thrashed out of his bedroll and leapt away from it. The seven adventurers watched something squirm out of the confining covers. It mewed plaintively. An orange fuzzy kitten.

No larger than a pair of breadrolls, it looked up at them with wide, curious eyes. It mewed again and stumbled toward the dwarf, who jumped back clutching his axe.

Lonsita came to the kitten's rescue and scooped it up. "Who left this precious little," she checked, "guy out here?" She looked over at Gillos, who was on watch. "Some watchman."

"I was looking for dragons and creatures that would threaten us. Not kittens," said Gillos.

"It is a long way from anywhere a domestic cat should be. Let alone a kitten."

"I agree," said Sarchos. "Perhaps someone lives nearby."

"Indeed, Sarchos," said Ino. "Perhaps you can lead us back along our fuzzy friend's trail to his owner. Someone who lives this close to a dragon should know about it."

Lonsita meanwhile fed the kitten some bits of cheese and milk, kept magically fresh; she was a vegetarian. This started the kitten rumbling like a small avalanche. She spent more time cuddling the kitten than listening.

"Do you think you can follow the trail now?" Ino asked Sarchos. "It is two hours until dawn, and we have but one moon left. But I doubt we will get much more sleep." The others murmured agreement on the sleep.

"Perfectly fresh tracks means no problem, even for a kitten and low light," said the hunter.

They broke camp and followed Sarchos as he retraced the orange kitten's path. Ino pulled out her necklace and put it around her neck, just in case. Intent on watching Sarchos and the sky, none noticed.

The path wound around rocks, leapt from trees, pounced on blades of grass, and led generally uphill. In a couple of places, the kitten made truly impossible leaps and Sarchos nearly lost the trail. Then the path led directly into a cliff with no sign of the kitten jumping. According to his tracks, he walked right out of solid rock.

They all looked at the dwarf.

"Do nae look at me," said the dwarf. "I be a priest, nae a miner."

Those with magic examined the stone. Absolutely plain and normal, with no enchantments.

"I do sense a chamber beyond, after perhaps twenty feet," said Lonsita. "I could melt a passage with about an hour's work."

"Do it," said Ino. She took the kitten from Lonsita and held it.

She watched as Lonsita drew elaborate runes on the rock face. Runes that mirrored the tattoos covering the winged woman's body. Then she placed her hands on the runes, chanted quietly, and *pushed*. The stone gave slowly.

Ino felt the backwash of magic and watched as the rune-covered stone receded like a pressed puzzle-piece. The walls around were smooth as ice, but radiated no magic or heat. The resulting tunnel was large enough for the knight's spider, but not enough for the knight to ride. When they reached the chamber beyond, Lonsita sagged against the wall, panting with exhaustion. The dwarf left his mount outside.

A natural cavern, now lit from their entrance and the rising sun, glittered with glistening stalactites and stalagmites. Ino gestured Sarchos and Jenkin to the fore. Torches were produced and lit. Sarchos again found the trail.

Ino suspected Sarchos could track a bird on the wing. A strange minty, yet spicy smell wafted to them, dragged by the draft of new cave opening behind them.

They felt it first. A low rumble that resembled the kitten's purr, but on a massive scale. The very stones carried the vibration.

A white kitten streaked out of the darkness, stood on its hind legs, waved its paws at them, batted Jenkin's foot, and then tried to run past them. Gillos swept this one up. It batted playfully at him with soft paws.

"Whoever lives here, she likes cats," muttered the magus. He skritched the kitten behind the ears, causing a purr.

"'Who says it is a she?" whispered Ino.

"Everyone knows it is women who live with many cats."

Ino chose to pet her kitten instead of killing him. For all his talk, he was not immune to kitten cuteness.

The rumbling grew as they went deeper. A light appeared around the corner ahead. They doused their torches and crept closer. Even those in armor were silent compared to the rumble.

They turned the corner, ready for anything. Anything but what they found. A massive, cavern, hundreds of feet deep, filled with kittens.

Kittens wrestled. Kittens climbed on carpets wrapped around wood poles. Kittens gamboled and tumbled over boulders. Kittens drank from a stream flowing across a corner (only paw-deep). Kittens climbed over each other to eat from troughs full of food. Kittens slept in a massive pile that seemed to breathe on its own. Kittens played with various shiny and jingling toys. Kittens chased each other. Kittens purred.

Hundreds, maybe thousands of kittens, and not a single adult cat in sight. A faint magic barrier separated the party from the cavern. A barrier to keep things in, rather than out.

They passed slowly through the barrier. Ino looked around for signs of Mittens, or the dragon. The cuteness of the kittens threatened to overwhelm her. Jenkin drew back a boot to kick a kitten.

"Stop," she hissed.

"A wise choice," rumbled a deep voice. A male voice. A dragon's voice. "Harm any of my little fuzzies and I will kill you as painfully as possible."

He rose from the pile. The sleeping kittens protested as they woke, streaming down his sides. Silver scales glinted in the light of glowstones in the ceiling. He kept rising. His leathery wings spread, wide enough to shadow huge swaths of the cavern. Fangs and claws the size of a giant's sword flashed as he turned his eyes on the party. Even without his tail—still buried in kittens—Ino guessed him over fifty feet long and probably past his third century.

Sir Kit mounted his spider and hefted his lance.

"You fool!" Ino shouted. "We are no match for him!"

The party disintegrated. Sir Kit rode his spider

up the wall and began a charge. Gillos set his kitten aside and took to the air. Sarchos turned and fled back down the corridor, dragging a groggy Lonsita (Ino thought that the sanest response). Jenkin ran to the right, heedless of the kittens. Ino stood frozen.

Gillos struck with his lightning, which raced down the glittering scales. The dragon replied with a cone of frost that rimed the mage and sent him crashing to the ground. Kittens scattered. Sergeant Erik ran to the fallen magus, a hearing prayer on his lips.

Sir Kit rode his spider as it leapt from the wall, aiming his lance at the dragon's exposed side. In mid-leap, the spider became spider bits from a claw-swipe. The lance still struck deep, drawing hot blood. A bite from the dragon removed the knight's arm at the shoulder. He fell.

Gillos and Sergeant Erik both threw spells at the dragon, to little effect. The dragon's silver scales now glittered with magic, making them stronger. Jenkin tried to stab the dragon's tail.

The dragon grabbed the elf with his tail and flipped him into his waiting jaws. Blood sprayed.

"Fly you fools!" Ino screamed at the magus and dwarf. They fled, leaving her alone with the massive silver dragon.

"Well, little sister?" He brought his head close to her.

She did not dare put down the kitten.

"You did not fight. You also helped bring two of my fuzzies home. You may leave unharmed."

"Why?" she demanded in frustration.

He left her to start gathering up his terrified pets and sooth them with deep rumbles and caresses. As he collected them, he tried to count them.

"Whoever complained about herding cats never tried to herd kittens," he grumbled.

She looked around for any trace of treasure. All she found were more kittens, toys, and items for their care.

"Shhh my fuzzy babies," he crooned. "All the bad people are gone."

"Why is this cavern filled with kittens?" she almost shrieked.

"Are you still here?" He turned to her once more. "How about proper etiquette at least?"

Seething, she spoke through gritted teeth. "Your pardon, great one. I, Inoth, request permission to speak."

"Better. I, Tarvinysh, give my leave."

Nine letters. She was right. Most dragons of that age and power were at least three centuries old and as large as the male before her. Dragons of metallic scales were rare; they tended to have a harder time blending in and thus fewer grew to this size. Only adventurers of great power fought dragons like him, not those chance-met in an inn.

"Would you please explain this? I do not understand."

"Very well. But put Bucephelus down please. He looks like he needs to use the sandbox."

She put down the kitten, who raced off. As she watched, she spotted a kitten that could only be Mittens.

"I am taking their age."

"What?"

"Kittens grow into cats quickly. Here in my lair, I take all the aging my furry babies would. Thus, I grow more powerful and they stay adorable." He returned to soothing the kittens.

"But why steal them?" She started sidling toward Mittens.

"As I said before, have you ever tried herding kittens? No matter how I ward my cave, they escape. They do not understand barriers. Some walk through solid rock walls. Then the animals of the forest get them. I try to keep them down, but the wolves in particular always come back. Thus, I constantly need to get more."

Casually, Ino scooped up Mittens and started edging toward the entrance.

"Do you think to steal from my hoard?" He was not even looking in her direction.

"Of course not, great one." She hastily set Mittens down. Then she had an idea. "You know, perhaps you need someone to herd kittens for you, or at least help. I know a little girl who is wonderful with kittens. Polite, and cute as a kitten in her own way…"

* * *

Ino the Swordswoman relaxed at the Wounded Strumpet. She sat in a dim corner and sipped her ale. Three coppers well spent.

Suddenly, a frantic woman burst into the room. "Someone must help me! My daughter was stolen by a dragon!"

The Swordswoman pulled her hood lower and settled deeper into the shadows. She was going to stick to peace and quiet for a while.

Realities

Story by
Lyn McConchie

Illustration by
Teresa Tunaley

She hated washing dishes, Aufreica muttered. She ate her dinner quickly as she dried the plates, managing unnoticed to slide a second stale pastry into her skirt pocket, then; with a nod to the owner of the cook-shop she was gone, merging into the market crowd. She reached her favorite corner, laid out her begging-bowl, dropped in five coppers to encourage passers-by, and began to sing.

She allowed the sound to flow out in one long sustained note, pure and sexless as ringing crystal. It cut through the market place sounds so that many stopped to listen. She sang a gentle ballad and waited. Here and there coins tinkled into the plate. There was the rent, the food, the clothing her younger siblings needed. She sang again and again until at last, weary and with her throat beginning to tighten, there was enough coin for her needs.

She gathered it up, counting quickly as she ate her stolen pastry. One in ten for the Buskers Guild. Two in ten for Aufreica. She bit back a curse. Her mother's last man had deserted them three years ago. Her mother had never recovered from the birth of the baby that had died. As the oldest at almost fourteen Aufreica must be the family's breadwinner. Her mother and siblings who lived on her voice trapped her, and sometimes Aufreica felt that they lived on her very soul. The worst of it was that she could be far more. Once a traveling Singer had tested her.

"You have the gift, child."

The girl had stared up at the bejeweled woman. "Then why doesn't it work. Those Singers with the true singing gift, they draw anyone who listens. Princes keep them." Aufreica had laughed bitterly, "Where is my prince?" she jeered. "Why do I sing for coppers?"

The woman had studied her. "Three reasons, girl. You are too young as yet for the gift to become active. Secondly you are under-fed. The gift draws on a singer's strength. The less you have, the less you can give to the gift."

"Three reasons you said?"

"The third is the training you need once your gift manifests. When it does, go to the teachers, they will train you to use it truly."

Aufreica stared. "They'll train me for my asking?"

"No. They'll want gold. The lowest level of teaching takes a year and costs a gold reni. For full training it takes three years." She saw the girl's face. "I know. 'Tis a huge sum, but put by coins each day. Eat better and save what you can. In time there may be enough for a year's training at least."

Aufreica returned thoughtfully to her singing. For

two years she saved. Then when she reached thirteen she felt the first deep stirrings of her gift. It terrified her. In a few years the gift would wither again without the training. She found herself a job in the cook shop. They paid her mostly in food, which allowed her to save faster. Yet time was running out.

She skimped harder on the coins she gave her mother. Aufreica would have sung longer in the market except for knowing that an untrained voice could be damaged that way. Every week she counted her saved coins. Almost enough, but something warned her that the gift might begin to fade soon if she did not begin training.

Then in the marketplace she saw him and blinked at so much splendor. She sang her best as he approached and gaped at the silver coin which he flung casually into her plate to lie gleaming royally amid the common coppers. Aufreica scooped the coins into her pocket staring after the giver. He passed and she saw the loose strings on his purse begin to unravel, she slid hastily after him. The purse fell and she snatched it up, her breath coming fast with excitement.

He was turning at the feel of weight lost from his belt, there was no time to hide the purse. She had the quick mind of a street-smart girl and she held it out shyly, all that lost glitter of gold thread and solid weight of coin. She could have wept at her opportunity which was gone, but she made her voice small and diffident.

"Oh, sir. My Lord. You dropped this as you passed where I sang. I ran after you." She raised her eyes in feigned admiration

He cleared his throat, noticing that the child still panted from her run to return his property. He remembered her voice. It had been clear and true with something else, an untrained gift perhaps? It was pleasant to be so admired and—if she had the Singer's gift it would bring him status to have recognized it. He reached into his purse before taking her hand.

"Give this ring to Mistress Anathea at the Street of Singers. Tell her Lord Tarran sent you for testing. The coin is for you." He closed her hand on the gold coin and the silver ring with his crest. "

Purse strings re-tied he strolled off leaving Aufreica gaping after him, this time in genuine adoration. She had an introduction to a Teacher of Singers and sufficient coin—with her own savings—to buy two years' teaching. She went home to her mother, and listened to the small events of the day. She looked over-tired so that her mother gave her the best of the bruised fruit and forbade the younger children to make too much noise.

They ignored their mother's command. Lasti charged about until he fell, howling for the pain of a stubbed toe. Torra stole Aufreica's fruit. Their mother allowed the younger girl to keep the fruit, soothed Lasti as she rubbed his toe and ignored her eldest daughter's silent outrage. Aufreica withdrew into herself hiding fury at the injustice.

She must go out to work and support all these idlers? Even when she came home there was no consideration. Why couldn't lazy Torra bear some of the burden? Lasti too, he was a sturdy boy and could find work around the market. Let him earn his own bread instead of battening on her. She scowled to herself, *and* her mother lay in bed most of the day claiming to be too weak to work.

What would they do without her? she wondered. An angry voice rose inside her to answer that. They'd have to manage if she was ill, if she was killed or died, they'd have no other choice but to support themselves. As she considered that, Torra grabbed for the coins in Aufreica's pocket.

"How much did you get? I want a new dress an' Lasti wants a knife."

Aufreica slapped the intrusive hand—hard. She listened with angry disgust as the girl set up a whining complaint. Their mother chided.

"Dear, that isn't kind. Torra just wanted to know."

The girl's temper flared abruptly out of control. "Then let her ask me politely. I work hard for that coin. I won't have it wasted or taken for granted."

Lasti jeered, "My Lady works hard. We should ask her gracious permission." He dropped to his knees. "Oh great Aufreica, please gift this humble one with a few miserable coppers."

Beside him Torra imitated his actions, holding out her hand as she whined the beggars cry for alms. Aufreica hid her rage at the mockery and their mother's refusal to call them to heel. She worked to exhaustion for them and this was how she was repaid? She stood, schooling her face to blandness, her voice to an icy calm.

"I'm tired. I'm going to sleep."

She lay down, wrapping the threadbare blankets around her. Her siblings jeered a few minutes longer before moving over to lie beside their mother. Aufreica smoothed out her breathing, waiting. An hour later as the other three snored, the girl sat up quietly, collected her stash of coins and gathered her meager belongings. She rose, bundle in one hand and glanced at her family. They'd manage, they'd simply have to

work for once, work as hard as she had these past few years. She'd given them enough of her life, now she had the coin, she would seek out Mistress Anathea.

Aufreica worked determinedly once she had found her teacher, for two years she strove to absorb everything she was taught, not to waste a precious paid-for moment. As the end of the second year drew near she was afraid. There was still more to learn, was she to lose that? She had some reason to hope not.

"Child, is it possible for you to travel?"

"Yes, Honored Teacher." Aufreica stood with her head bowed politely. Lord Tarran had continued to take an interest. She had given him only admiring looks and occasional sweet stolen kisses. He had given her far more. This was to be his greatest gift if she was correct in her hopes.

"Well, my dear, Tarran has agreed to pay for your third year. As you know that will be at the school in Mirray. The caravan leaves in two days."

She eyed Aufreica thoughtfully. A gifted girl, but calculating. Tarran seemed to think that if he paid for this last year it would buy him a Singer for his house. Anathea could have told him it was unlikely. She wondered about the girl's people. Some tale Tarran had told her of having found the girl busking in the market in the poor quarter. But the child had arrived well fed and decently enough clad.

"Tell me child, do you have a family?"

Aufreica nodded. By now her mother should have recovered her health. Torra would be fourteen and likely betrothed, Lasti would be beginning training as a guard perhaps. She murmured something of this. Anathea nodded. As she'd thought, a middle-class family, poor but respectable.

"Why were you singing in the market?"

Aufreica thought swiftly. "My mother didn't wish me to be a Singer. There was a man she planned for me once I was older…" she allowed her voice to trail away artistically. Anathea filled in the gaps. Likely a man older or ill favored—and the gift was a demanding mistress. The child had chosen to earn the money for training instead.

"Your father?"

"He was killed."

Anathea was soft-hearted for all her strict teaching. She asked no further, putting together a picture in her mind. If the son was learning to be a caravan guard most likely the father had been one too. After the man's death the family would have been poor. Many places paid no pension to a guard's family. Probably the child's younger sister was betrothed to the man Aufreica had spurned. She nodded to herself, satisfied with her conjectures.

"Tarran has paid for your journey and sent money to the school. I have a small purse from him to help you." She handed it over. "You have studied well, continue to do so. Those who have trained at Mirray may rise high." She saw the flicker of hunger. Yes, whatever Tarran had hoped, this one would not be returning. She patted the slender arm.

"Work hard, my dear Sherra. I expect great things of you."

Aufreica packed quickly that night. Taking another name had been a sensible precaution. So had pausing to change into her only good dress and shoes and purchase a once-expensive secondhand cloak from a used-clothing stall. During her two years here she'd kept her mouth shut except when she sang. She'd continued to save where she could and with Tarran's purse added, she had sufficient to buy better clothing for her arrival in Mirray. Clothing that would mark her as a step up again. She'd listened to the girls here and learned what to say—and in what accents to say it.

Towards the end of her—increasingly successful—Mirrayan city year she was again asked of her family. She brought them into her mind's eye. Her sister Torra, now wed to the middle-aged merchant Aufreica had rejected. Her brother Lasti, rising steadily in rank among the merchant's caravan guards. Her mother who lived with them to keep house. She sighed.

"I do miss them but the gift can't be ignored. My betrothed was happy enough to take my sister in my place. Father left sufficient for my first two years. Then his employer took an interest."

Those around her nodded. Sherra had been fortunate. Not all employers were so kind, all betrothed so sensible.

"Where are you going once you leave?"

"I have a position offered. I'll decide when I must." They understood that too. If a better chance came she would accept it—as would they all.

For Aufreica the chance did come. Her voice had matured into vibrant beauty with her Singer's gift in full flower. When she sang her voice drew all who heard, transporting them to sorrow or joy according to the song. She was offered a place at Mirray's court and took it, being sensible enough to continue her training. She reveled in the luxury and respect a court singer enjoyed.

Occasionally she was asked about her family. She would smile as she remembered them. Her mother, now with a servant of her own as Torra's merchant husband prospered. Her brother Lasti, soon to head the merchant's caravan guards. And her sister, Torra, grown a little plump but happily wed with three small children. Aufreica would touch lightly on her home, how happy they'd been.

It was fifteen years before she returned to her homelands at last. Mirray's King had asked her to travel to another court, to sing at his sister's wedding and she had done so, now she was on the way home again. Her route took her past the town of her birth and on impulse she ordered her guards to halt. She would spend a day or two here. Let them seek out two people and announce her.

"Yes, Singer Sherra."

As she'd expected Tarran had long since forgiven her defection. She was kind to him and gracious to her old teacher. In fact her return was quite a triumph, Aufreica thought. In the morning she would take a stroll through the markets. She'd never *had* to sing there of course, her father had left sufficient money to pay … she shut off her thoughts; feeling oddly confused.

At the market Aufreica strolled past stalls bright with goods. Behind her marched two guards. A Singer was very unlikely to be harmed, but even so, there were occasions when guards might be necessary. Her feet took her down an alleyway. She glanced about, shuddering delicately at the smell and filth. Revolting, how anyone could bear to live here! From a doorway there came a sudden cry.

"Frey! Aufreica!"

A figure staggered towards her. A bony hand seized the Singer's wrist. The guards closed in; to be waved back. Whatever the creature wanted Aufreica doubted it intended her harm. It was babbling something at her.

"And when you didn't come home again we had no money for the rent an' the landlord threw us out. Lasti went thieving to feed us. Mother got sicker and died and he was caught a year after that 'n executed. I went into Mother Deggo's House, there wasn't nothing else I could do. Last year she said I'd lost all my looks and threw me out. I'm starving since an' I got nothing pretty to wear so I don't get the clients no more. But you'll buy me a new dress and all the food I can eat, won't you. I told them, Frey, I knew you'd be back to look after me one day."

Sherra looked down at the babbling fool indifferently. Aufreica? Oh, yes. She remembered some girl of that name now, but it was nothing to do with her. She recalled the tale, of how the girl had left a family who used her, ridden on the back of an overworked child and would have left her gift to wither. But that was nothing to do with Sherra whose family prospered. Her brother was head of his Lord's caravan guards now, her sister was happily wed with three half-grown children. Sherra's mother lived in comfort. She shook off the clutching hands casually.

"My name is Sherra. Singer Sherra of Mirray."

"Aufreica. I know it's you, I'm hungry. You have to look after me." There *was* something familiar enough about that whine to irritate the Singer to a tart reply.

"I *have* to do nothing, woman. Certainly I do not have to feed and clothe some gutter-bred whore. If I look after anyone it will be myself."

Those words too seemed somehow familiar. Sherra brushed the idea aside. The town was boring, the market was boring, and most of all this grubby scrawny woman was boring. She turned to depart as the woman shrieked desperately, grabbing for the swirl of silken skirt.

"Frey? Please. Frey, I'm starving!"

Sherra nodded to one of the guards. With brutal efficiency he detached the sobbing female and shook her.

"You know the penalty for laying hands on a Singer. Get gone and count yourself lucky."

His shove sent the woman sprawling into the stinking mud. Impulse sent the Singer's hand to her purse. She tossed a handful of coppers to the cringing figure. At least the woman—whoever she was—should eat well for a few days and Sherra's purse was lightened of that rubbish. The Singer walked gracefully away down the street, her guards a pace behind her. A day later she left the town of her birth—never to return.

Some dreams do not survive well in the daylight.

Fisher Brother

My brother wearing Fisherman's armour,
bright as the scales I scrape from dead fish.
In the gutting hut, I smile accepting
the congratulations.

My brother flashing in the ocean
of Mother's admiration,
and Father's quiet pride.
The children in the street shout:
"Fisherman! Fisherman! Bring us a dreamer's sword."

My brother, armoured in certainty.
A righteousness man of the shoal.

I am the bird that flies in shade.
I dream of the dreaming tattered man sowing death;
of men gutted like fish,
of bones bleached under the foreign sun,
My secret dreams, my infidel dreams.
I see my brother's future laid out in my heretic's gift.

"I will kill all the dreamers," says my brother.
I kiss him goodbye.
The sun shines all angles on his silver coat,
I listen to the screech of the bad omen birds.

I'm glad he goes to kill the dreamers,
those with the future, desolate knowledge,
I only wish that he could return for me.

— Deborah Walker

The Dreams of Dragons

She moved swiftly down the echoing corridors of light,
seeking a passage through the labyrinth of visions,
walking on refracted feet,
dancing between transparent walls,
or soaring on wings like a luminous bird
with effortless delight.

At times she carried a staff of light,
at times a wand of crystal fire
that sent forth coruscating sparks
and cast dancing shadows
around her winged flight.

The dreams of the dragon seemed to flow around her,
creating the shimmering maze
she shifted with her own thoughts,
as though she too were dreaming
and being dreamed.

The sense of having a distinctive body
flickered in and out like a candle,
as did the shimmering threads of memory
and the contours of a clear purpose to guide her.

Memories far more ancient seemed to emanate from an
invisible source,
untraceable yet pulsating all around,
giving a strange shape and depth
to her own more slender strands
of vision and association.

Now the walls seemed to completely dissolve
and she was in a sky filled with glittering stars,
flying in spirals on great iridescent wings
almost without weight
beyond the sensation of shifting momentum.

Another dragon sailed in front of her,
luminous blue scales reflecting the myriad points of light.
At the same time she was conscious
that every star in the sky was a vast consciousness
gazing out of fathomless eternal depths,
and that every star was conscious of her,
watched her exultant flight,
and reflected it between infinite rippling centers,
even into the constellation of tiny stars
that formed her dragon's body
and her ceaseless flight,
and the very sky full of stars

mirrored in her eyes
themselves infinitely mirrored.

The sense of time was vast and empty,
rippling infinitely in all directions,
taking shape through movement
like the path of her own flight,
or the twinkling of stars
that are no more than flickering fire
and dancing light,
infinitely mirrored, and felt, and echoed
by all the other dances.

— Nicolo Santilli

The Copperroof War

Story by:
Megan Arkenberg

Illustration by:
Tom Kelly

If a house is divided against itself, that house cannot stand.
— Mark 3:25

It began in the south wing, near the long cold Hall of Empires and the chambers of the Duke of Cloud. Helene, the Duchess, woke at midnight to the metal sound of marching in the corridor, and farther away, the hollow ring of drums.

"Paride," she whispered, shaking her husband's shoulder. The cold was bitter, even in the Duke's bedchamber, and her breath froze in a puff of white. The distant marching became louder, and she reached for the dagger on her bedside table.

Before Paride had fully awakened, the Duchess was flinging a silk dressing gown around her and fumbling for a candle. The fire had died—strangely, as the maids of Copperroof were known for their diligence—but the air smelled faintly of smoke.

"Ghosts," the Duke murmured, pulling on a pair of trousers. "But I'll be damned if they burn down Copperroof in the King's absence."

"Ghosts never enter the south wing," Helene said. She climbed up on the chair by her writing desk and took two trophies from the wall: an ancient Imixian saber, curved and wickedly sharp, and a bastard sword from the brief reign of Socorro XI. She handed the saber to her husband and led the way—candle and dagger in one hand, sword in the other—into the smoke-choked corridor.

Night in Copperroof was never silent. There were the usual noises, lovers' muffled laughter, the echoes of a duel in the basement tunnels, a drunk violinist playing a half-remembered tune. And there were some noises that were only usual in Copperroof; whispered conversations of which only a word or two could be understood; footsteps pattering in a walled-up staircase; the mechanical organ in the Salon of Cats humming itself to sleep. Even the south wing housed the parlor where the pen of the Marquise von Argent whispered silkily on invisible pages, rewriting the infamous letter that drove the Marquis to hang himself in the tunnels.

But that night, the night the war began, the sounds were different. Even the Duchess's footsteps as she slid along the corridor echoed like the clang of iron boots. The smoke was thick and white, swallowing vision, swallowing breath. Helene had to listen for the rustle of her husband's dressing gown only inches behind her.

"My father told me a story when I was a child,"
Paride said softly; the Duchess shirked to admit how much the warmth of his voice comforted her. "He said that in the days when his grandmother was Duchess of Cloud, a war broke out in the Library of Cadmus."

"North wing," Helene said contemptuously. She was south wing only by marriage, having been born to a humble tailor in the Via Theatre, but distrust of the north wing came readily and hard. "They'd fight for a dropped glove."

"I don't know what they fought for, but my father said it began like this; smoke and drums. The armory had been rearranging itself for days, and some of the suits had gone missing, but the archivists were too afraid to let anyone know." Something hit the marble floor with a heavy clang, and the Duke and Duchess froze like two suits of armor themselves. A round object was rolling towards them in the dark: *clang-bringa-bringa-clang-bringa-bringa-clang.*

"The King had been gone then, too," Paride said.

The thing halted at the Duchess's feet. She flipped it over with her toe, gripping her sword tightly. It was a brass helmet, polished for display, but with a brutal dent in the left cheek. Two green lights seemed to gleam in its depths like a pair of drowned eyes.

"Reign of Albinus," said Helene, who was almost as well versed in arms as the archivists. "From the Gallery of Spears."

"North wing," the Duke said.

A blast of ice struck them from behind, extinguishing the candle. The Duchess swung her sword and felt it connect with something hard and smooth. She raised her dagger, but something cold sliced across her cheek and she stumbled backwards. Paride's cry of pain was the last thing she heard before her head struck the floor.

The war had begun.

* * *

Of course, the real trouble began three days earlier, when the King announced that he was leaving Copperroof.

"It's ridiculous," the Duke had said—and it meant something, as his was the most powerful voice in the south wing. "His child will be born any day now, and he wants to leave Copperroof. For the love of God, why?"

Room by room, Copperroof took up the cry of protest. How could the King wish to leave? His house had the finest theatre, the finest poets, the finest gardens, the finest paintings and books and horses and playing-fields in all the land. Every play worth seeing was performed in Copperroof; every salon worth attending was hosted there. Men and women spent their lives trying to breach those marble walls. From the monstrous canvases in the Hall of Empires to the sulfur pool two miles away in the Bath of Virgins to the sun-heated orangery and the Grotto of Austerity, everything a King could desire was there to be had.

And there was the Queen: Arete, youngest sister of the Duke of Cloud. Tall, slender, as dark as her brother was fair—and heavy with the King's child. But while the Duke fumed, then wheedled, then begged, she said quietly that her husband would do as he pleased.

The day before he left, she retreated with little ceremony to the chapel on the west façade. It had been built in the reign of Consolata III, and crouched over the orangery like a buttress-clawed panther. Even the King could not miss the significance of this gesture, as the Queen famously loved neither God nor oranges.

Nevertheless, the King left. It was the first sign of trouble in Copperroof.

* * *

Paride was screaming; he could not get enough air; everything was smoke and bitter cold. He heard Helene grunting as she swung her sword, then the sickening thud of iron and marble against bone.

Then he was awake, lying on a velvet couch in the Chartreuse Parlor, and Helene was smoothing his forehead with a damp handkerchief. A bandage covered her left cheek and eye, pinkish-white against her brown skin. Her right eye was red from smoke and weeping.

"Thank God," she said when he caught her hand, pressing his lips to her cold palm. "If something had happened to you, I'd tear those metal bastards limb from limb."

"Someone already did," said a dry voice from the doorway. The Duke turned his head, wincing as a bandage peeled away from his shoulder. Madame Chloe Saré, the senior archivist of Copperroof's armories, was stripping a pair of blood-stained gloves from her hand fingertip by fingertip. Though educated in the north wing libraries, she was born above the Catacombs, and her gestures always carried the air of a torturer.

"We have the suits mostly reassembled," she continued, as though it should reassure him. "The complete ones are laid out in the tunnel beneath the Arborie. Now we're working on the … miscellaneous pieces."

"There's one even I don't recognize," Helene said, "and I know every sword from the Gallery of Spears to the Broken Nautilus." She lifted something from the rug by her knee and handed it to Paride.

It was a sword—that much was clear. But of what metal, in what tradition, from which room was harder to determine. A marble hand still gripped its hilt, stained and fractured cleanly at the wrist.

Paride shook his head. "I've never seen it before," he said. "Don't you have a guess?"

"Well, we know one thing for certain," Saré said. "It's not from the north wing."

* * *

Then again, perhaps the trouble began earlier than the King's departure. Perhaps it began when Yvon was thrown out of Copperroof.

It had been an unsightly but well-attended tragedy at the time. No one could imagine a worse fate than exile, and Yvon, beautiful and cruel and lion-proud, had never been popular in Copperoof. Most of the house turned out that pale winter morning to watch him flung down the long flight of stairs at the east end of the orangery. His head left streaks of red on the snow-powdered marble—blood or strands of his famous hair, it was hard to say.

He scrambled to his feet at the base of the stairs, trembling with cold and the pain of wounded dignity. His shirt billowed in the wind, snow-damp and translucent as his skin. When he had stood there for a moment, staring at the King's metal guards like a fox cornered by hounds, the King took pity on him and came down the orchard stairs. Yvon reached for his hand, bending to kiss it. The King struck him across the face, and Yvon fell sprawling in the snow.

* * *

Three days into the war, the north wing armor disappeared from the tunnel beneath the Arborie. Madame Saré left a card, brief and tactfully worded, pasted on the Duke and Duchess's door. She thought it would be best, her precise calligraphy said, if the Queen was left uniformed until the last possible moment; Arete had gone into labor that morning.

It was the last anyone in Copperroof heard of Madame Saré.

* * *

Two weeks before Yvon was thrown out, Arete said an interesting thing to the Duke of Cloud.

"I want the key to the Globe Library." She stood by her boudoir window, one hand on her mounded belly, the other pressed against the frost-speckled glass. Her cheeks were red as peach-skin, soft and blotchy.

The Duke sat on the floor across from her, laying

cards against himself. It was a game he and Arete had played as children: Kings and Queens, odd and even cards dueling each other, with the Knaves calling for a reshuffle. Paride had been explaining for nearly an hour how he would teach the game to his nephew.

He frowned, laying the Queen of Crowns on his north-hand pile. "The Globe Library is locked?"

"Unlocked," the Queen said. "I wish I could lock it. The King spends all his time there now."

Paride's frown deepened. He remembered the story now: how King Bastian had the lock made for the library at the far end of the north wing, after Queen Nausicaa VII took to cataloguing the shelves instead of ruling her kingdom. The catalogue had survived, saved in a golden casket near the Hall of the Catafalque. Nausicaa had died of apoplexy within the year.

"What is he doing there?" the Duke asked. "I thought it was an archive of obscure texts." And not the interestingly obscure ones—those had a salon to themselves, east of the Via Theatre.

"It houses the collection of Gertrude the Surveyor," Arete said. "I'm told he's been reading that."

"Tax records and travel logs?"

"And maps." She stroked the black velvet stretched over her abdomen. "I am so tired of hearing him talk about mountains and the sea."

* * *

Five days into the war, the Count of Belphoebe was drinking ginger tea in the Arborie, leafing through the collected poems of Téo von Blum, when he saw them.

He thought at first they were the Ash Children, a trio of phantasms who often appeared near fireplaces on the ground floor. He was about to offer them tea—the customary offering was three drops of brandy, but Belphoebe hadn't touched alcohol in seventy-nine years and wasn't about to start now—when he saw that there were at least a dozen of them, and none were less than seven feet tall. He remembered the missing armor—but the Duchess of Cloud had said they clanked as they marched. These were silent, and their eyes were flat and red.

That night, something broke into the northern stables. Two of the horses were slaughtered, their eyes ripped out and their legs snapped like firewood. A third horse died convulsing, apparently from fright.

By the sixth day, the things were sighted all across the north wing, red-eyed shadows that smelled of musk and dead violets and lilac turned to dust. A maid went missing; nine hours of searching uncovered her at the bottom of a little-used stairwell, her neck twisted at an odd angle. There was blood beneath her fingernails, and worse things, a whitish substance veined with red. The dead girl's hair smelled like musk and lilac.

Pasiphae of Blois, whose family was the oldest north of the Gallery of Spears, sent a letter to the Duke and Duchess of Cloud offering the north wing's unconditional surrender. The Duke's reply was curst, as his messenger preferred not to linger: *They aren't ours.*

On the seventh day, Frances, Lord Oberon saw them in the Via Theatre, running on two or four or eight legs across the catwalks in the Opera House itself. But by then, no one cared.

* * *

When Arete announced her pregnancy, Copperroof erupted in spontaneous displays of joy. The mechanical organ in the Salon of Cats began a waltz that would last almost two months, the orangery blossomed until the petals fell thick as snow. Even the Bath of Virgins bubbled with excitement, filling the adjacent corridors with pungent steam.

But the greatest victory came at the masquerade the King declared to mark Arete's third month. No one knew how it happened, but suddenly Yvon and the Queen were dancing with the rest, their foreheads pressed together, their hair spilling over Arete's bare shoulders, entwined crimson and coal.

"The wolf and the lamb have made peace," Paride whispered to his wife.

"Yes," Helene said, "but which is which?"

* * *

"I'm sorry, your grace," the girl said, "but no one is allowed within." She was a tiny thing, dark-skinned like the Duchess, and seemed to melt into the twisted ebony carvings on the chapel doors. But her voice was firm, sharp-edged as the dagger hanging unsheathed at her hip.

The Duke of Cloud moved his hand to the hilt of his own dagger. "She's my sister," he hissed. "Step aside and let me speak to her."

"The Queen is exhausted from the birth. She has no energy to waste on these foolish squabbles."

"Squabbles? Copperroof is destroying itself!" Paride gestured broadly at the hall around him, the Hall of the Antechamber of the Most Holy Presence. The red-eyed shadows had swept through in the night, tearing canvases and breaking swords from the statues of Kings and Queens. The smell of dead violets clung to the marble shards. "The world is breaking around our heads. This isn't a squabble, it's a war."

"A war started by petty men who have not the courage to kill with their hands." The maid raised her eyebrows, like a pedantic archivist at a salon. "If they cannot make peace among themselves, it must wait until the King returns."

"Look at this place. Look at this." The Duke unwound his cravat, showing the long mark of an ancient spearhead along his neck. "Do you think *men* began this war?"

The girl lifted her chin, a perfect imitation of Arete. "Be reasonable, your grace. It is men who fight wars, not houses. And for all that Copperroof is, it is still only a house."

* * *

They gathered in the Candlecomb on the last night of autumn, the King and Queen, the Duke and Duchess, Arete's ladies and attendants, and Yvon clinging to the King like a second shadow. The Candlecomb was a handsome room, small and warm, filled with honey-colored light and mirrors and the sweet mingling scents of wine and cinnamon. Paride held a deck of cards in his hands, and one by one the gathered company drew from it.

"The Ace of Roses," he said, checking Arete's hand.

She lay the card on the game table. "And what might that mean, brother? Am I to name every Empire that rose and fell between Remus and the Lampade? Or sing the seven songs of the Nephelean service?"

"Not that last, please," the King said, smiling. "God would fall in shock from his throne, hearing His name on your lips."

Paride bowed to his sister. "It means you must name a man whose love means more to you than your husband's."

The King's smile faltered, but the Queen waved a long-fingered hand and laughed like the cracking of ice. "Is that all?" she said. She turned to the King, curving a hand around his knee. "My son. Our son."

The King's eyes widened, golden in the candlelight. "You're certain?" he whispered.

Arete nodded. The King lifted her hand and kissed it, closing his eyes tightly. Yvon, standing with one pale hand on the marble mantelpiece, swept up the Ace of Roses and handed it to the Duke of Cloud. "You will have to devise a more difficult task for the next player," he said sharply.

Paride flushed scarlet and offered the deck to the King, who rose slowly, gripping a card as though it were a struggling viper. "The Queen of Crowns," he said.

"Well," Paride said, glancing at Yvon. "A more dif-

ficult task? I charge you—before God, who damns all falsehoods—to kiss on the mouth the man or woman in this room whom you love above all others. Is that difficult enough, my lord Yvon?"

"Yes," Yvon said. "But I motion that all present close their eyes to keep the King's choice a secret."

"Agreed," said the King, and all closed their eyes.

In the silence that followed, they heard the King stand and move about the room. It seemed to Paride that he went to the fireplace and stood there for a long moment before returning to his chair at Arete's side.

"It is done," the King said. "You may open your eyes."

Yvon and the Queen stared at each other and the gathered company glanced inquiringly about the room. At last Helene spoke, her voice cool. "Who was it?"

"Not I," Arete said, equally cold.

"Nor I," Paride laughed. "Give the King some privacy."

"It was the bust," Yvon said. All turned to him. On the mantle at his elbow, a handsome white bust of the King stood gleaming in the candlelight.

"Yes," the King said, "it was the bust. Now someone draw the next card, or let us be done with this game and retire. My wife and I have a child to celebrate."

While the others filed out, Yvon lingered near the fireplace. The King felt his eyes on him and paused in the doorway. Slowly, as if performing some act of great moment, Yvon went to the bust and placed a kiss on its cold white mouth.

* * *

By nightfall on the seventh day of the war, all Copperroof knew what the Queen had said. Conversation in salons and parlors was subdued; guests returned to their chambers in groups, and once there they locked their doors and moved armoires for barricades. All manner of arms disappeared from the archives, this time by less supernatural agencies. Now and then a scream would echo in a distant corridor, but no one wanted to investigate.

The Duke and Duchess of Cloud sat before their fireplace, playing a slow game of cards. Helene winced at every unfamiliar sound, though she had believed herself broken of the habit. Paride stared solidly at the cards in his hand.

"Do you really think a man is doing this?" Helene asked. "I thought so at first, but not with all of Copperroof terrorized. Who could be gaining from it?"

"No one in Copperroof." The Duke lay his card

on the wolfskin rug: the Knave of Roses. "But Arete is right. It can't be the house itself."

"Perhaps the ghosts…"

"The ghosts have fled, Helene. Listen." The only sound was the crackling of the fire. "There's the armor, which is … memories, old bloodlust. But it answers to men." He shrugged roughly. "Or it used to. No one's seen so much as a gauntlet since Saré disappeared."

Helene lay her card on top of her husband's: the Ten of Swords. "What about *them*?" she asked.

Paride shuddered. "The shadow-things? They aren't ghosts in their own right. Ghosts—human ghosts—have never caused us harm. But perhaps they too answer to someone." He did not look at their door, barricaded by a dressing table and the volumes of an old Encyclopaedia. "Someone outside of Copperroof."

"Paride, I think they *are* Copperroof."

He narrowed his eyes, still staring at the cards. She leaned over and pressed her fingers to his knee. "Can't you feel it, when they're nearby? They feel so angry, so betrayed. And there's a bit of fear, too—fear that the King will return."

"Why would Copperroof fear that?"

"Because it knows the King would stop it. It doesn't want to be kept on a leash."

"A feral house," the Duke said, laughing without humor. "But there is another possibility, love. It could well be a man outside of Copperroof who doesn't want the King to return." He raised his card: the Queen of Crowns. "Can you not think of one?"

* * *

Standing in the corridor outside the Candlecomb, Helene had overheard Paride and Yvon whispering as they lit candles for the King's gathering.

"You know it is Arete who lets you near him," the Duke said. "She is more forgiving than I. Given half a chance, I would turn you out in the snow."

"The King would never allow it," Yvon said. His voice was quietly rough, like the rustling of book pages. "Unless you would invent something—some unspeakable crime. Would the noble Duke of Cloud stoop to calumny to protect his Queen?"

"I would," Paride said. "But knowing you, you snake, I wouldn't have to lie. And I wouldn't trust your King so far."

Yvon made a muffled sound in his throat, halfway between a moan and a laugh.

"One word from Arete," the Duke said, "and he would slit your throat with his own hand."

The Duchess, hearing the ice in her husband's voice, stopped her ears and shivered.

* * *

On the tenth day of the war, Helene found the missing armor.

There was a helmet in her writing desk, a greave in her armoire, a glove in the case of her harpsichord. Breastplates filled her bath, and chainmail jangled when she opened the bedroom curtains. Laid across the bed she shared with Paride was the strange exotic sword, its hilt still gripped by a marble hand. She did not have to look in the shadow of her wardrobe to know that a pair of red eyes was there, watching.

She lifted her own bastard sword from its place on her bedside table, took the helmet from her writing desk, and went to see the Queen.

"I will not be stopped," she said to the maid at the door, "by a half-grown chit who hides behind a throne and a cradle while Copperroof falls around her head. I do not care if Arete is tired or sick or ready to brood a litter of dragons, she will hear me speak." And with the sword in one hand and the helmet in the other, the Duchess of Cloud pushed open the chapel doors.

The light in the chapel was cool and green, the light of water running beneath ice. Windows taller than seven men standing on each other's shoulders made a strange cage of the marble room, seeming harder and more substantial than the lengths of white stone between them. In the center of the harlequin floor was a cradle, and standing over the cradle, a tall woman in gray.

"So angry," the Queen said, gently chiding. "You'll wake the princess."

"If I heel like the dog you think I am, your child will have bigger concerns. Namely a house filled with corpses, one of which will be your brother."

Arete snapped her mouth open and shut, a clicking sound of disbelief. "My brother. And what does our fond superstitious Duke fear now? Are the walls caving in on him? Are the floors clamoring for his overthrow?"

"You know Copperroof is more than walls and floor," Helene said. "But the threat I fear comes from outside the house. *He* is trying to kill us." She flung the helmet at the Queen's feet. It rolled lopsided around the base of the cradle.

"Have you realized that?" the Queen said.

"All this time, it's been Yvon. Paride told me three nights ago, but I couldn't believe it, couldn't believe one man's anger and betrayal would be enough—"

"Yvon? Of course that's what he'd want you to think," Arete said. She bent and caught the rolling helmet on one finger. Helene could see the flash of her ring in its depths, like a single emerald eye. "But for all your prattling about Copperroof, you know so little of it. The archives, for example…" She leaned her head against the helmet's crown, eye to invisible eye. "While most of the armor is in the north wing, it belongs to the Dukes of Cloud. Did you know that?"

"It tried to kill us, whether it belongs to us or not."

"It tried to kill you, love." Arete let the helmet fall with an echoing clang. "Poor Helene. Armor is incapable of treachery. Like ghosts, and houses—and Yvon, in the end. It always obeys its master." She shrugged, sending black curls tumbling down her rigid back. "Its master is Paride."

"No." The Duchess of Cloud clenched her sword. Its weight felt too great for her arm. Her cut cheek stung, her injured eye burned with tears. "No. Not Paride." But the question burned in her mind; *Would the noble Duke of Cloud stoop to calumny to protect his Queen?* Did he hate Yvon so much?

The Queen smiled quietly, rocking the cradle with her foot. "No?" she said. "As you wish. It is very easy, I find, to keep one's illusions in Copperroof."

* * *

Yvon had approached her before the wedding began. He was all in black, with garnets on his fingers and in his ears. He did not smile, but neither did he weep, as Helene had seen other bitches do when their hounds changed collars.

"Your grace," he said, bowing over her with one hand on her chair arm. His hair smelled sweetly of orange blossoms and rain. "Would you give your husband a message from me?"

Helene nodded, glancing at the back of the hall. Paride stood beside the bride, brushing a black tendril of hair behind her ear.

"Tell him Arete must never know," Yvon said. "She would not bear it … gracefully. I suspect, in fact, that she would do something rash."

The Duchess tossed her head. "What must she never know?"

"Something I told Paride when we first met. Nothing to concern yourself with, your grace." He kissed her hand, his lips dry as paper. "Tell him also that I do not worry. He is very good at keeping secrets."

In the back of the hall, Arete laughed brightly. Her fingers worked deftly to braid a strand of hair with her brother's, midnight and gold.

* * *

Paride found her in the Hall of Empires. Helene stood very still, hands resting on the pommel of her sword, like a marble Queen in the Antechamber of the Most Holy Presence. It seemed she had been waiting for him for a long time; he could not say why he thought so, or why the thought frightened him.

"The noble Duke of Cloud," Helene sneered. Her breath looked like steam pouring past her copper-colored lips. "I should have guessed. But how was I to know your hatred ran so deep? Even when he is gone, you would bathe his name in blood."

Paride flinched, holding his hands as if to ward off a blow. He had heard that voice before, but from crueler, redder lips. "Where have you been?" he asked. "Who were you talking to?"

"Forget where I learned it. I want to know if it's true." Helene pointed over his shoulder at the length of the war-scarred hall. "Do you command the soldiers in the archives? Do you hate Yvon enough to murder in his name?"

The air in his lungs froze, became solid ice pressing against his heart. He took a step closer and caught her scent in the air, musky and bitterly sweet.

"Did you start the Copperroof war?" Helene asked.

He stopped in front of her and placed his hands over hers on the iron sword's pommel. "Yvon was a cruel man who took pleasure in tormenting my sister and my King," he said, "but no matter how much I hate him, you know I would not stoop to lies."

"But secrets and games are permissible, aren't they, your grace?" Helene bared her teeth, a cornered wolf. "Maybe it isn't Yvon you aim for. You've always been a jealous man, Paride, and most of all you envy your sister. She married a King, after all, and what are you saddled with? A poor tailor's brat."

"A tailor's brat I wouldn't trade for all the Kings in the world." He felt his heart breaking itself against the ice in his chest. "Believe me, love, I did not start this war. Not to hurt Yvon, and not to hurt Arete. I don't wish to command soldiers or wear a crown. I don't know how you came to suspect me—"

Helene ripped her hand from the sword and pressed it against her injured cheek. "The sword that gave me this belongs to the Duke of Cloud. Who but you has the right to that title?"

He caught her scent again—musk, and dead violets, and lilacs turned to dust.

"Where were you?" he whispered.

The Duchess drew herself up. "The chapel," she said.

Paride's grip tightened on the sword. "Arete."

* * *

The night before her wedding, Arete came to

her brother's study. Her face was white above her waistcoat checkered blue and gold—the colors of the Dukes of Cloud. Already her features seemed better suited to royal black and white.

"I had a terrible dream," she said. "I dreamed a voice was calling to me from the walls, begging me not to marry the King."

Paride pushed his chair back from his writing desk and folded his hands in his lap. "You're nervous," he said. "It's understandable. Before I married Helene—"

"I'm marrying the King, Paride. There's no reason to be nervous." Her teeth flitted across her lip. "Besides, it wasn't a normal dream. It felt like a warning. A warning to run away."

"A warning from who?"

Arete closed her eyes. He saw at once that she had already begun to look like a Queen; she seemed unbearably tired. "From Copperroof," she said.

Copperroof is only a house, he thought, but the words died on his lips. If Arete was to be Queen, there were things it would be better if she never knew.

* * *

Before he entered the chapel, Paride matched the strange marble-gripped sword to the King's statue in the Antechamber. His heart did not sink; it had already fallen to the deepest part of him. He lay the sword at the King's feet, like an offering, and went into the chapel.

Arete still stood over her daughter's cradle, the evening sunlight making a long needle of her shadow. She did not look up when the Duke entered, though she must have heard the door slam behind him.

"Why, Arete?"

She knelt slowly, brushing her child's cheek with one silky fingertip. "Why you?" she said. "Because it fit. It's perfectly true that the armor only answers to the Dukes of Cloud—I was a Duchess before I became Queen."

"You know what I'm asking."

"And how would you have me answer?" She looked at him for the first time, her eyes red in the setting sun. "This palace is a prison, love. Can I be blamed for playing a game to while away the time?"

"You tried to kill Copperroof!"

"I tried to kill you," Arete spat. "Copperroof is a *house*, Paride. It can't fight and it can't die."

She stood, leaning heavily on the cradle edge. The scent as she came near him was almost unbearable, as sweet and heady as rot. "You think I was jealous of this place because my husband loved it. As you think

I was jealous of Yvon. But I am incapable of jealousy, brother. The kindest thing I ever did was cast Yvon out of this place."

"Why would you show kindness to him?"

"Because I knew the King would follow him out." She did not smile, but her pale face softened. "I saved the man I loved most, and the man who loved him most. Now he will see everything he dreamed of—the mountains, and the sea."

He saw a flicker of movement in the shadows behind her, the flat red gleam of eyes.

"I must admit," she said, "that in the end Copperroof surprised me. I thought the north wing and the south wing would tear each other apart. I thought that old wounds given time to fester would poison this place anew."

"The hatred is yours," Paride said, watching as the shadows emerged from hiding at the feet of columns. The princess began to cry, a healthy sound of fear. Unthinkingly, Paride crossed the chapel and lifted his niece in his arms. "Why do you hate so much?"

"What else is there to do here?" Arete closed her eyes for a moment, sighing wearily. When she opened them again, they were flat and red.

Paride ran. He heard the hate-things running after him, and the sobbing of the child against his chest. The doors held for a moment, heavy as fear, but he pushed them open with his shoulder and ran to reclaim the King's sword. He thrust the blade through the handles like a bar on a prison door and leaned against it, heart pounding.

All was silent. Then Arete screamed.

The Duke stopped his ears, hunched over the sobbing princess. He felt the weight of the house around him, its anger, its betrayal. Its warning, stronger than all of them, not to open the chapel door.

It was a warning he heeded, even when the screaming stopped.

* * *

Yvon first appeared in Copperroof on a warm day in early spring. Paride walked with him through the halls, through the galleries and gardens, playing guide as the King had asked. Yvon was very quiet, until Paride paused by the chapel windows and asked him what he thought.

"It's pleasant enough," Yvon said, "but really, it's only a house. There's a whole world outside of Copperroof." He smiled, dazzling in the sunlight. "Didn't you know?"

* * *

The Duchess of Cloud paused at the edge of the

rose garden. She looked at her husband on the path beside her, his pale hair loose in the wind, his arms folded tightly around the child sleeping against his chest. The shadows that had darkened his eyes when she found him weeping at the chapel door were still there, like ghosts against a marble wall.

"This is the farthest I've ever been from Copperroof," Helene said.

Paride glanced over his shoulder. She knew what he saw in the distance; the great dead bulk of Copperroof, its windows curtained and dark, the rays of morning sunlight gilding its roof in fire.

Helene took his hand. "The King is never coming back," she said.

"It's only…" Paride began, but whatever he had to say died in a puff of ice on his lips.

Before their feet, snow stretched like a linen sheet to the black hills on the horizon. A road ran through the distant shadows, like a strand of silver in a woman's dark hair.

First Published in the June 2010 issue of *Ideomancer*

Let the Fire Decide

"We want to dance!"
Said orange and red,
"Anytime we get the chance,
We dance, and dance, and dance, and…"

White and blue sunk and sighed.
The wise ones, pale, thin and hot,
Were used to being pushed aside,
By the vaudeville show living on top.

Yellow pulled back,
Mulling it over,
Always last,
Thick and hot—
From in-between,
The base beneath the fire's blast.

The fire was lit for fairy tales,
Behind the local mega church.
Around the front, a child wailed,
As Brothers Grimm was ripped away.

"Who cares?" said red.
"For fire to dance, it needs to be fed!"

"You should care, you crazy beast,
You'd turn a Library into your feast."
That was blue piping in,
Then it disappeared and came back again.

White hissed, black smoke was forlorn,
Orange writhed its serpentine form,
It never cared once red was born.
Yellow couldn't really decide,
Either burn fairy tales or prepare to die.

White and blue already said nay,
Orange was for it, as red said yay.
That left the black, wispy carbon remains,
That spun off the top and always complained.
It was always yellow who had to decide,
To burn things up or refuse to light.

Should we stab the lore with a Baptist stake?
Yellow thought to itself amidst internal debate.

Before the pile of fantasy books,
The preacher preached and the children were hooked.

Men came to the fire with torches unlit,
But yellow pulled back and that was it.

Red shrank and screamed in bloody protest,
Orange beneath shut up and acquiesced.
Said Blue and White with a sigh of relief,
"Good call on that one.
That's why you're the chief."

Once the fire had put itself out,
The men couldn't figure what that was about.
It wasn't raining and plenty of air,
But for years to come no fire would burn there.

— Sarah Wright

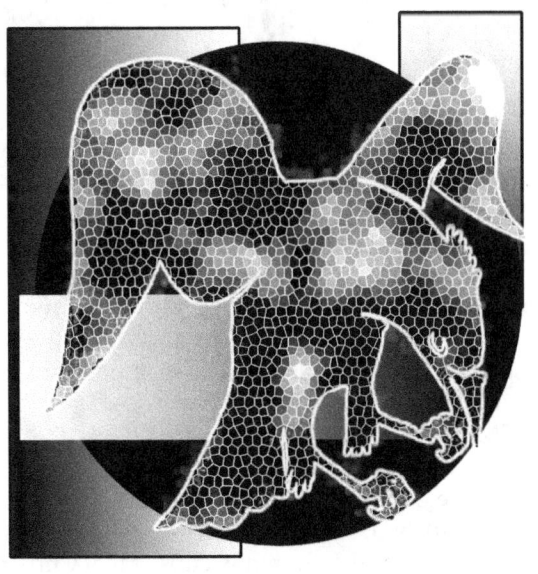

Nativity

Story by Frances Silversmith
Illustration by Shoshana Holl

"Meow."

Kris ignored the cat and continued to stare at her cup of Wassail. A tear dropped into the drink. Her divorce had gone through yesterday. After two years of separation, it shouldn't hurt so much anymore, should it?

"MEOW!"

This time, Kris did look up. "What…?"

:Come on, let's go out to the stable:

She flinched, startled, and looked around for the source of the voice. How many cups of that Christmas punch had she had? It couldn't have been more than two, surely.

"Meow." The cat walked towards the door, tail up. When Kris opened the door, Whiskey stayed where she was, tilting her head up to look expectantly at her human.

"You want me to come out with you?"

Well, why not? It wasn't as if she had anything better to do on this lonely Christmas Eve. "All right, let me get my coat."

Why was she talking to her cat?

:Get the Wassail bowl and two cups, while you're at it:

Kris looked around once more. She was alone with the cat.

Feeling more than a bit silly, she went into the kitchen and collected the required items. Why two cups? What cruel tricks was her subconscious mind playing? But she took the second cup.

Once outside, Whiskey led the way to the barn. Kris opened the door—and froze. The horses had gotten free of their stalls, as had the donkey. The sheep had come in from the meadow, and even the chickens had joined the party in the open area reserved for the cows.

Kris stepped all the way into the stable. She stared at the old hearth, left over from a time when the barn had been part living area. Someone had swept the straw away from the hearth, and a merry fire burned in it. Two piles of horse blankets lay close to it.

:Welcome, Kris. Come, sit. It's a special night, let's celebrate together:

That was a different voice than before. Kris turned and met the eyes of … Dusty, her riding horse.

She shook her head, attempting to clear it. Wasn't there an old story that told of animals talking to people on Christmas? A special night, indeed. She would try to understand all this—later. She set the Wassail bowl down next to the fire and sat down on one of the horse blanket piles.

The barn door opened. There stood Paul, her old High School sweetheart who lived on the neighboring farm. When her husband had left Kris, Paul had offered to assist her with the farm work. He adamantly refused to accept payment for the considerable time he spent helping her.

"Hello, Kris," Paul said. "You'll think I'm silly, but I could have sworn that the animals called me. I had to come here and check on them."

"Come on in," Kris said, glancing at the animals in the barn. To the last chicken, they were watching Paul and her. Dusty and Whiskey both looked smug. "You know, I believe they did call you." She watched Paul step in and close the door. "Would you like to have a cup of punch with me?"

"I'd love to," he said and smiled, unexpected tenderness in his eyes.

Kris smiled back.

The Expanding Universe

Seven eons following the Big Bang
Quark, the great sea monster,
rose from the waters into the darkness of the land.
He plucked his string like scales
Ethyl, a copper serpent, surfaced next to him.
Quark commanded, "Acclaim my strength and beauty."
Ethyl touched vibrating strings
whispered in his ear,
"I think dear Quark this space is much too dark."
As Ethyl spoke the egg of wisdom
from her vibrant body burst.
And Quark said, "Nourish the egg of wisdom
upon this spinning rock which I shall call Earth"

Then Quark created man and woman
and decreed, "admire my stringy scales."
And they did speak, "I think dear Quark
your earth is much too dark."

They fooled around until
their first child was born on earth.
Quark was dismayed by all the fuss of birth.

Quark created god and said, "Oversee my Earth.
I've new galaxies to generate."
Quark disappeared into the dark universe.
God told Ethyl to fry the egg of wisdom.
"Sunny side up is good," he said.
"I want my wisdom bright."
Then god created light so humans could adore him.

Quark seeds new rocks
in expanding space
and wonders still why no one will
admire his golden scales.

In far off Earth
humans wait for wisdom's birth.

— John Hayes

Story by:
M.E. Garber

Illustration by:
Tom Kelly

Survival of the Wolf

Darra twitched awake. Her racing heart slowed as she took in the crude roof overhead, the familiar scents of home. Safe. She blinked, relief washing tension from her body.

She rolled to standing. Pain radiated from her left shoulder, and her right hip ached. Her breath hitched as her ribs moved.

Damn-the-gods. That one would take a while to heal.

At least she was home. She couldn't count the number of times she'd woken in some strange field, miles from home. Or worse.

Her cabin door banged open. She spun and crouched in a defensive stance, naked but for a pelt covering her shoulders.

From outside came crunch of stone, a familiar stink of corruption. She stood straighter, but her back remained tense and every suppressed ache set her teeth on edge.

The witch stepped into her doorway, surveyed her battered body.

Even after all this time, some eight years, she didn't know his name. Didn't care. He was just 'The Witch.' And her master.

He looked down his lean frame at her and his lips twitched. It was as close as he came to smiling, and it raised the hairs on Darra's neck and arms.

"Good. You're relatively unhurt."

Darra said nothing, just kept her eyes on him the way a beaten dog watches the man with the stick.

"Come to my cabin tomorrow for dinner. I have a new assignment for you."

"Why not just send me now?" She couldn't keep the anger out of her voice. She didn't want to do this anymore, hadn't wanted to from the beginning.

The witch didn't flinch or react in any way. His reply was complacent.

"I need you strong enough to survive. It's hard finding one to wear the cape so long, and I don't want to abuse my privilege."

"Get me killed, you mean." She spat the words at him, shaking with fury.

"Correct. A dead guardian does me no good."

"But my *pain*, my *suffering*—none of that matters?"

"You accepted the terms."

"I had no choice!"

Darra stepped closer and stood before the witch, her shoulders hunched and her head low before her body, elbows splayed and arms wide. Her joints ached in that familiar way, and her jawbone creaked and snapped. The protective enchantment was too strong. Still she tried, and her skin buzzed and stung as if a cloud of biting flies had settled upon her. She couldn't harm the one who controlled the pelt.

The witch looked down at her, a thin frown creasing his brow before he turned and walked back the way he'd come. "Tomorrow," he said loud enough for her to hear as he disappeared into the dark shadows of the woods.

Darra's eyes followed him, finding the weak points to rend, to shred. Finding ways to bring down her prey. She ignored the lancings of pain such thoughts brought her. *This* pain she was used to.

She remained vigilant until she heard him enter his cabin on the other side of the small wood. Then she sagged against her small table, just for a moment. With a soft sigh, she went to wash.

The greasy wolf's pelt cape swung around her shoulders as she poured water into her small basin. Seeing it, Darra's lips pulled back in a snarl. Its curse kept her tied to this horror of a life. It haunted her days, marking her for all to see as the witch's beast. She wished for the thousandth time to be rid of it, to be free of its stink and corruption.

Shaking her head, she turned away and rinsed herself. The water in the basin ran brown with dried blood. She threw it out, rinsed herself again, paying special attention to her ragged fingernails which were thickly embedded with blood and gobbets of flesh.

She kept her mind blank. When she finished, her hands were clean again. Innocent-looking. She dressed in a coarse homespun shift—she'd long ago given up caring about clothing—and limped outside.

She made her way to the sunny patch planted with soft sweet-smelling grasses and eased to sitting among the plants. Sunlight washed over her, soothing her aches and baking the stinks out of the fur. She drowsed as her body mended.

Her mind drifted to her family. She watched again as her nephew's color changed from blue-pale to healthy-pink, as his painful rasps turned to soft, steady breathing. Morg, her sister, collapsed onto the bed, weeping her relief.

A grasping hand had fallen onto Darra's shoulder.

"We must go," the witch said.

"Kellar will live?" she'd asked, trying to buy time. The answer was obvious. With Kellar healed, Morg and her daughters wouldn't lose their holdfast. They would continue to live under the protection of a male. They were safe. Now Darra had to fulfill her bargain with the witch.

She'd hugged her two young nieces, pretending not to notice as they shrank away.

With this last look at her family, she had ducked out the door and into a nightmare.

Now *she was* the nightmare.

Darra never remembered being in wolf form, but bits of memory floated into her consciousness. Half-remembered scenes toyed with her, as they always did after a run. She glimpsed a woman in a cabin's dim half-light, her arm raised to protect herself as she pulled away. The woman's face was familiar. Darra blocked out the features she knew too well, and the memory flowed on, the stink of fear exciting her in unnatural ways.

The wet, sucking sounds of rending flesh overlaid onto fading screams. A scent she could only describe as 'terror' filling her mouth with saliva and making her heart race and her paws twitch with anticipation. The wild joy in shaking and shaking *and shaking* the thing in her jaws until it stopped squirming, stopped scratching at her muzzle, beating at her neck and shoulders. The ecstasy of her strength and power surging through body as she ran prey off its feet and made a frenzied kill.

The memory-flashes kept on until Darra moaned under the weight of them. Still half-asleep, she panted with her anxiety to be away, to not recall. Her human mind would not cope....

When she'd begun, Darra had put these thoughts out of her mind, refused them. They'd built up until she couldn't deny them, or the evidence of her eyes—bloody mouth, gore embedded under nails and between her teeth, her aches corresponding to the dreams' injuries. She'd retched and gagged for weeks. Then she'd begged the witch to release her from his service.

"Please take it off. I'll do anything else. *Anything.* But don't make me do this. You *can't* make me do this."

"But you're doing it. You agreed, and now you have no choice," had been his dismissive reply.

And so she'd stopped thinking, stopped wondering who or why. The repressed memories remained firmly repressed. After all, as the witch said, she had no choice. It was *his* sin. She was merely the tool.

One day, she promised herself. One day she would be free. Still sleeping, she growled.

* * *

Darra stepped into the clearing before the witch's stone cabin. As always when she approached this place, unease slid between her shoulder blades, and cold dread settled into the pit of her stomach. She sniffed at the air, worried at the smell of roasting meat

that wafted out to meet her. The better the meal, the worse the assignment that came after.

She stomped into the cabin, not bothering to knock. A roast haunch of venison and root vegetables covered the table before the fire. The witch waited for her there, and scowled as she gorged herself. She couldn't help it. Her body healed quickly, but it needed great reserves of energy to survive the transformations. She might hate herself, but she still wanted to survive, to find a way to freedom.

Darra tamped down her anger as the witch spoke.

"Tonight someone is coming. I do not trust him. You will remain here, prepared for trouble."

Her hand gripped the edge of the scarred table, her nails curling into the wood. Even the hint of threat brought the tingle of transformation to her edges. Pain twisted through her as fingernails became claws.

"This man would try to kill you here, in your lair?" She couldn't believe anyone could be so foolish.

"His name is Damballa. He is another witch."

The prickle of unease rippled down her spine. She felt the muscles elongate, the bones shift slightly in her shoulders and hips. She suppressed the whimper of pain, but a small gasp escaped.

The witch nodded in approval. Her human eyes would not have been able to see the slight curve on his mouth, but her half-changed eyes saw. And she smelled the emotions on him—pride, anxiety, and a forced calm overall.

Darra leaned back and bared her teeth in a tight smile, enjoying the power of these half-wolf senses. If his increased pulse-rate meant she scared the witch, well, so much the better.

The moon rode high above the trees when the other witch drew near. From a distance, she smelled the threat of his magic like smoke and flame. And something else. Someone came with this witch. Darra paced to the door and back, nervous with the unexpected change.

"Guardian. Go sit in the alcove," her witch ordered.

Darra slunk to the small niche by the hearth and curled herself within. She hovered at the edge of transformation. Tension trembled in her muscles, her bones ached. She longed for the release transformation would bring—the pain for an eyeblink, then she'd be free.

She shook her head. *No!* She wouldn't let herself look forward to being the beast, the tool of the witch. She curled more tightly into the alcove, trembling as she hugged furry knees to her chest.

The cabin door swung open. The other witch, Damballa, was a thin young man, his head shaved smooth. In one hand he carried a glowing birch staff which illuminated the cabin like daylight. Two round-eyed twelve-year olds accompanied him, one gliding in before him, the other drifting after. They too were lean and bald, and they wore thin robes that glittered in the light. A scent of salt and fish wafted in with them.

Damballa's head swiveled until he found Darra. She saw him smile, then turn to her witch, dismissing her.

"I see you are not alone after all, Sconsious."

"And neither are you." Darra's witch gestured to the children.

The children were given mugs of water and sent to sit by the door. Their wide eyes roved the room as they sipped. Darra knew they sensed her, but they refused to look at her. She yawned her unease and focused on the two witches, now seated at the table.

They spoke in soft voices. Even with her acute hearing, Darra couldn't make out their words. The tension fizzing in the air sputtered out. She relaxed as the minutes stretched into an hour, then longer. The scent of sweetgrass washed over her, and she leaned into the warm stone. Her eyes blinked, then closed.

A scream shuddered through the air. Pain knifed through her body. She howled in agony. The transformation ripped her muscles and bones, re-knit them according to their needs. Mercifully, her mind blacked out.

But the howl carried on until a huge werewolf scrambled to its feet where Darra had collapsed. Its eyes glowed with hate and fury, pain having sent it mad. It leaped to defend its master, the one smelling of death and decay, snarling as it threw itself onto a small shimmering thing that hung onto the witch's arm.

The shimmering thing turned a wide mouth filled with needled teeth toward the wolf and lunged. Darra-wolf snarled, then yiped as another set of teeth ripped into her haunch. Swirling around, she saw the air ripple around the small things. The barracuda-changelings darted around her, snapping and ripping her flesh. They flashed through the air as if it were water, there and gone before Darra could turn.

A maddening fury overwhelmed her. She became a whirling ball of teeth and claws. She leaped, smashing her weight against the smaller barracudas, scoring their scaled sides with her claws. First one, then the other barracuda-child was seized behind the head, shaken and flung onto the hearth. The impact released the magic. The lean predator-fish shuddered, then shimmered. In their place, children in scaled tunics lay upon the stones.

Werewolf-Darra flung herself upon them, ripping them to shreds as scales and flesh flew through the cabin. Turning about, she sought more prey.

Her master lay gasping by the door. She crept toward him, fear and duty warring within her. His right arm was sheared off just above the elbow. The missing arm lay by his feet, the hand still clutching a broken wand. A lingering smell of brimstone made her rumble deep in her chest.

"Darra. You must...." He trailed off, his eyes blinking closed.

The werewolf panted, confused and conflicted. The blood coating the room excited her. Her master lay wounded, and needed her to be human to help him. She felt the tingle that preceded transformation in her ears-tips. She whined, then backed away as she bared her teeth in a silent snarl.

Humans nursed their injured; the werewolf understood this. But wolves killed them. And the werewolf wanted to kill. If she could only hold off his command.... She sensed a way to freedom.

Darra whirled toward the door and growled as if she'd sensed an intruder.

The witch jerked his head off the floor. "Attack him!" He gasped, pointing his remaining hand toward the open door.

The werewolf bounded out the door, eager to be gone, to pursue and destroy. The scent of her prey lured her onwards, through the night and into the dawn. The essence of his magic lingered, kept her fear strong and her anger fresh, while the quivering edge of her transformation buzzed her muscles and etched her brain like acid. She raced away from Sconsious, towards liberation.

The glare of mid-morning stung, but she did not stop. She whined and raced onward.

Villages passed in a blur. People screamed and ran; some after her, most away. The werewolf wanted to race them down, to shake them until they stopped—stopped running, stopped screaming, stopped taunting her with their freedom. But the compulsion to do her master's final bidding kept her pursuing her target. Her pursuers quickly fell behind.

The sun rose higher. The urge to run faltered, gave her a moment's reprieve. Darra paused at a streamlet trickling through the deep shadows of a forest. Here it was cool despite the heat of the day. Her sides heaved and her tongue sagged to the side.

The pine scents eased her anguish. The chill water soothed her throat as she drank. But a strange tingling filled her skin, racing like fleas in her fur. She took a step, shaking herself like a wet dog. Then she was down, howling as pain wracked her body. She flung herself about, but the biting and stinging drove deeper and deeper, until the world went dark.

* * *

Darra sat up. The world spun. She put a hand down to steady herself, touched pine needles, sticky and deep. A forest, near dusk. She inhaled, smelled the resin of pine and a distant brine. The sea must be near.

Her body ached everywhere. Her legs trembled, too weak to allow her to stand. Gashes ripped her buttocks, her thighs. Great scabs covered her cheeks and hands. Her feet and palms were raw and sore. She had run far.

A breeze ruffled her hair and made the trees above her sough. Darra shivered. She felt more naked than usual. Her dress was shreds, barely holding together—typical. But her back felt … cold.

Darra raised a shaking hand to her shoulder. No fur cape met her fingers. She slapped her hand across her back and neck. The pelt was missing. It wasn't attached to her. Ignoring the pain knifing through her body, she whirled into a crouch, patting the ground around her.

Pine needles, small branches, a stone … and there! Fur, greasy and rough. Darra pulled it toward her, lifted the small cape into her lap as she stared down at it.

It looked so small, so paltry. Her shoulders itched without its accustomed weight and warmth. It lay like an ancient dead thing, smelling of decay. She shook her head, unable to understand.

A flash filled her mind: the witch was dead! Without his command, it was merely a pelt, an artifact.

She was free!

Her heart flew at the thought. Freedom….

Darra quailed.

She had no one, nothing. Whatever family was left, they were dead to her. The village knew her for a monster, the witch's thing. Without his protection, they'd kill her on sight. *His* was the sin, but she was the tool they'd seen. They'd settle their vengeances upon her. Fear and hate: she smelled them still.

Darra scuttled into a tighter ball, cradling the pelt in her lap. Her tears watered and washed it as she clutched it to her. Freedom smelled of cold and fear, hunger and death.

Around her, the forest was settling to sleep. Darra curled into a tight ball and pulled the pelt over her, inhaling its aromas, finding comfort there.

The witch Damballa couldn't be far now. His guardians were dead. He'd activate the enchantment on her pelt. He'd grant her that solace in return for her fidelity. He had to. She had no other choice.

Darra rose to her feet, swaying as the pain caught at her. Slowly, stumbling over roots and tripping in the darkness, she made for Damballa's. She would not sleep. She did not want to dream or remember. Not tonight.

She only wanted to survive.

Gambling in the Magickian's House

I was a card shark, quick with the cut—
hard deal, fast turnover, ace up the sleeve—

working the Magickian's House—full-court
gentleman's club, steeped with occult flavor.

Just past the ballroom, hard at a table with
the rougher crowd, I played magickians

for their trinkets, small spells, played the
swells for their rings, finer things. My

hat tilted, garter clear and ribboned, silk
stockinged feet slipped free of shoes.

Champagne, fine and chilled, spilled into
crystal; jack of hearts, suicide king,

shuddered under my sharp, clear gaze, drank
up, paid dear. He was no trump, though,

standing suspendered, jacket slung over one
shoulder, full beard. He also was no hand at cards.

Smiling, no diamond, no club would turn him
to win; he called spades first, brushed the table

with hearts, queening. Still, he lost. It was
a shame to steal him, beautiful, hat in hand,

the hat he took with no little grace from off
my head. I cajoled him to another game,

gambled for the ring on his finger. When
his last card fell, I thought I heard him

moaning. No, his mouth quirked. Deftly,
he placed the ring on my finger, hat

on my head. His hand molded the air,
suddenly, arching the aethyr. The room

stilled with a plaintive jerk. The room
tilted. Too late, I knew his eyes. Play

the Magickian's House lightly, dears.
Weavers lie there, and rings are tricky things

for removing. Moving in the ballroom now,
I miss the messier days at the card tables,

stand still and branded on his arm, let
his mouth move me to laughing, brief

gestures, like moaning, tangling my heart
in his sleeve. The ring on my finger

a sparkling, royal flush.

— Alicia Cole

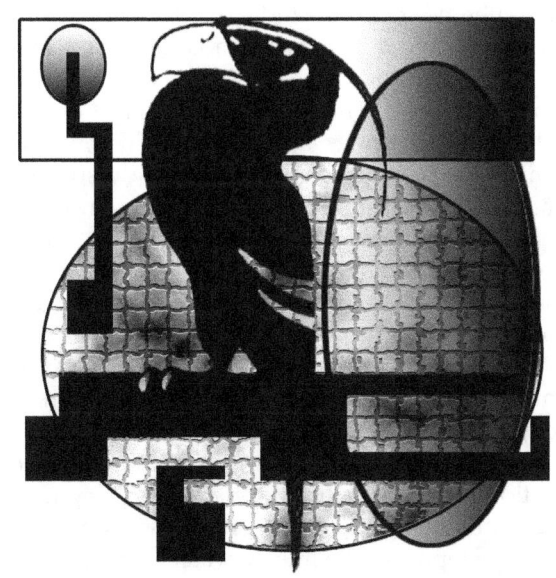

Dear Cthulhu

by
Patrick Thomas

Dear Cthulhu,

I'm seven years old and this summer, my family and I are going to spend a couple weeks up in the Finger Lakes area. My brother tells me that they're called that because they're filled with real fingers. I think he's lying to try and freak me out.

What's the real story?

— Curious in Cortland

Dear Cortland,

The Finger Lakes got their name many years ago because of a bizarre human courtship ritual. Beautiful women would go to stand near the lake shore. Gentlemen callers would approach them and attempt to impress the women, often with gifts of gold, jewelry and sometimes tracts of land.

There came a time when a competition arose among two determined suitors about who was more in love with a certain young woman. Each of them pledged their fortunes and their very lives, but the woman was unimpressed. After many displays of wealth and privilege, one man was driven to such desperation to prove his love and devotion that he stood over a lake, took out a knife and cut off his own finger. He let it fall into the water. His incredibly idiotic act of self-mutilation won of the lady's heart and they were soon wed. As is apt to happen among humans, this stupidity inspired more and even greater idiocy. For years thereafter men—and the occasional woman—would attempt to prove their love and devotion to their significant others by coming to the lakes, cutting off a finger and letting it sink down into the black depths of the murky waters. This is one of the reasons they say the fish there still have a taste for human flesh. This was despite the fact that the original couple's marriage did not last. She cheated on her husband with their milk man. The husband in his rage decapitated his wife and put her head in the man's milk vats. Strangely they did not change the brand name to Decapitation Milk or the like.

Sadly, in recent years the finger slicing tradition has fallen out of favor and is frowned upon. But now you know the reason they named them the Finger Lakes. That or because they look like fingers when viewed on a map. I often get the two explanations mixed up.

Dear Cthulhu,

My baby's mama is getting to be a real pain in my rump if you know what I mean. I've been living here with her for the last three months, ever since our little bundle of joy—and by joy I mean misery—was born. The ho and I met in a bar one night. I'll admit she's a little bit out of my league, but the fact that she was drunk and some guy slipped a ruffie into her booze didn't hurt my chances. I saw the guy do it and I told him if he didn't leave the bar I'd blow the whistle. He took off for the hills, which is good because there's no reason he should benefit from such a heinous act. But since it was already done, there was no reason I shouldn't, especially since I was doing the right thing by running him off.

When the ho woke up the next morning, it took me about 15 minutes to get her to stop screaming. She didn't remember anything about the night before, so I showed her a video I took. The ho was ticked, screaming that she was a virgin and had been saving herself for marriage.

I told her it's her own fault for not keeping her pants on and that she really wasn't that great in the sack and if she wanted to be better she needed to practice a lot more. I even offered to help. The ho had the nerve to threaten to call the cops. I took off, figuring I'd never see her again. Unfortunately, I left my wallet behind and she found my driver's license. Pity, because otherwise she never would have found me, even if for some reason she didn't believe my name was James Bond.

I got a call from her a few months later, saying that she was pregnant. I told her there's no way that baby was mine. She said I was the only guy she ever did it with, which was a crock far as I was concerned. I mean, I never met a virgin over fourteen. I told her I watched talk shows and wanted to go on one to get a paternity test.

We went. Unfortunately, the paternity test showed that I was indeed the baby's daddy. This particular ho believes in family values and that kinda crap. She thinks that every baby should have a mommy and daddy. She even offered to marry me. Apparently in her religion it's a big deal if parents aren't married. I told her no way, that I wasn't gonna be tied down.

Then I told her she would have to pay me for child support. Using a recording of the show, the court took money out of my welfare check to pay *her* child support. That's what I get for doing a good deed and helping her out in the bar that night. I shoulda let her go home with the guy who ruffed her. That would've taught the ho a lesson.

The ho offered to let me move in with her so I could help her raise the baby. I figured free rent and free nookie was a deal I couldn't pass up. Turns out she's making me sleep in the guest bedroom, so there ain't no hanky or panky going on. She breastfeeds right in front of me, which makes me nuts because her knockers got so freaking huge. The ho won't let me near them, but she lets the baby. I told her she shouldn't be showing her boobs to no baby and I was going to call the cops and report her as a child molester if she didn't let me have a go at them. She didn't, so I called 911. They laughed and hung up.

After that, she says I need to carry my weight. She wants me to do chores, wash the dishes, clean the house and have dinner ready when she gets home. And she had the nerve to say I wasn't doing a good job watching the brat. Every morning after she leaves for work, I put him in his crib, throw in a couple of bottles and duct tape some cardboard over the top so he can't get out. The brat cries all day long, but do I complain? No I do not. I just turn up the volume on the TV to drown it out like any good dad would.

Then the ho has the nerve to accuse me of not changing his diaper all day. I tell her that all that poop and pee happens right before she gets home. Might be true even since I never check. What would be the point? I ain't touching no dirty, stinky diaper. It's enough that I remember to take the cardboard and duct tape off before she gets home so she don't have to do it.

The ho's given me a week to shape up or ship out. I don't think it's fair. In fact, I think she should pay me for providing day care. Can I sue her for alimony and child support? Maybe back pay for being her day care worker? Can I get a judge to make her do all the chores that interrupted my day with all this nonsense? Or fake an injury and make her pay me for worker's comp?

— Proud Pappy In Peekskill

Dear Proud,

In nature, many animals eat their young. In your case, I think the reverse would be justified. Sadly human babies have neither the teeth nor jaw strength to make that practical.

In order to get alimony, you have to first be married. And in order to get child support you have to be the one taking care of the child. Since you are not wed and what you are doing with your offspring sounds more like neglect and abuse, you qualify for neither. No reasonable judge will make the child's mother do those chores and since you are the child's biological father, not only are you not an employee but have an obligation to take care of your offspring.

Your options are simple. Do what your child's mother requests or move out. I recommend the latter, because it sounds like they would both be better off without you in their lives.

Dear Cthulhu,

I'm five years old and I got a kitten for Christmas. It was the most wonderful little cat in the world. He would play with string and let me pet him all day long. I named him Buttons. One day a month ago, Buttons got out and we couldn't find him. It was a snowy day and my family had been making a snowman and we didn't see where he went. We looked for weeks, even put up flyers and signs, but no Buttons. Then we got a warm day and the snow melted. We found Buttons dead on the lawn. We had a funeral and buried him. After the funeral, my big sister whispered in my ear that the snowman we made had come to life and eaten Buttons, then pooped him out onto the lawn underneath the snow. I think she's making it up, especially since all the snowman on the Christmas specials are happy, friendly and don't eat pets.

I've been having nightmares about snowmen chasing me and trying to eat me as a herd of cats run by me. They all have Buttons's face. I need to know the truth. Can snowmen come alive and eat cats? Or kids? The weatherman is saying we're supposed to get a big blizzard this weekend. My parents are already talking about making another snowman. I need to know whether or not I have to stop them.

Thank you.

— Five years old and Missing Buttons.

Dear Missing,

Most snowmen do not even have a chance of doing anything but melting. For a snowman to come to life, it requires dark magic far beyond what the average human could manage. However there could be an evil wizard or witch in your neighborhood that is going around and bringing snowmen to life. And if that is the case, you are lucky all it ate was a kitten. One evil snowman broke into a family's house and devoured them all. He almost got away with it too, but made the mistake of crossing in front of the fireplace and melted.

I checked the weather report for your area and they are saying it is going to be good packing snow. I suggest putting the heat in your house up to ninety degrees and sleeping with an acetylene torch instead of a Teddy Bear just in case.

Have A Dark Day.

Dear Cthulhu welcomes letters and questions at DearCthulhu@dearcthulhu.com. All letters become the property of *Dear Cthulhu* and may be used in future columns. *Dear Cthulhu* a work of fiction and satire and is © and ™ Patrick Thomas. All rights reserved. Any one foolish enough to follow the advice does so at their own peril. For more *Dear Cthulhu* get the collections *Dear Cthulhu: Have A Dark Day* and *Dear Cthulhu: Good Advice For Bad People* and *Cthulhu Knows Best* from Dark Quest Books. Learn more at www.dearcthulhu.com.

Changeover

The creature is old,
new ones will supersede it.

It's not the wrinkles on the face,
it's the contortions of the mind.

It's not the great achievements,
it's the miserable shortcomings.

The path has come to an end,
a whole new one is brewing for others.

— Alessio Zanelli

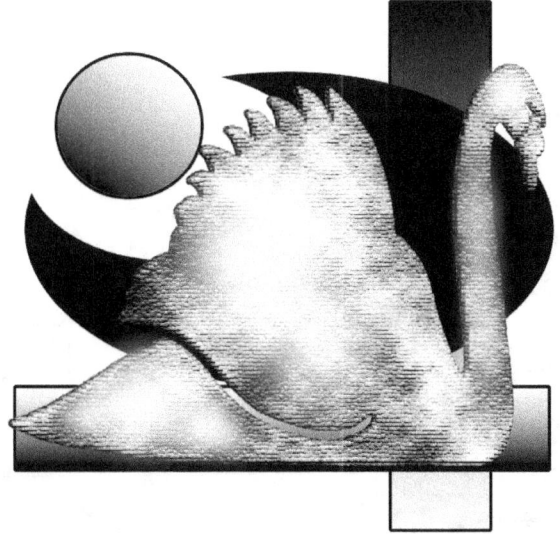

Intelligent Illusion

They stretch out pseudopods—
interlacing, interconnecting, becoming
a vast mat of intelligence
beneath the red surface sand.

An amoeboid brain subsiding on
soil perchlorates and nitrates.
A colony of individual cells,
independent thoughts …

Another object is falling!
Then we have mere moments!
What do we do?
Slide out of the way—like before.

And when they don't find us?
They'll give up—eventually.
Or come here themselves.
But how many? What shape? What size?

We can't hide forever.
Some will be caught.
Or killed—
Our intelligence diminished.

I've got a plan—let's vibrate
to generate heat.
Yes! We could melt this ice …
And flood their object!

That might discourage them!
But there's no time.
It's too close.
Scatter!

To Earth's disappointment,
the rover Curiosity
finds only
barren ground.

— Lauren McBride

Breaking Down

Story by Edward J. McFadden III
Illustration by Jag Lall

Lester Troupe sat with his back against the wall, watching the procession as it made its way through the throng of onlookers. Unmodified humans weren't allowed to participate in the ceremony, or enter the nave, but there was a separate viewing area in the rear of the church for anyone who wanted to watch the proceedings up close. The area was cordoned off, a glass wall separating the congregation from those who wanted to witness their traditions, or just gawk at what some considered nothing more than a collection of freaks. The viewing area was required so the *Gathering for the Future* could maintain its tax exempt status—even in 2062 the United States tax code was still king.

Lester's face twisted in a scowl as a pain shot up his spine. He winced, bending backward in an attempt to stretch his contracting muscles. His neck hurt, and his morning breakfast was having a party in his stomach that was chasing bile up his throat.

The sanctuary of *Gathering for the Future* looked very little like a traditional church on the inside. There was no altar, but a stage. No gold chalices or candlesticks, but detailed schematics of various transhumanist body modifications hung from the walls between old patchwork stained glass windows. Instead of pews, folding chairs filled the open space in organized rows. There was nothing special about the place except its people.

Some members didn't look any different than normal human beings, their skeletal enhancements, eyelid view-screens, tattoo displays, and internal computer and communication implants hidden or invisible to the naked eye. Then there were those who wore their transcendental ideals on their sleeves, sporting yellow ultra-vision eyes, modified limbs, various weapons enhancements, and more than a few skin pigment colorations.

Pain throbbed in Lester's right knee, and he felt the tendonitis in his elbow begin to act up. He closed his eyes, taking in a deep breath of air and letting it out slowly. His ex-wife liked to call him Less, with an emphasis on the double S. Linda was a modi-human who kept her enhancements private, and Lester hadn't even known about them before they were married. Linda came from middle-class roots, and he had no idea how she had managed to afford her enhancements, or the system upgrades that she got every six months, but none of that was his problem any longer.

Body modifications were usually installed to either correct or prevent a problem, or to enhance the human body's rudimentary design and function. These modifications, while extremely expensive and accessible to only a fraction of the population, served to create an upper class that not only had fiscal superiority of the masses, but now physical advantages as well. Internal nano-computers which grew titanium reinforced bones, or devices that could inject chemicals into the body to enhance performance in a variety of ways, were common amongst the upper class and those who had mortgaged their futures for a better now. Life extension, gene therapy disease prevention, and a multitude of energy and brain power enhancements created a subset of the human race that was quickly pulling away from the rest of Earth's inhabitants. These were the people who stared mortality in the face and said, "Screw you."

Then there were those who had motion-tattoos covering every inch of the exposed portions of their bodies. These motion-tattoos advertised numerous products, from body enhancements to the newest designer drugs. Often, these ads were used to pay for legitimate licensed modifications, or to enhance underground modifications that could be had much more cheaply than the licensed and regulated upgrades. Black market upgrades created a sub-class within the modi-human community, where no-frills, cobbled-together upgrades often failed at the worst moments.

Lester's neck ached, and he slowly rotated his head in a counterclockwise circle, stretching and trying to be casual about it. It was no secret that those who sat behind the viewing window wanted to be on the other side of the glass, and each had their own reasons, but none of the reasons qualified for a government incentive, or a job related upgrade. In fact, most of the folks who sat alongside Lester were like him: out of work, and addicted to their virtual realties that they wasted their lives in. On the nets, modifications didn't matter: everyone was equally desperate and pathetic.

With a sigh, Lester leaned forward and rested his elbows on his knees, watching intently as the night's speaker made his way to the front of the seated guests. No one spoke, and all of the ceremony's participants had shut off their data feeds, amped down their sensors, and were doing their best to fight and enhance their paper-thin attention spans.

The speaker wore a blue tunic and, had it not been for the lack of a long grey beard, Dr. Nikolai Fyodorov would have looked like a wizard missing his trademark pointed hat. When he reached the podium, utter silence fell as he shuffled through a thin stack of papers, selecting one to his liking, then looking up and measuring the crowd. A smile spread across his face as he looked at his flock, and Lester felt the pit of his stomach go cold. The man's dark eyes paused briefly on the tiny throng gathered behind the glass wall, and his face changed from pride and appreciation, to one of disgust and loathing. Most modi-humans felt superior to unmodified humans, but still managed to be human enough to feel sorrow and pity for others less fortunate than they, but there were those—hardcore transhumanists like Dr. Fyodorov—who felt that they were the future of humanity, and those who had chosen not to join them in their transcendence were nothing more than peasants created to serve their higher goals.

"My dear friends," began Fyodorov, as he shifted from one foot to the other. "Today I am here to talk to you about the next step. The next action that will put us that much closer to transcendence. Not to heaven, or any other crude representation of bliss, but closer to a world in which there is no hardship, no death, and no suffering." Fyodorov stopped there, letting his words sink in.

That was Lester's cue to leave.

He rose and moved quickly from the viewing room, pushing his way through the large wooden doors of the old Catholic church that had been purchased by the *Gathering for the Future* when the Roman Catholic Church went broke and was forced to close and sell more than half of its worldwide holdings back in 2032. He enjoyed watching the modi-humans, but once they started preaching, he felt the crap running a little high around his boots.

The air outside was thick with pollution and Lester coughed, thinking how great it would be to have an internal breathing filter installed in his windpipe. The air smelled of chemicals, human sweat, and shit. The stars were blotted out by dense clouds of pollution, and Lester looked up into the gray-brown murkiness, searching for answers to life's questions. He sat on the steps of the church, his tailbone aching under his weight.

Pulling his PDA from a hip pocket, he scanned for messages, both from real people as well as his virtual friends and acquaintances, but there was nothing from either. For an instant, Lester's eyes blurred, and he shook them back into focus with a wag of his head.

"Hey," a voice said from the shadows. "You Lester Troupe?"

Lester turned to see a man who had so many visual modifications that he barely looked human. His skin had been dyed light green, and multiple advertising tattoos hawking everything from cStar—a new bio-enhanced sex drug—to Rudy's Strip Club, danced about his skin. His yellow enhanced eyes stared through Lester, muscles pushing against the man's pants and shirt, and Lester saw titanium body supports running up the man's arms. Lester also could see the tiny tips of dart pistols protruding from two of the man's fingers, but they weren't pointed in his direction—yet.

"Yeah. Who wants to know?" Lester rose, his knees cracking loudly, and the man giggled.

"Coming apart like a rag doll, are we?" said the man, his yellow eyes flashing red as he accessed a data feed on the inside of his eyeball. The man's clothes appeared to be changing colors as he moved, and as Lester looked closer, he could see the tiny silver lines of titanium reinforced skin.

Lester didn't answer. Instead, he circled behind the man, searching his body for any additional enhancements that might prove fatal. After he completed his circle, Lester asked, "How did you know I'd be here?"

"You're usually here for the Wednesday ceremony, no?" When Lester didn't answer, the man said, "My name's Templar."

"So," said Lester, still eyeing the man. Unmodified humans—or what modi-humans called Amebas—weren't normally very trusting of the technological upper class, and dealt with them as one would deal with a government enforcer, or a battle droid—very carefully.

"So, today's your lucky day," said Templar. "Today you can start the rest of your life. Leave everything you hate and despise behind." Templar was smiling broadly, and Lester frowned. He couldn't trust this man, not even if he really wanted to.

"How so? What could I possibly do for you?" The question was pathetic, and Lester knew it. He felt his stomach grow cold, and his back ached with renewed vigor, as if his body were telling him to pay attention to what this man was saying.

"Ever hear of a mind dump?" asked Templar, his smile growing so wide it almost split his green face.

Now Lester was really suspicious. "Sure. The entire data contents of a brain implanted in a newly grown, bio-enhanced body that will allow its owner to live—for all practical purposes—forever. The most experimental and expensive upgrade available. Even some of the folks in there don't buy it yet," said Lester, as he pointed toward the church.

"Yep. And what would you do for a mind dump? Think of it, Lester. A new body that wouldn't ever break down, no pain, no disease." Templar took a step back and he appeared to be receiving a message over his internal communication network that was linked to the nets at all times, exchanging information and making requests. This constant connection to an almost infinite data stream was believed by some transhumanists to be extremely dangerous, as they believed eventually modi-humans could take over the nets and become a collective consciousness.

"What would I have to do? Kill the emperor or something?" asked Lester.

"Nothing so drastic. All I want you to do is kill your ex-wife, Linda. Can't imagine that would be very hard for you," said Templar, as he watched Lester.

As an unmodified human, Lester wasn't very good at hiding his emotions. He had no skin temperature control, or mood enhancing drugs in his blood. So the confusion on his face was easy for Templar to read. "I…" stammered Lester, his eyes glazing over. Then the idea began to sink in, and a thin smile spread across his face. "I've never killed anyone before, never even hurt anyone intentionally. But…" again Lester trailed off.

This time, Templar picked up where he left off. "But you hate her, right? The bitch used up all your good years, she never told you she was a modi, and you didn't find out until the divorce proceedings. She took all your credits, your home, your dog, and left you for dead while she spent her evenings screwing her new boyfriend. Can't be much love lost there."

"That doesn't make me a killer," said Lester, as he looked out at the throng of bicycles and motor scooters in the street. *Or does it?* he thought, his brain already starting to justify actions he hadn't taken yet.

"No. But she does deserve it. No?"

"I don't know," answered Lester. "Does this have anything to do with how she pays for her enhancements and system upgrades?" asked Lester, and Templar's thin evil smile returned.

"It has everything to do with it," he said, and this time Lester smiled along with him.

* * *

Templar's TramCar glided along its track soundlessly, and Lester stared out the frosted rear window, looking for anything that would remind him of the Chicago he had known as a boy. Many of the buildings still stood, but were nothing more than hollow shells for the homeless, or worse. Most of the large

US cities took a major hit when the economy totally collapsed in 2019, and two-thirds of city dwellers left everything behind for a new life beyond the metropolis, where the air was cleaner and certain crops would still grow in the polluted soil. Lester's family had been in the one-third minority that had decided to stay, and they had paid for that decision.

Chicago had become a street nightmare. Gangs controlled and policed most areas, but even these wayward violent groups couldn't hold a candle to NewMafioso, a group of criminals so strong and powerful that none of the propped-up governments claiming control over all the United States' 72 states and 19 provinces would consider challenging them. It was to the executive offices of NewMafioso that Templar brought Lester.

Templar pulled his TramCar into an empty spot, released Lester's door lock, and the two men headed for an elevator with shiny steel doors. Lester whistled. "Piss on me. A working elevator? Haven't seen one of these in a while." Templar didn't acknowledge him as the elevator doors opened. They stepped inside as Templar pressed his thumb to a fingerprint scanner, and once cleared, pressed the button for the top floor. The elevator doors slid closed with a rumble.

"So why do you want me to kill Linda?" asked Lester. He was becoming more comfortable with Templar. Clearly if the man meant him harm, he'd already be hanging from the roof by his toes. Lester's right knee chose that moment to lock up, and he staggered and almost fell, but was able to steady himself against the elevator's wall. Templar just shook his green head.

The elevator opened into an expansive foyer, which had several couches, a large wall screen, and several pieces of early 2000 American art which were tastefully displayed about the space. A guard with an old-style gun on his hip, and a nerve-snarlor wand held by his side, stood by a closed silver door. The officer had a variety of upgrades, many of which were clearly military issue. When the guard saw Templar, he smiled, but when he saw Lester, he frowned.

"You have papers for this?" he asked Templar, motioning toward Lester like he was a sick dog.

"Yeah. He has a meeting with Hiram," answered Templar, as he brushed past the guard with Lester in tow. Beyond the door, a long hallway led to a white room with no windows and no color accents. A folding table and two folding chairs stood empty in the center of the room. They entered, and Templar closed the door behind him.

"Where's Neo," asked Lester, but Templar didn't

get the joke, and simply shook his head; his yellow eyes turning red as data scrolled down the inside of his eyeball. Several seconds passed and Templar laughed, his search finally finding the movie reference and applicable visuals.

"Sit," said Templar, and Lester complied. "I like you. You seem a good sort. So listen up. Remember when the US had presidents? Guys that some said ran the world show?" Lester nodded. His father used to rant about the political battles of old. "Well, this guy that's going to be watching you," said Templar, and he paused, pointing at the video camera above the door. "He's ten times more powerful than any president ever was. He can make you disappear with a nod of his head. This is not the time for jokes, self-deprecation, or any of that other bullshit you try and use to manipulate people. Just shut up. Answer the questions as simply as possible, and don't editorialize. Just what you *know,* not what you think you know. You got me, Ameba?"

Lester nodded. Templar got up and left the room, and he sat there for a long time, sweat dripping down his neck, his lower back aching. The bright light reflecting off the white walls hurt Lester's eyes, and he covered them with the back of his hand. The door opened, and a man in a black suit entered and seated himself at the folding table.

"I'm sorry, sir, the light," said Lester, as he looked across the table at the man. Lester rubbed his eyes and shook his head, trying to focus on what might be the last conversation of his life.

"No, I'm sorry, Mr. Troupe," said the man, as he handed a white linen handkerchief to Lester. Lester held it in his hands, rubbing between his fingers. He was old enough to remember real fabric, but Lester hadn't seen cloth spun from actual wool in years. "Mr. Kutzu's men can be a little rough. It's their business, and we tolerate their crudeness due to the necessity of the times. Can I get you anything? Food? A drink? Some whiskey, maybe? I'll join you," said the man before Lester could respond. A wave of his hand brought forth a guard carrying a tray with two glasses, a decanter of whiskey, and a bucket filled with ice. The guard worked silently, stuffing the two tumblers with ice, then filling them half way with whiskey, and retreating without a word.

"My name is Hiram Locke," said Hiram, as he held out his hand and Lester shook it. He lifted his whiskey and took a long pull, closing his eyes as he savored it. Then he placed his glass on the table and watched Lester. The silence seemed to press in on them, and

Lester began to grow nervous. Finally, Hiram spoke. "You didn't know Linda had spy upgrades when you married her? That true?"

Lester looked at the floor, embarrassment coloring his cheeks red. "Yep. I had no clue."

"Don't beat yourself up about it, Mr. Troupe. Only a handful of trained professionals have the skill to detect her upgrades," said Hiram, as he took another sip of his drink.

Lester's stomach tingled, and he lifted his glass and drank some whiskey, trying to settle his nerves. "How do you … I mean, why do you know about her upgrades? Why do you care?"

Hiram rose and walked behind Lester, putting his hands on the back of his chair. "Do you know what your ex-wife does for a living?"

"I thought she was a teacher, but obviously I don't know shit," answered Lester.

"No. You do know shit, or some shit," said Hiram, and he chuckled. "She's a teacher all right, a private teacher for the children of former Congressman Benjamin Bass, who served the fifth district of Pennsylvania East, our country's esteemed 63rd state."

Lester looked confused. "So."

Hiram shook his head. "Not too bright, are we?" Silence and a heavy sigh from Hiram. "Bass is a lawyer now for one of the biggest investment houses in the world, and—"

"Piss on me! You funded her upgrades so she could steal insider stock information from this guy?" shouted Lester.

"Light dawns on yonder head," said Hiram, as Lester watched him in amazement. "And now the bitch is trying to extort money from NewMafioso, and no one does that."

"Why not just send one of your goons to do the job? Surely they'd be better at it than me," said Lester.

"She'll be looking out for us. She'll never see you coming," said Hiram, and Lester nodded in agreement. She wouldn't believe he had the balls to try to hurt her, let alone deal with NewMafioso.

"I've wasted enough time here. Are you with us? Shall I have Mr. Kutzu's personal secretary make the appointment for your mind dump?" asked Hiram.

Lester stood, his hands by his sides. His mind was racing in an attempt to justify murder, no matter how many spins he tried to put on it. Then Lester held out his hand, and said, "Yeah. I'm with you."

* * *

Getting Linda to meet him wasn't difficult. A free meal at her favorite restaurant, Griffy Masons, plus his promise to sign the final divorce papers, which he had been holding up for almost two years, had been enough to convince her. In Masons, seated at their favorite table, Lester would poison her. Hiram had given him a small vial of serum, which he claimed would kill her within minutes, with very little pain, and was medically undetectable. Lester turned the vile over and over in his pocket as he pushed through the heavy wooden doors of Griffy Masons.

The bar was packed with modi-humans, but Lester was able to wedge himself to the bar's edge and order a drink. He was on his second when, looking in the mirror above the bar, he saw Linda arrive. She looked gorgeous; her blonde hair pulled back, large blue eyes bright, the signs of a slight tan visible. She made several stops along the way, pausing briefly to kiss and hug male admirers. She smiled broadly, laughed at all their jokes, and there were more than a couple of glances thrown his way as she explained to her friends why she was there. In that instant, Lester wanted to kill her, to clamp his hands around her throat and squeeze until that energetic light left her blue eyes.

Then she was tapping on his shoulder, and Lester turned. She pecked him on the cheek and said, "Shall we sit?"

"Sure," said Lester, the pain in his back causing him to grimace. Her sensors picked up his pain and she turned away, half embarrassed for him and half disgusted. Lester's knees cracked as he rose from his bar stool. He was feeling good, the whiskey pushing blood through his veins, when he felt the glass vial in his pocket. Like a quarterback calling a play, Lester sensed the clock start to tick.

Linda turned and looked at him, but her face was impassive. Most likely her mood modification controller releasing a variety of drugs to make her appear any way she wanted, and what she wanted to look like tonight was soft stone.

Lester watched her ass as she followed the hostess to their table. She wore a loose fitting sun dress that hid her shapely figure, but he could still admire her legs, which looked the same as they had twenty years prior, thanks to her system upgrades and rejuvenation treatments.

When they arrived at their table, Linda sat, and her face remained emotionless. "You want a drink?" asked Lester, trying to get things going. He knew at some point she'd want to go to the bathroom, and he needed her drink to be ready.

"Yeah, sure. What do you have there?"

"Whiskey on the rocks," answered Lester.

"Whiskey? You?" She looked at him. "Whiskey?"

"A newly acquired taste," said Lester, as he flagged down a waitress and looked at Linda.

"Martini. Straight up. Olives." The waitress nodded and scampered off.

"So." She reached into her bag and retrieved a manila folder. "The pages you need to sign are marked. I'd like to take them with me, if you don't mind." Lester picked up the folder and placed it next to him. He had no intention of signing anything. Once he did, she'd be gone.

Linda frowned, and when her drink arrived, she took a long pull, downing half the glass. "Why did you want to have dinner? What do you need?"

"Funny you should ask. First thing would be a skeletal enhancement package. My joints are killing me." Linda laughed, and when Lester didn't, he continued, "You have big bucks, right?"

Linda's face went white for an instant before her enhancements kicked in. "Is this some kind of joke? Because if it is, I don't get it. I don't have the money…"

"Don't waste my time. I know you do." Lester turned the vile of poison over and over in his hand under the table. She would only need to look away for a moment, and he could poison her drink.

"Where'd you grow these stones? I know you for years and you're a total ameba. Now what?" They stared at each other, the chatter of the restaurant filling in the silence. Her blue eyes had lost some of their luster, and she looked uncomfortable. She dropped her napkin on the table as she rose, and locked eyes with Lester again, distracting him as she deftly passed her hand over his whiskey glass. "I need to powder my nose. I'll be right back," she said, and left him alone.

Lester looked about him, and his head started to pound. There were mirrors everywhere, and he wanted to make sure no one saw him. Then he casually picked up Linda's martini, pulled it under the table, poured in the poison, and put the glass back where he had found it. He looked around, and it appeared no one had seen him. He was home free. He picked up his whiskey and took a long pull as he searched for a mirror that would give him a good view of the ladies room exit. The whiskey felt silky in his stomach, and it warmed his heart.

Linda exited the ladies room and made her way back toward the table. So it was that she saw Lester rise from his seat in pain, grabbing his chest as though something was eating him from the inside out. He looked manically at the half-full whiskey glass, wondering how she had managed to poison it. Then he looked across the room at Linda, and fell in a spastic zombie-like motion that left him face down on the floor beside their table. Linda knelt beside her husband, feeling for a pulse, but it was already too late. Head bowed, she rose and sat down at the table, her eyes glazed.

"Sorry sweetie," said Linda, as she picked up her martini and downed its contents, including the olive. "Poor bastard."

* * *

350 years later...

Rip Silver sat at a table in the front of the Yesteryear Café, sipping a coffee blend he had never experienced before. He had made up his new name from a combination of Rip Van Winkle and Lee M. Silver, a scientist who pioneered the concept of genetic divide. Though most people who knew him in Old Chicago called him Old Lester, and they spoke his name with awe.

The café stood on what was once Our Lady of Perpetual Sorrows Cemetery and Sanctuary, where Linda had been buried. Hiram Locke had been at Griffy Masons the night Linda died—the same night Lester died—but Hiram said a deal was a deal, and he had the mind dump performed minutes after Lester's death, while the fireworks of his brain were still working toward their finale. The docs had told him something might be lost, but how would he know? All the aches and pains were gone, but the one thing his enhancements hadn't been able to fix was his heart. It

didn't comfort him that Linda had poisoned him. She had failed, and he hadn't. It was really that simple, at least that's what Hiram always said. He had worked for Hiram for years, his service being the real reason Hiram had saved him.

Lester vowed to himself that he would visit Linda's grave every 50 years of his life, to pay tribute to the fact that it was her life that had made his eternal. When he had arrived last time to find the cemetery destroyed and a building constructed in its place, he simply made his peace at the café. And when the café was ground to dust, he would shop in the store, sleep at the hotel, or climb the mountain that replaced what was before it. He would do this forever, or until he forgot his darkest deed, the one that had brought him eternal life.

Searching back in his mind, Lester finds many good memories of he and Linda enjoying life and each other, and it is these memories that over time Lester comes to believe are the true history of their lives. Even Hiram, who hadn't survived the plague wars of 2314, had believed that love could change reality.

Rip smiled.

Granpa's 6502

Like the old Ford pickup
polished and cherished
past its working days,
released from the garage
for special occasion jaunts,
Granpa hauls out the old Atari,
with its 8 and 16 bit buses,
dusts off the keys
that click when you press them,
and teaches his grandchildren
to program in Basic.
He tells them stories
of the old days of microchips:
"Held only one thousand transistors,
they did," he says
and they sit open-mouthed.
"Went to the moon on just 64 kilobits,"
we did," he says
and astonishment widens their eyes.
"We're waiting for the wonders
of qubits," they insist.
"They're gonna burst out bubbles."
Sure will," he agrees
and pats their artless little heads.
"But it's nice to know
where you came from."

— Karin L. Frank

Where'd That Come From?

Story by
David B. Riley

Illustration by
Morland Gonsoulin

Sarah's eyes couldn't focus on the clock. The numbers were so blurry. That was the problem with Martian Red Ale, at least when you drink a huge amount of it. That chirping sound was getting annoying, too. Finally, she realized it was the terminal. It was Gompers, Mars City. No, it was Gompers, but not Mars City. She sat up. Gompers HQ? They never called her direct. She tried to remember how to answer. "Whuluh?"

"Sarah Meadows?" some guy was asking.

Sarah wondered if she had any clothes on. She wondered who this guy was. "What do you want?"

He seemed to be saying something about Fremont Station. "Why do I have to go there? I'm tired. I want to sleep."

"Dragon says to get up to Fremont Station on the next available shuttle," the guy was saying. "Now!"

"Who's Dragon?" she asked, though the name seemed familiar.

"He owns the company," the man said. This man seemed a little testy.

"Oh, him. Dragon always wants stuff," Sarah said. "I'm going back to bed." She turned off the terminal and let her head fall back to the pillow. She noticed that she didn't have any clothes on and she'd flashed some guy she didn't even know. "I'll bet he'll remember me." She climbed out of bed and struggled to find the shower in the tiny apartment. It was proving difficult to find. She finally found it next to the bathroom. The hot water hit her face. She wondered what some guy she didn't know was thinking about some strawberry blond girl sitting in front of the terminal stark naked. She wondered where it was she was supposed to go. "Fremont Station," the voice inside her head told her.

Sarah had no idea how she got to the Mars City Space Terminal. But she was there. She accepted the boarding pass and staggered over to one of the orange plastic chairs in the waiting area. Sarah wondered what the guy from Gompers HQ was worried about. She'd made it with five minutes to spare. Lord, she wanted to pass out. *Can pass out on the shuttle. Can throw up on the shuttle. No, we can't.* Some man was talking to his lady friend. Sarah grabbed his carry on and upchucked into it, then put it back unnoticed. *Enjoy your lunch, sir. Can't believe I just did that.*

They were boarding now. She staggered through the airlock and grabbed hold of the first seat she saw. The shuttle was swirling around. They didn't used to do that. The attendant was waking her. They were there. That was fast. She wandered out into Fremont Station.

Some short little bald guy was standing by the window holding a sign that read Sarah Meadows. "Are you Sarah Meadows?" she asked.

"No. I'm Smedley, from finance."

"Well, Smedley from finance, I'm Sarah Meadows, too."

"There's an MDF transport waiting at Level D," Smedley said.

"Lead on, my good fellow," Sarah said, though she knew the way and could probably walk it blindfolded. She was feeling much better. Sleeping on the shuttle and the simple passage of time was eliminating the effects of lack of sleep and too much Martian Red Ale. "Uh, where are we going again?"

"Pittsburgh," Smedley replied.

That didn't seem right somehow. "I don't go to Earth. I hate Earth."

"The other one," Smedley explained.

"The space city?"

"That's the one."

"But, it disappeared 20 years ago?" Sarah asked. She sort of remembered the guy from HQ might have mentioned some of this.

Smedley nodded. "And yesterday, it suddenly reappeared."

"The biggest underwriting loss in the history of Gompers Insurance Company is suddenly back?" Sarah pointed toward the stairs that went down to Level D. "No wonder Headquarters called me. Why are you here?"

"They said to come. Beats me. I work in a cubicle," Smedley replied.

The airlock was open. Two crewmen clad in the khaki uniforms of the Martian Defense Force looked them over.

"Sarah Meadows and Smedley from Gompers," Sarah said. She wondered if Smedley was a first name or a last. She decided she didn't really care.

"Welcome aboard," one of them greeted. They were both quickly strapped in to the space couch things by the crewmen.

An officer climbed down from the cockpit. "I'm Lt. Commander Skip Ferguson. Folks just call me Skip."

"Sarah Meadows. This is Smedley."

"Pleased to meet you. My orders are to head out to the Pittsburgh Station and try and figure out what the heck is going on," Skip explained. "I got called out of bed by the Minster of Defense himself for this one."

"Sounds like a plan," Sarah agreed.

"There's a small group of five MDF engineers

already on board Pittsburgh Station," Skip added. "They got there a few minutes ago."

Fremont Station, from where they were disembarking, was obsolete the day it opened—too small, too limited in its features and services, lacking the space for cargo transfers and not enough hotel rooms for people to sleep during layovers.

Pittsburgh Station was to have ended all that. Massive in size and scope, grand and sparkling in appearance, and simply too far from Mars, many said. It was so big it had to be placed in a parallel orbit around the sun, rather than in orbit around Mars. It was feared that, over time, it would alter the orbits of Deimos and Phobos and perhaps cause them to crash into Mars itself. So, it was going to be more of an independent city in space than simply a space station. Two days before its planned opening, the entire facility vanished without a trace. The cost of building it had been astronomical, with much of the materials coming all the way from Earth. And the Gompers Insurance Company had made the unfortunate decision to insure it.

"I've never been on a mission before," Smedley said.

"Why are you here, exactly?" Sarah asked.

Smedley explained, "If it really is back and operational, Gompers owns it unless the Martian Government wants to repay the millions they got from the claim and have long ago spent. They may decide to lease it. That's what I do, negotiate leases on property Gompers owns."

"Makes sense," Sarah agreed.

They could see Pittsburgh Station long before they arrived. It was a glistening little star in space. As they got closer, it was not all that little. Its docking area was bigger than the entire station they'd just left.

"Prepare for docking," Skip said over the intercom. There was a gentle thud a few moments later. "Welcome to Pittsburgh."

The docking area opened out into a huge atrium with large skylights and pleasing indirect lighting. "Wow," Sarah said.

"The operation center is four flights up, if the elevators work," Skip said. "Let's check in with the engineers."

"Lead on," Sarah replied.

One of the engineers looked up from a heating duct. The others kept on working. "Hey Skip."

"Anything interesting?" Skip asked back.

"Heck yeah. There were 23 construction workers on the station when it disappeared. There's no sign of any of them. And," he paused for just a moment,

"some of the escape pods are gone. No idea where they went."

"Place looks brand new," Skip said.

"That's why we were checking the ventilation. It's hardly been used. Thing is, everything was running when we got here."

"It's been running on empty for 20 years?" Skip asked.

"I'm not so sure what's going on," the engineer explained. "I want to check out a few more things." He started back for the ventilation system. "Hey, one more thing. The bar's fully stocked."

"Well, then maybe this won't be a wasted trip after all," Skip said.

"Wasted?" Sarah asked.

"It's not a military station. I don't know what I'm doing here. This is the future of space commerce," Skip explained. "It's not an MDF facility."

"Well, for Gompers, this is a big deal. But we've got to figure out what happened or people will be afraid to come here." She gazed out one of the many enormous windows for a moment.

"Where have you been all this time?" she asked the station. There had been plenty of theories from falling through a wormhole to being stolen by aliens. Truth was, no one knew for sure. It had simply reappeared at the precise location it had vanished from 20 years earlier. The Gompers HQ guy had told her that. She was starting to remember things, including the billions Gompers lost.

"Hey, Smedley, let's go check out one of the penthouses. I used to dream of living in them when I was a little girl. They told us about this place in school. It was going to be this wonderful city. Then, it was gone."

Smedley cautiously approached an elevator. The doors sensed him and opened. "Penthouse please." The doors closed and they were quickly taken up to the penthouse level.

"Ooh." Sarah looked around in amazement. The entire ceiling was an open skylight view of space. She touched a button and the windows instantly clouded up. "Ooh." Then she saw the bathtub, in many ways it looked more like a little pond. It even had its own cascading waterfall. "Ooh." She turned it on and the warm water began to cascade into the tub. "If a man wanted to sleep with me, all he'd need do is bring me here. That'd work." For a space station, this was beyond fancy.

Smedley seemed uncomfortable with that revelation. "Hey, it's got its own bar." Smedley poured himself a glass of Martian Red Ale and took a sip. "Not bad for 20 year old brew. Want one?"

The thought made Sarah's head start hurting again. "Uh, not right now."

"Not bad at all." Smedley collapsed into one of the big comfy lounge chairs that filled a conversation pit next to the bar. The little terminal at the edge of the bar started chirping. "May I help you?" Smedley asked.

A rather sexy computer voice asked, "Shall I put through a call for a Smedley?"

"Nobody ever calls me. Uh, okay, put it through," Smedley decided.

"Smedley?" A face appeared on the tiny screen. Smedley pressed a button and the face also appeared on half of the wall. He pressed it again and the image went back to just being on the small screen. "Smedley, are you there?"

"I'm here, sir," Smedley assured him.

"Is the station salvageable?" There was something odd in his speech, like it was taking too long between words. "I've," there was a quick skip, "got a meeting," another skip, "with the Chancellor."

Sarah recognized the man, though she had never actually met him in person. He was Malcolm Collier, Director of Finance for Gompers Insurance. "Sir, Sarah Meadows with Special Ops, we're hopeful. Everything seems in good shape, but it's a big station. A lot to check out." She looked back at the bathtub. "Water system is in great shape."

"Who's in shape?" he asked. "You're not coming in too good. Maybe it's sun spots."

"We'll keep you informed, boss," Smedley said. He terminated the call from a new bunch of controls he found underneath the armrest of his comfy chair.

"Damn, I so wanted to take a bath in that tub," Sarah said.

"Oh?" Smedley asked. He wasn't really sure if she meant by herself or not.

"Sunspots my ass. We've got to get back over to operations," Sarah said.

"What for? I haven't finished my beer."

"I didn't like that call clarity," Sarah said. "I want to check something." Sarah headed for the elevator. The doors opened. "Central Operations." The doors closed. She noticed Smedley was still with her.

The engineer looked up from his work doing whatever it was with the vents. "These vents are amazing."

"Do you have a name?" Sarah asked.

"Chuck."

"Well, Chuck, I need help with something," Sarah said.

"Oh?" Chuck looked anxiously.

"Can you set up a hyperspace link with the MDF Research Lab in Mars City?" Sarah asked.

"We're not that far away. A regular link is all we use," Chuck explained as he looked longingly at his vents.

"Can you set up a hyperspace link with the MDF Research Lab in Mars City?" Sarah asked for the second time. "The Martian Defense Force Research Lab? In Mars City?"

"Yes, it's no different than calling some other planet. System here was state of the art in its day." He went over to a station next to a window that overlooked the main promenade down below them where shops and recreation were going to be. He touched a panel. "But, why a hyperspace link? It's really not necessary."

"Just connect it," Sarah said.

Marshall Fenton, civilian director of the lab, appeared on the screen. He looked curiously at them.

"It's your party?" Chuck said.

"Dr. Fenton, Sarah Meadows with Gompers," Sarah explained.

"How," there was kind of a skip, "help you?" he asked.

"Behind you is the atomic clock. Can you show, not tell, us the time? I know it's an odd request," Sarah explained.

He spun his terminal around to a digital display on the wall. The time was 6:22.

Sarah pointed to the clock in the operations area. It was 6:43. "Doesn't this clock align itself with that very clock we are looking at on Mars?"

"I don't understand," said Dr. Fenton.

"I went to the Martian School of Economics. Time theory is not my strongest area, but I think this station is existing in a different time than Mars. Doctor, is there any possibility that some sort of rift in time is going on? This station does not appear 20 years old. It is brand spanking new."

"Possibly. Frankly … know," Dr. Fenton said.

"I think we missed some of that, say again?" Sarah asked.

"I don't know. It may be possible … may be fluid. Not much … research." He looked kind of blank.

Sarah pointed at the clock. It now read 6:58. The one on Mars was reading 6:44. "Either we've got a defective clock or we are in big trouble," Sarah said.

"What should we do?" Smedley asked.

"Abandon ship!"

"This is not a ship," Chuck pointed out.

"Evacuate! Get the heck out of here." Sarah pressed a red button that was labeled ALL STATION ADDRESS SYSTEM. "All hands, this is Sarah Meadows. Evacuate! Evacuate now!"

"Madam, I think you're over reacting," Chuck protested. "I'm going back to my vents. This station looks rock solid to me."

"Suit yourself, Chuck." She started running for the elevator. "Coming Smedley?" She noticed he was right on her heels. The bidirectional elevator whisked them directly to the docking ring.

The MDF crew were already on board. "What's wrong?" Skip asked.

"We need to get away from this station, pronto," Sarah said.

Skip looked down the hallway toward the docking airlock of the transport the engineers had used. There was no activity. "Aren't the engineers coming?"

"I don't know what they're doing," Sarah said. "If I'm right, this station is going to do another vanishing act."

Skip pressed the talk button on the communicator clipped to his shoulder. "Get us out of here now. Straight away course, maximum speed."

"Aye, aye," came the reply. The airlock door slid shut. "All hands prepare for departure. I'll get us in hyperdrive as soon as we clear the station."

"No!" Sarah yelled.

"What?" a confused Skip asked.

"I think it's worse in hyperspace than regular space," Sarah said.

"Stay in regular space drive," Skip ordered, "maximum thrust."

The shuttle jerked as it pulled away from the station. "I'm heading topside. Get strapped in." Skip bolted up the ladder to the cockpit on the top level.

Smedley managed to get himself buckled in. "I don't know much about hyperspace."

"Neither do I, frankly. It's just a gut feeling. I've got this rudimentary vision in my head of holes in time that I can't begin to explain right now. It's like my brain is solving this, but can't quite explain it to me yet." The shuttle craft jolted hard as the pilot blasted into full speed. It was a violation of the Uniform Space Act to use anything besides thrusters within two kilometers of a docking space station.

"I may puke," Smedley said.

Sarah was so glad the Martian Red had worn off. "Think happy thoughts. These shuttles are pretty tough."

Time went by. Sarah wasn't sure how much, or which time. Were they in Martian time again or something else?

"Sarah Meadows, topside," Skip announced over the intercom.

Sarah floated over to the ladder and held on. Small transports didn't have artificial gravity. Gravity ceased the instant they uncoupled from the space station. She grabbed the ladder rung and pulled up. She easily floated up into the cockpit, which was very dark, illuminated only with the greenish glow from some of the instrument panels. She looked expectantly at Skip.

He pointed out the window. Pittsburgh, the space city of the future shined in the sky, directly ahead of them.

"I don't understand," Sarah said.

"This ship also has an aft view." He pointed behind them. There was a small porthole style window. Sarah floated over and looked out. Pittsburgh, the space city of the future shined brightly in the sky, directly behind them. "Care to explain that?"

"I, uh." She looked back at the front, then again at the same image behind them. "Uh."

"Yeah." Skip looked at some of the reading. "I don't know where to turn."

"Think three dimensionally, commander. They're both on the same plane. Head up or down."

"Might as well," Skip agreed. He nodded to the helmsman. Take us down 90 degrees. "There's really no up or down in space, they say at the academy. Down compared to Mars, anyway."

Then, in an instant, the station behind them was gone.

"This is getting weird," Smedley said.

Sarah wondered how long Smedley had been there. "That's for sure."

"Golly," Skip said.

Sarah looked back to the front of the ship. Because of the change in angle, the station was now high up on the front window. Then, it was gone. "Golly."

"What just happened?" Skip asked.

"I think the one in front was yet another view from a different time, of the same station," Sarah said. "Though I could be wrong."

* * *

Sarah noticed that Dr. Fenton and the two men who were never actually introduced to her were no longer looking at her drawings that tried to depict how her brain had tried to tell her what was happening with time and space and the enormously expensive Pittsburgh Station. "Maybe, in time, I'll figure out what my brain was trying to tell me. It's hard to explain."

"There is no known link between hyperspace and time," Dr. Fenton said. "Why did you think the hyperlink would be no different than the regular com transmission for such a relatively short distance?"

"I didn't. I knew it would be immune to interference from the sun. That's all. I could rule out solar interference with a hyperlink call. The rest started coming together when we called you," Sarah explained.

"I sure wish the engineers would have believed you that they were in danger," he said.

"So do I," Sarah said.

"That will be all, Miss Meadows," Dr. Fenton said.

Marketing Strategy

Corporations now sell products
made from real Human® milk
as health foods or beauty aids
(remember placenta shampoo?).
Cheese and yogurt—and recipes.
Martha Stewart chats with Oprah:
low-fat human ricotta cheesecake
and colostrum facial masques.
Of course the milk is imported
from underdeveloped nations.
It's really expensive here, but
Whole Foods carries it. They pay
the mothers it came from enough
of a pittance to enable them
to buy replacement formula
from multinational corporations.
Women are given hormones,
like dairy cows, to maintain peak
lactation. Culinary reviews compare
taste, color, and butterfat content
from producers of different races
and national origins. Any woman
who wants to get top dollar
for her milk must sign a notarized
affidavit, promising to exclude
onions and garlic from her diet.
Or else they promote that milk to
specialty markets, for ethnic cuisine.
Trade associations hold banquets
where top producers get medals
pinned to their chests.

— F.J. Bergmann

Cunjerred

Story by
Sarah M. Lewis

Illustration by
Shoshana Holl

"Chicken! Chicken!" That was what people called bird meat. There was bird meat in the garbage bin which was a container people kept food they wasted. This was better than he'd hoped for when he went prowling in the dark around the houses of the furless ones who called themselves men dodging the puddles of light created by their small suns. He could open this container unlike the box men had trapped the Forever Cat in.

"I told you and I told you before your eyes were even open, eating their food gives the furless ones power over you. Do you want to be cunjerred?" Mamou spoke sharply between his pointed ears even if in his reality she was only a memory.

"I don't want to be hungry." He thought it was a good argument while using his stubby opposite sixth toe on his front paws to get a good grip on the garbage can lid.

"What if people see you walking about on your back legs? Do you want to be boxed up and maybe gassed which is what men intend to see when they open the Forever Cat's prison?"

"The chances the Forever Cat will be gassed are 50/50. Even boxed up all possibilities exist for the Forever Cat." He grunted while jumping and pushing up on the lid. He was going to flip it open yet. "It makes no never mind any of the furless ones see me walking on my back legs. They knew some of us walk on two legs like people. They might even think I'm one of their mindless Doderrie."

"Keep thinking that way and you will end up Doderrie." Mamou hissed in his head.

"Mamou, do you mind? I'm trying to get this thing open." He wondered if other cats' Mamous talked to them in their heads.

She ignored him. "If people ever understood how they change reality. If men ever find out us walking upright became reality when in faraway time men observed the Forever Cat walking on his hind legs. They cause enough harm without knowing."

"I'll never tell." He knew people must never know all cats and all cat possibilities came from the Forever Cat ever since the Cosmic Creator dreamed the Forever Cat into being. He now had the lid raised. One good jump on his back legs and he could flip the lid back.

"No!" The lid banged down. He barely got his front paws out of the way.

He was going to have to tip it like a dog. Angrily he charged the garbage bin. It rocked back and forth. Again he threw himself against it.

The can rocked backward. He put his front paws against it and pushed. It went over on its side. He pulled the lid open with his front paws and slashed the bag open with his claws. He backed out of the can and sat on his haunches with a big drumstick with plenty of meat still on it in his front paws.

He bit into the meat savoring its sweet taste. "Chicken is too good to waste."

He tore off another strip of meat.

Suddenly he was caught in the glow of yellow light. He grabbed his prize in his teeth and fled into the darkness on all fours. He could run faster that way. He heard the big furless male yelling spells at him.

"He's knocked over the trash can and torn the bag apart! One of those God damn Coon Ass Cats!"

He felt the unleashed curse following after him. One of the many destructive gifts the Cosmic Creator had given people, the power of their words. He lifted up his tail showing his Grwr-Chakus. That stopped the pursuing curse dead.

He might have escaped that furless one, but there was no escaping Mamou's scolding. "I told you to stay away from people!"

He growled. He couldn't talk back to Mamou even in his head while he was running carrying a chicken drumstick in his mouth. There was no staying away from people. They were everywhere, casting their spells and using their power to change everything, draining the swamps and cutting down the trees.

He kept running till he gained the safety of the trees beyond the peoples' houses and climbed up his tree for the night where he made himself comfortable in the abandoned Storne's nest he'd found. It wouldn't have been worth his life to go near a nest a Storne lived in. Those birds with their terrible teeth and claws hated cats. A Storne would disembowel him and feed him to its young.

An unused Storne's nest was a find like the chicken he was eating. It was like the empty Storne's nest he'd used to paddle around the swamp catching fish and avoiding gators before the men drained the swamp and all his fellow cats had to scat.

* * *

He was sitting in front of the bright yellow bowl with his front paws full of the dry brown pellets. The screechy voice female put out food for her Doderrie. Lots of furless ones did for his enslaved kin. Her slave didn't eat it all. She was wasting food like people.

"If you eat that, the furless ones will cunjer you

for sure." Mamou told him.

His stomach growled like an angry ravenous dog. He sniffed the pellets and stuffed some in his mouth.

"Mmmm. Crunchy."

He put more pellets in his mouth and began crunching them. They were dry. He needed a drink from the Doderrie's water bowl.

"Mine! Get away!" The Doderrie she cat hissed at him.

He'd been busy eating and hadn't noticed the black and white Doderrie glaring at him through her slitted green eyes, her tail lashing back and forth.

"When I'm finished. Your master will put out more for you." He told her reasonably around another mouthful. She was smaller and not one of the cats who could get up on back legs or grasp things with front paws.

She growled and spat. Then she came at him with her claws out taking him completely by surprise.

"Shame! Letting a Doderrie jump you. I raised you better than that."

"Mamou, I'm trying to fight."

"Yeeoww!" the Doderrie lashed out raking his ear. He barely avoided a swipe at his eyes.

Goaded, he sprang and landed on the Doderrie. She rolled and they were both trying to get their claws and teeth in each other. He felt her kicking at his underbelly and Grwr-Chakus with her hind claws.

Beneath his panic he could hear Mamou. "You have six grasping digits on your front paws. Use them!"

He wrapped his front paws around her neck and began to squeeze. She kicked and scratched him with her back claws. He tightened his hold on her neck choking off her air. She had to give up and then he'd let go.

"Had enough?" She glared at him through her green eyes and stopped struggling.

The instant he let go she righted herself and attacked. He clenched his six digits together and swung at her, hitting her hard upside the head.

"Betsey! My baby!"

"My name is Elizabeth!" the she cat said.

Screechy Voice didn't seem to understand what her Doderrie said. She came running screaming protective charms for her Doderrie. Her voice hurt his sensitive ears. He turned and ran, making for the back fence. He wasn't fast enough.

Screechy Voice grabbed the long green water spitter. Water from it hit him hard knocking him off the fence. He lay on the ground wet, panting and bruised.

"Get up!" Mamou told him.

He got up and looked around. Too bad for Screechy Voice. She'd knocked him into the next peoples' territory. Furless ones only respect each other's territory.

This was an interesting territory, full of trees, bushes, all sorts of interesting places to explore. Most furless ones' territories were open and nothing but grass. The same kind of grass. No variety to nibble.

Curiosity got the better of him. He walked up to the house and looked in through the big door made of almost invisible material. He didn't see any furless ones. He noticed a seat where they could look out at their territory instead of facing the box with moving images. He wondered if this was the Forever Cat's prison. He'd looked into enough houses to know hairless ones spent a lot of time watching the box.

"What was that?" He heard sharp angry footsteps. Screechy Voice was coming looking for him. He dashed under a bush into its shadow. He tucked his white legs under him and hunkered down. "Don't see me. You can't see me if I am still in shadow."

He saw her feet from his hiding place. Then he heard the see-through door open. Two furless ones, a man and a woman, came out of the house.

"What's the ruckus about, Ms. Adams?" He heard the man ask.

"I'm looking for the Louisiana Swamp Cat that attacked my Betsey!"

"Your precious Betsey killed a bird off my birdfeeder the other day." The other woman said. At least her voice wasn't shrill.

The man's piercing gaze swept the yard and settled on him under the bush.

"Don't see me. Don't see me." Too late, that man saw him, truly saw him in a way most hairless ones didn't. Then the man looked away and said, "I saw a Nova about the Coon Ass Cats."

"Angus!" That was the other woman speaking again.

"Sorry. Louisiana Swamp Cat. They've been proven to exist. They can use their front paws almost like hands and sometimes they walk on their hind legs. Experts think they're the results of pirate ship cats mixing with some unknown native wild cats."

"Run while they're talking." Mamou urged. He knew the man had spotted him even though the man pretended not to see him. He dashed out from under the bush and up the tree by the fence and over it while Screechy Voice shrieked, "That's him! Get him!"

As he ran, he heard the man acting surprised. "You mean the big gray striped fellow who was under the holly? It's a shame he's so shy. He's a pretty cat and he needs a good home."

* * *

He stayed away until he was hungry again.

"Haven't you learned anything?" Mamou's voice in his head sounded weary. "Already you're being put in a box. The man said you're gray striped. Now you can only be gray."

"This time I'll be more careful." He told Mamou and himself. He examined himself all over when he stopped running and it was true. "Gray is the best camouflage color. I still have all the possibilities of gray from deep shadow to shining silver."

The man's territory was a good way to sneak into Screechy Voice's yard to eat from Betsey's food bowl when it was left unguarded. He peeped through a hole in the fence. No sign of Betsey and her food bowl was full.

He was happily filling his stomach when Betsey showed up.

"Mine!"

He sadly got up to leave. He hated to back down, but he didn't want Screechy Voice after him again. He looked longingly over his shoulder at the food bowl before turning away. He heard Screechy Voice's door open and he began to run when the sound of a food bag being shaken stopped him. He felt a powerful presence that wasn't Screechy Voice. He turned back and saw the man filling another food bowl.

"You hungry?" He felt the man's power pulling at him.

"Don't! Never accept food people offer." Mamou told him. "Especially from a man who sees you."

He was caught between the man's spells and Mamou. His stomach growled and he realized the man's power was stronger. He approached the man slowly, keeping an eye on him. Each wary step brought him closer to the food.

Betsey hissed and laid her ears flat. "Just wait till my woman gets back."

"Quit your fussing." The man told her. "You have your food."

He licked his lips and started eating. He got so busy eating that he forgot to watch the man, until he felt the man's hand barely brushing the top of his head. "That good, Pretty Boy?"

"No! You touched me! You gave me a name!" He felt the world compress around him, boxing him in. All his possibilities narrowed down to a choice.

He took off like gray striped lightning. Later up in his tree he washed himself again and again trying to get the man's smell off him.

"I'm not cunjerred! I'm not cunjerred!" He told himself over and over. But he knew it was too late.

* * *

"Here kitty, kitty, kitty. Pretty Boy, here kitty, kitty, kitty."

He could hear the man summoning him. He ignored it. He resisted it. He couldn't fight it anymore. He wanted to obey.

The food bowls were out. Betsey was glaring, but she let him alone.

"What's going on?" Screechy Voice was back. He jumped, but the man stepped between him and Screechy Voice.

"You're feeding that cat! I asked you to feed Betsey."

He peered out from behind the man's legs. "That cat comes here all the time. I thought you'd taken him in too. After all, you have Betsey and all your indoor cats."

Screechy Voice fumed. "I'd never have him. I'm calling Animal Control tomorrow."

"No, you're not." The man sounded angry. He looked down at him. "Pretty Boy, do you want a good home with a full food bowl, where you'll be treated right?"

"You'll never be the same again." It was the first time he'd heard Mamou's voice in his head since the man had touched him. She sounded sad and faraway.

He thought about the swamp being gone. He thought about the Forever Cat and how even in the box possibilities existed. He thought about being hungry and alone. Then he spoke the word of consent. "Meow."

He held still and allowed the man to scratch his ears. It felt good like when Mamou licked him when he was young.

"Come along, Pretty Boy." He followed the man to the man's house. Slowly he stepped over the threshold one paw at a time. Then he looked back at the man.

"I'm keeping my Grwr-Chakus."

Gentle Push

Story by John C. Conway
Illustration by Laura Givens

I encountered the leading edge of retreating human vessels 20 light hours from Delta Pavonis—a steady column bound for Earth, where they believed we could protect them. My mission would determine if that faith was justified, and if so, for how long.

As I skirted the system's rocky halo, I spotted the small starship drifting quietly in the mid-outer dust cloud—a tug with strong field generators fore and aft. It was not preparing to flee. I looked closer. Its artificial environment was intact. Its engines were functional. It had a single human occupant, alive and well as far as I could tell.

I hailed it. "Do you require assistance?"

It responded abruptly: "Leave me alone."

It was my first direct conversation with a human, and not what I expected. I was intrigued. But with no sign of emergency, I continued and found the blue-shifted forward wake of the Akridi fleet one light year beyond: 22,410 heavy ships moving at 0.9 C, including hard-shelled battle cruisers capable of demolishing small moons and misshapen population transports bulging with the next generation of Akridi workers and soldiers. They fired. I spun, outran the weapons, and returned to Delta Pavonis well ahead of the armada. Because of my velocity, my two-day round trip was two years relative local time.

No humans remained on the surfaces of the worlds and the last orbital stations and skyhooks were dismantled. Stragglers accelerated to solar escape velocity. But the small tug still drifted. It still had life support and one occupant. I routed enough power to project me steadily into the ship in as close to a human form as I could manage.

Its occupant sat in a small observation lounge near the engine section. Thrusters were off, but warm. The main power unit hummed at low output.

Humans were a two-gender species, and this one was female.

"Hello, Angel." She said. "Thanks for visiting." She remained seated.

"I'm not an Angel," I said, hoping she was sane, and wondering why the Council wanted to protect this particular species.

"Yes you are," she insisted. "More than you know."

"I saw you drifting here two years ago. Do you have a malfunction?"

"No," she said. "Everything's fine. Why don't you help yourself to some food or drink?"

"No thank you," I said. I was not certain whether she knew I was not physically present, although

humans had sufficient knowledge that she should. "The Akridi are close behind. They could bombard within weeks, maybe days."

"I'm meeting George," she said. She settled back into gazing out the observation lounge window.

I positioned myself—except for my projected image—well above the plane of the solar system, watching and waiting. I expected the Akridi to start with high-energy gamma-ray bursts, annihilating most unprotected complex life.

"Who is George?" I asked.

"My husband." She tapped the table, activating a small holographic representation of the man's head and shoulders. Humans, like most physical, reproducing species, age quickly and obviously. The image of George appeared considerably younger than the woman here.

I compared her to the human data norms available to me. Her mass significantly exceeded the female average for her length—5' 5" and 314 pounds. Her metabolism was unbalanced and she suffered atypical complications, including internal cancerous tumors. Because of the cancer—a condition human medical science could correct easily, if she sought treatment—she was sick and dying.

"Where is he?" I asked.

"Close," she said. And more quietly: "Very close."

She took two steady breaths, and then disengaged the holographic image. She grabbed the handle of a delicately designed teacup on a matching saucer—a uniquely human trinket out of place on a tug, but perhaps not entirely so here.

She sipped. A masterfully-crafted ring reflected the ambient room light. It was a gold wedding band—a symbol of human partnership-mating. She was clean and well groomed. The hair on her head was artificially colored.

I scanned the chamber interior. It was decorated intricately with neatly-placed, non-utilitarian objects on most flat surfaces. Some surfaces existed for the apparent purpose of holding the objects. There were living plants in small, ornate pots with glass marbles and water.

"There are still over 10,000 humans in system evacuating," I said. "I can help you locate your husband if you can you tell me how to identify—"

"No. He'll meet me. Don't worry about it."

I was surprised by the amount of information conveyed through demeanor. I was told humans communicated verbally. But it was clear now that, despite her words, George was dead. And based on the holographic photo, it was at least 25 years ago, maybe more. But if so then her behavior was irrational. She might be in denial; she might actually believe George would arrive soon. She might have divided her mind, which, to my knowledge, was not a healthy condition for a human. I resolved to be gentle. I did not want to cause more harm.

Past her, on a shelf above the console, a flat photo depicting two young humans in ceremonial garb. Next to the photo were books—a primitive, physical means of semi-permanent communication. I scanned them. Their contents were unique—information not reflected in the ship's digital storage devices. But it resembled, in structure at least, the fictional dramas portrayed in the data stores, with the notable exception that these written records conveyed detailed information about the internal thoughts and emotions of certain characters.

"This collection," I said, gesturing toward the books, "is for entertainment?"

"No." She let out a short, sharp guffaw. "Nothing so trivial. Those are inspiration. They remind us what we know about life."

"Some convey sinister circumstances."

"The dark side of the human soul," she said. Her tone and posture said that was just as important, and possibly more important, than any other aspect of humanity.

I scrutinized the unusual records further. Every tale, in one way or another, dealt with a condition or challenge, emotional turmoil, and in each case, those issues resolved in a more or less fitting way. Humanity seemed far more self-reflective than the Akridi.

The forward wake of the armada was still not in sight. Good. I needed a moment to think. The similarities between humans and Akridi still outweighed the differences. Both travelled in metallic craft powered by anti-matter drives. This vessel utilized most of the same technologies employed by the Akridi, although the Akridi, in power and speed, were superior. They both exploited the physical properties of nature and their origins were eerily similar: fast evolution after dramatic global catastrophes. Clearly, the human personality was more complex and idiosyncratic. But was that better? Or would they eventually self-destruct?

I wondered if these volumes revealed redeeming qualities. I nodded toward them and tried to elicit comment. "But there is also forgiveness, acceptance, sacrifice, mercy—"

"Yeah, yeah," she said, flopping her palm upward. "The things we strive to achieve. Believe me, Angel,

we rarely manage it." She was deliberately conveying nonchalance. "Read the stories about war."

I did. "Those values appear there as well."

She leaned toward me. Her chair creaked. "It all means just one thing, Angel. We forget it all the time. But it's just one thing."

I did not see it.

"Purpose," she said. "We all need purpose."

It was an interesting proposition. I had only ever had purpose in the context of a mission. The Akridi had a collective purpose. Individual humans apparently had individual purposes. At least they did in their fiction. But there was a theme. The common thread throughout the stories was an aim to improve, one way or another, through flaws and conflict and struggle.

Hidden in her gesture, her temperature, her tension, was the truth—she valued those concepts, treasured them—she believed in their existence and attainability. Although humans engaged in war, they believed it was tragic. They wanted to be better. And they could be better—wiser, gentler.

The Akridi could not.

"Where are you from?" I asked her.

"George and I are both from Beta Hydri. But we left there in our twenties for the frontier at Alpha Mensae."

I nodded. The journey from Beta Hydri to Alpha Mensae would have taken almost 15 years. The Akridi took the Alpha Mensae system 18 years ago. The humans failed to heed our warning at the time. It was their first encounter.

They listen now.

"Did George fight the Akridi at Mensae?" I asked.

"You're a nosey Angel, aren't you?" she said. Her expression was, I am certain, a grin. It appeared she was warming to me, and it dawned on me that she used sarcasm—a human form of harsh irony—not only as a defense mechanism, which was common, but also as a mode of familiarity, which might also be common, I wasn't sure.

As we spoke, the last of the largest human ships—miniature worlds in themselves—approached solar escape velocity. "You should leave."

"You gonna make me?"

"I'm here to observe the Akridi advance," I said. I could not force her to leave.

"And I'm here to meet George," she said.

I tried to explain her options. "There is a caravan of smaller vessels organizing at Beta Hydri. And that system will be safe for several years. If you cannot make it to Earth alone, you could—"

"Don't worry. I can make it to Earth if I want to," she said. "And there is no one for me at Beta Hydri."

She was right about her flight range. Her engines, although currently idle, were in good condition. She had sufficient power and her ship was light enough that she could probably catch the leading wave of Earth-bound refugees.

But I felt in her profound loneliness; also deep resolve. I considered leaving, but tried once more. Perhaps she could come to her senses with a gentle nudge. Without expressly saying George was dead, I told her, "There are no humans between Alpha Mensae and here. Only Akridi."

She looked at me with a half-sneer. "What kind of a sap do you think I am? Do I really look that hopeless to you?"

It sounded like hostility. But I wasn't sure. "I'm just saying—"

"Yeah, yeah, you and every armchair psychologist in human space," she said. "Look, Angel, you're a nice entity. You really are. But you've got a lot to learn about human nature."

"I don't understand it at all," I said.

"I know George is dead," she said. "He's going to meet me here because *I'm* going to meet *him*. *Capiche*?"

It was clear she did not expect a response.

"You think I've been just sitting here?" she asked.

"Had you left while I was gone?"

"No. I haven't *left*," she said. "But I haven't been just *sitting* here, either. Do your math. Am I where I should be if all I did was drift for two years?"

I checked. She was not. She was in the same belt of ice and dust. But the orientation of her orbit was entirely different.

"What have you been doing?"

"I've been planning a welcome-to-the-neighborhood party. Did you chart the paths of the comets out here when you passed?"

"No."

"Why not?"

"They do not affect my mission. They are small. This is a stable planetary system—"

"Because they're not important," she said, interrupting me.

I was puzzled. But I suspected she had a point.

She lifted a marble from the little flower pot on the shelf closest to her and studied it.

"And how important is this?" she said, tossing the marble at my image. It passed right through. "Well, you know what I mean. If it hit you—how important

could it have been?"

"Not important," I said. As we spoke, I separated a fraction of my mind and set it to the task of mapping the icy bodies in the dust cloud and then throughout the system.

"You could even have dodged it if you wanted," she said. She grabbed a small handful of additional marbles. She held them in front of her in her fist. "But if I tossed ten thousand of these little things at you, and if they were coming from all directions … fast … then what?"

My review of the system space revealed an extraordinarily high number of icy bodies on unusually sharp elliptical paths—each in the early sun-bound swing of its orbit. None of them were close enough to the sun yet to sprout a tail.

"Comets," I said.

"Hey, they *do* make smart Angels," she said. She threw her handful of marbles at my image. They bounced on the floor and rolled. A small cleaning robot darted about gathering the glass spheres.

"I'm going to make it rain comets!" she said.

I shook my head. "That will not be enough to have a substantial—"

"You're still underestimating me."

I reviewed her navigation logs. She had indeed been busy. And the calculations were more complex than I had expected.

"Impressive," I said. She let out a short, vengeful burst of laughter, and then sat, grinning, while I continued to work out the plan. There were collisions with asteroids and slingshot flybys for acceleration. There were almost 10,000 icy bodies falling inward.

"It looks like you've done what you can here," I said. "Shouldn't you consider leaving?"

"Look closer," she said, still smiling. Her eyes were gleaming with anticipation.

I considered her formulas and the trajectories of the various bodies. Many of the objects would pass close to where the predictable Akridi would place their outposts—in this case, very close to the cold, sub-giant star. But many would miss, unless … Her calculations reflected an interesting assumption—she seemed to expect the comets, asteroids, and chunks of moons to be influenced by a subtle outside force; something that was not currently in position in the system.

"Well…" I said.

"It all just needs a little push," she said.

She was right. I looked closer. There was a path that could be followed. A single vessel with a drive the size of hers could sweep into the system at maximum acceleration, and could route these cascading pieces, one after another, into a sharp focus. She planned to drive her ship into the solar system. The Akridi would be in place by that time. They would see her. But before they did, or could do anything about it, she will have executed her plan.

"I'm going to play a game of billiards out here. And they are going to be sitting right on the eight ball."

She was right. But there was a serious problem with the plan. "You can't survive it," I said. "They will—"

"Give me a break, Angel," she said. "It's what I want to do. It's time for me to meet George, and this is how I'm gonna get there. You got a problem with it?"

The challenge was rhetorical. She was firmly committed to her plan. I did offer an insight—a slight modification to her trajectory that would enhance her effectiveness. I also suggested a technique that would strengthen her shielding against gamma-ray bombardment.

She thanked me, and told me she'd say "Hi" to George for me.

I terminated my image on her ship. She needed nothing from me; and my orders required observation for six months from a standard distance of four light-hours.

From my perch, I watched her plan develop. First, the Akridi swept over the system, flooding from their ships onto every planet previously terraformed by the humans. They devoured all they found. In the meantime, an unlikely number of comet tails filled the region. The Akridi took note, but saw no danger. Then a comet changed course, and another. They saw the subtle course changes—dangerous course changes; a dead giveaway. They scrambled, but too late. In one 24-hour period, the rubble of the outer system rained on the inner planets, demolishing the new Akridi colonies, and avenging the death of George.

Delta Pavonis was not the end of the Akridi. And that trick would never work again. But *something* would. And the blow slowed their advance.

My report confirmed the wisdom of the Elders who felt humanity might be worth protecting. More importantly, as ancient and unchanging as we were, it carried a new message to our numbers that we now embrace. The flawed but striving humans can stop the Akridi—and *will* stop them—given time.

At all cost, facilitate the human retreat. Protect the cradle Earth. Allow them to struggle and rise.

That, alone, is our purpose.

First published in *MindFlights*, September 2012.

Millinery Dogma

'They all look the same to me'
has proved to be a universal truth
the silicon lens, the aqueous filled eye,
the photosensitive gaseous spot cannot
resolve differences into species.
So, it has been decreed that all
aboard The Floating Diplomacy
should wear distinguishing hats.

Alice dons the human bonnet.
"You look charming," says her husband.
"Can I try yours on?" she asks.
A bonnet may be charming,
but a top hat has more gravitas.
"Certainly not. They're only for human diplomats,"
says her husband, adjusting her cherries of wax

If you're not a diplomat,
It's boring on The Floating Diplomacy.
Alice explores the servant floors of the spaceship,
where the clones oil the machinery of peace.
One day she finds a Charonite helmet
lying, abandoned, behind a crate of peculiar meat.
She stuffs it in her handbag, and beats a hasty retreat.

"I look just like medusa," Alice thinks.
The helmet suits her.
The assimilation tentacles,

(presumably neutered according to galactic treaty)
Waver like floating weeds.
She caresses the hypnotic tentacles,
feels a strange stab of disappointment,
instead of nano-tech hive-ability.

What a difference she finds when she enters
the subordinates/wives luncheon club.
instead of the usual courtesies
she faces stares of outright hostility.
How unfair, she thinks.
It's just not right that the Charonites should
be judged on the action of their ancestors,
that small solar system assimilated aeons ago.

Even her husband, her human husband,
cannot see through her disguise,
(although admittedly the helmet is rather large
and almost covers her eyes).
He passes her in the corridor with a 'humph' of
disdain.
What power is held in a hat.
Diplomats and subordinates, alike,
see only what they expect to see.
And Alice finds herself longing for a galaxy where
all could be hatless and free.

— Deborah Walker

The Alien Recruiter

Story by Marge Simon
Illustration by Teresa Tunaley

There's a time for moving on, she knew it was coming soon. It always came too soon. The mist kissed her cropped hair, made it too curly—she hated that, always hated anything that might have made her too attractive to the natives. But she'd been picked for her good looks as well as her brains.

They had her name in Glasgow. The artist had done a bad job on her face, but it was still out there on bulletins. Of course, she'd changed her credentials, passport, time and time over. The cramping had returned. She flexed her toes, pushing them up to relieve the pain. She missed the sea, missed the stroke of webbed feet, leagues below the surface. Her kind had visited for centuries, and so the legends of the Selkies, changelings of the seas. Amphibian, or they'd never have reached the stars. Absently, she scratched the scars behind her chin. The operation was a small price to pay for the prime directive. It would be easily reversed, once home.

Down the beach from her, a young man squatted, looking out to the horizon. She walked until she stood beside him, but he didn't seem to notice. *Like a young messiah, a young, long haired Dylan, maybe?* She stifled a smile.

"Penny for your thoughts?" Startled, he looked up and stood, wiping sand off his pants. His eyes were an amazing deep cerulean, like that of the ocean farther out. He just stood there, so she put out her hand. "Lara. And you are?" Hesitantly, he took her hand. His answer was almost drowned in the crash of a breaker. "Stefan."

"Well, Stefan, tell me where I can get a decent cup of coffee." She grinned, adding "I'm new here."

He smiled back. "Sure! Um, are you with the college?" She shook her head. "No, but I was thinking of taking a class or two this summer. I'm just visiting relatives."

They moved on to the boardwalk, past the greasy spoons and fishy smells from stalls. He stopped in front of a modest cafe proclaiming *Beer & Sundry.* "This is it. Best coffee in the state, so they say." Once served, he opened up a little. He was majoring in philosophy, but had just dropped out that morning. "What can you do with a degree in that?"

She laughed softly. "I hear you. Teach it or preach it?"

"I wasn't expecting that from you." Stefan's face lit up. He ran his fingers through his tousled hair. "Say, if you're free Friday night, would you like to split a bottle of vino, maybe listen to my collection? I'm into Celtic music."

"Sounds like a plan." She smiled back at him. Enya? She'd briefed herself hastily on Gaelic history and modern music trends, but not needed much of it. The pubs were noisy, the youth cared only for what was current. It usually wasn't necessary to know more than that. Or was it? Gazing into Stefan's eyes, she felt inexplicably unprepared.

Back in her apartment, she stood staring into the grey-gold New England dusk. *Get a grip! What is it about him? The way he says something that means much more? A pliant mind, but strong.*

She glanced around the room. A few books, some papers and photos. An iPad, fairly new. She ran a finger over the keyboard. The wifi connection didn't work, but she rarely used the internet. Certainly not for communications with Command Central. Nothing personal on the shelves unless you count the shell collection. Most of them got broken as she moved from place to place. She'd toss the damaged ones and add more, depending on her location.

Her job as an agent was to recruit from a planet rich with supplies. Young minds to bend to a cause, it never mattered what cause. Just make them angry, make them care. She was good at that. She prided herself on her skill. It was always the same. Once taken, they'd be programmed as servants of the State. A government indifferent to independent minds. From what she knew of this world, it had happened here times over. *Make no entangling alliances* was the operative, no matter where she was, no matter what she felt personally. It had worked out okay, just part of the programming for the most part. A few times, she'd cared for a recruit more than she should have. But such thoughts were easily erased by the CC technician. Besides, that was years ago.

Friday morning came, and with it storms that lasted most of the day. In the evening, the skies cleared. The seas were scored with froth, the air clean. But heavy clouds hung motionless, the rain was not yet done.

Stefan was waiting on the steps of his small apartment. Once inside, she noticed a medium sized aquarium with several species of tropical fish and a few mollusks. "Nice selection," she said casually. "That lionfish and the mollies are a good choice."

"Thanks. It's the closest to them I'll ever get. They're so beautiful."

She raised her eyebrows. "Ever been to the Keys? Or can't you swim?"

Stefan shook his head. "Asthma. My father thought I was a being a wimp and threw me in a public pool. It was a close call, I almost died. Anyway, that's why I can't—*won't*—swim. Lucky I can breathe okay most of the time. Excuse me a sec." He disappeared into the kitchen and returned with two glasses and a bottle of chardonnay.

He held up a CD. "You familiar with Enya?" She shook her head. What she knew about Celtic music was current rock, little more. A few moments later, she decided she did, indeed, like the Enya group. It was a far cry from the abrasive current pop. Sipping the wine, she lay back on the cushions, letting the music of "Orinoco Flow" wash over her. A song of the sea within the notes, the upward waves, the booming depths.

When it was over, Stefan had returned with a bowl of pentagonal crackers which she found divinely salty, perfect with the garlic in the side dip

"You mentioned your father. That's just awful," she said between bites. She felt sure that this would elicit some straight reply. Some kind of rebellious angst.

"Yeah," he said. "He did that, and some other stuff." Stefan's eyes darkened. "I don't want to talk about him. Tell me about the sea. You said you've scuba dived on the west coast."

She found herself telling him things she'd not shared before. Things like how it feels to be one with the sea, how the sights below the surface one never takes for granted, the colors. Ocean currents satin soft.

He was looking at her strangely. "I've never heard any divers talk about it quite like you do. It's as if you enjoy the ocean like a seal or a dolphin or something. Where did you say you're from?"

She frowned, *TMI, watch it!* and drained her glass. "Born and raised in Florida."

"Oh? You don't have a Florida accent. My aunt was from there, and she talked with a twang. A real Florida cracker, Aunt Em…" His voice trailed off, but he didn't take his eyes off her face. "Lovely Lara, my mystery girl. Have another?" he asked.

"No, thanks. It's getting late, I'd better head back home." She stood up quickly, almost knocking the bottle over. Tonight wasn't going the way it should have. But she stopped at the door and turned.

"Next Friday? Treat you to my amazing hot dogs."

Stefan smiled, but his steady gaze didn't change. "All right. See you then."

Time to prepare for the swing, as she'd always thought of it. A week, a little research and she'd have him nailed to volunteer. Yet for not the first time lately, she found herself reluctant.

* * *

Friday came and she did her best with the hot dogs. Even got the grill marks right, rather than burnt. Cooking had never been her forte, nor had she much interest in it. Heinekin seemed a good choice for drink, according to the liquor store guy. Stefan seemed to like the fare, consuming three dogs and two bottles before declaring he was full. They made small talk over another beer, sitting outside on the steps until darkness consumed the ocean view. When his hand crept over hers and closed, she squeezed it back. Realizing what she'd done, she pulled away, saying she was chilly.

They moved inside to sit on her divan. "Lara, I—" he drew her in for a kiss. After a moment, she moved back, shaking her head to clear it. "All right, I like you. But—"

He laughed. "Everything you say before 'but' isn't important. So?"

She narrowed her eyes. "You didn't drop out of classes. You're not even enrolled here."

"How—how did you know? You've been spying on me?"

"No, not spying. Never mind. I'd like us to be friends. That means no more lies, okay? You don't need to make up a life just to entertain me."

"I wasn't trying to entertain you. I'm crazy about you, but you keep pushing me away."

She moved back to him, running her hand down the side of his face. "Stefan, where are you going now? What do you really want out of your life?"

His smile faded. "Don't know. My grandfather's trust fund works fine for me—in fact, he was overly generous. But I don't plan to wind up like my dad. Fighting a war he didn't believe in. Coming home less a man. Wheelchair and booze. Looney, most of the time, after. All for a cause he didn›t care about."

"So—what do you want? I can offer you a life that gives you meaning, a cause. My agency has need of the brightest minds, like yours. There's so much to be done, to make this world a perfect place, and it's so easy to join. Trust me. You do trust me, don't you Stefan?"

"Trust you for what you can offer me? I thought we had something. Now you're talking like you're selling me something." He turned to look at her. "You know, you're pretty sharp yourself. Somehow you seem to know I've been at a crossroads for months. I just don't care about getting a degree. Maybe I don't want to commit to anything. He stared out into the night, drumming his palms on the windowsill, then turned to face her.

"I don't give a crap about causes. Yours, especially. You know how I feel—felt about you. Maybe I still feel something, but I'm not stupid. You're not from Florida, are you? Not from here, not from anywhere remotely near here, are you." It was not a question. His eyes widened. "You want me to serve your people—whoever or whatever they are—don't you? That's your cause, your great, god damned cause!"

He swallowed and continued. "I can't be like you, and I'm damned sure I'm not going to be your next recruit. It's all wrong."

She hadn't known what to say to him. How could he have sensed the truth? Why did it suddenly matter so very much that he was telling her goodbye?

* * *

This time was different too. She squinted, shielding her eyes to the sun, searching the boardwalk crowd. No, he wouldn't be there, she should have known, their last talk made that clear.

The wind rose, and with it a keening sound, not of the sea, but the soundless cry of a human soul between life and death. So he'd kept his word. Maybe Stefan had a cause after all, if it was to protest her mission.

All she had to do at that moment was dive in and save him. Prove that her cause was righteous, no matter how much longer it might take. But she simply stood there, looking out over the water until the sun passed below the horizon.

Come daylight, the beach would fill again with fishermen readying their boats. She shuddered, feeling the pain in her legs, the longing to let go. It wasn't natural, keeping human form so close to the rhythm of the tides. Yet it wasn't natural doing what she'd been programmed to do, either. Stefan had been right.

Slowly she began to undress. Naked, she waited until the moon was full above the waves.

Taking a last breath of air, she dove in.

Never Been Kissed

Medusa has never been kissed.
She reads cheesy romance novels.
She sits in the back row
Of movie theaters, a scarf
Around her head and
Sunglasses at night,
To watch chick flicks.
She can imagine what
It feels like, soft lips
Touching the daring
Slither of tongues.
Yet she remains virgin
To the experience,
What with the turn
To stone thing and
Her unfortunate hairdo.
She tried dating blind men
But the snakes kept biting.

— K.S. Hardy

Rocket to the Morgue and the Problem of "Fair Play" in Science Fiction

Article by Robert E. Porter

When *Rocket to the Morgue* came out in 1942, it had H. H. Holmes in the byline. Holmes was a cover for mystery writer and critic—and future *Fantasy & Science Fiction* editor—Anthony Boucher. The pseudonym was taken from a real-life serial killer in Chicago who was written up in the book *Devil in the White City*.

Boucher's *Rocket* was a send-up to the science fiction that had recently swept him off his feet. It was also a roman à clé with some fictional characters standing in for people that Boucher knew personally. One of the more interesting characters was science fiction writer and suspect Austin Carter.

Carter was "utterly true to [our] perception of what Heinlein was like in person," said The Heinlein Society's D. A Houdek and G. E. Rule. "Boucher ... gives later readers a time-machine glimpse into Robert Heinlein's own living room, hearing him speak—more or less—as himself." (Houdek)

And, during the course of a murder investigation, Austin Carter said, "we can't have detective stories in science fiction." (Boucher 77)

Why not?

Faced with a locked room mystery, Carter proposes the following SFnal solutions:

1) "The Dagger was conveyed through space and plunged into the victim's heart by teleportation."

2) "[T]he murderer dissembled his component atoms on one side of the wall, filtered through by osmosis, and reassembled them on the other side."

3) "[T]he murderer simply entered and left through the fourth dimension of space."

4) "He committed the murder, set the dials of his trusty time machine back an hour or so, and left the room ... He could then call on the detective in charge of the case and be visiting with him at the exact hour when the murder was being committed." (Boucher 76-7)

Carter goes on to tell the detective, "So many maneuverings are logically possible [in science fiction] that you could never conceivably exclude the guilt of anyone." (Boucher 77)

He's right, of course—on those premises. But I disagree. It depends on how you'd answer two basic questions:

What is science fiction?

and

Can a science fiction writer "play fair" with his readers?

What Is Science Fiction?

When I was about 11 years old, a cousin gave me Jerome Bixby's *Space by the Tale*. This was my introduction to science fiction. I was hooked. Bixby is still one of my favorite writers. You probably know his story about a boy with godlike powers. "It's a *Good* Life" was included in *The Science Fiction Hall of Fame*, "chosen by those who know better than anyone what the criteria [for the best science fiction stories] should be—the Science Fiction Writers of America." (Silverberg ix)

In Philip K. Dick's *Time Out of Joint*, pieces of paper with words on them construct "reality" in the minds of brainwashed characters. In *Ubik*, the dead man helping the heroes may very well be more alive than they are. These are a couple of my favorite novels. Are they science fiction? Of course. You'll find them ranked among the best. But Dick was no popular scientist, no philosophical naturalist; if his Berkeleyism and mind-blowing, schizoid hallucinations are compatible with science, so is the Creationist's god seeding the young earth with dinosaur bones.

I could go on and on. But I mean to say that Carter's "solutions" to a locked room mystery seem typical of science fiction—more diverting than possible, practical, or likely.

Wrap the fairy godmother's wand in foil, give it a blinking red light, and *voila!* It's science fiction. After all, wishes really *can* come true. Technology becomes magical at some point, according to Clarke's Third Law.

And the gods were ancient astronauts, according to Erich von Däniken.

Readers come to science fiction as True Believers, or at least willing to suspend their disbelief. This is a fundamental difference in the approach to science fiction and mystery/detective stories.

Established in 1976, CSICOP was like a detective agency. Members included Isaac Asimov and L. Sprague de Camp. They popularized science and the scientific method by investigating the stuff of science fiction, fantasy, and horror—psychics, talking with the dead, Big Foot, alien abductions, crop circles, poltergeists, spontaneous human combustion and so on—when they wound up on the evening news, in the tabloids, or the nonfiction section.

Whether Asimov and de Camp did anything like this in their science fiction is debatable. Both had stories in the magazine that launched L. Ron Hubbard's Scientology. Their editor John W. Campbell also promoted "The Science of Psionics" in *Astounding*, the flagship of hard SF, which he later renamed *Analog Science Fiction and Fact*.

"Judging by the number of Campbell's readers who are impressed by this nonsense," said Martin Gardner, "the average fan may very well be a chap in his teens, with a smattering of scientific knowledge culled mostly from science fiction, enormously gullible, with a strong bent toward occultism, no understanding of the scientific method, and a basic insecurity for which he compensates by fantasies of scientific power." (Gardner 348)

Tough criticism. But that was back in 1957.

"I think SF fans are more scientifically literate today than they were in those days," J Alan Erwine told me, "but I also think there are fewer fans than there used to be—at least of literature." Erwine had just come back from MileHiCon, where he had joined the "Lunatic Fringe" panel to discuss the science in science fiction. Other members of the panel included Hugo and Nebula award-winner Paolo Bacigalupi and USAF space command's Doug Beason. It sounded like a fun panel, but not a very critical one.

"They also discussed that planes were really teleporters, because it really should be unthinkable that we can get on a plane and ten hours later be halfway across the world," said Science Fiction Analyst Alison Baumgartner. "Naturally, this makes one wonder, if we do indeed live in a science fiction society, is there really such a thing as science fiction?" (Baumgartner)

If planes are teleporters, sure, we're living in a science fiction society. But a ten-hour transcontinental flight is not only thinkable, it is do-able. It is, in fact, routine. Teleportation, à la Carter, is only thinkable.

If anyone says that we live in a science fiction society, that's a falsifiable claim. Why not put it to the test:

How many stories in *The Science Fiction Hall of Fame* described a world like ours? How many Hugo and Nebula award-winners of the 60s, 70s, and 80s? How many stories in the annual Year's Best? And how many of these stories were off the mark? WAY off the mark?

Crunch the numbers.

If we're going to give the writers credit for their hits, we'd be dishonest not to also hold them accountable for their misses.

But science fiction writers aren't necessarily trying to predict the future. They're often trying to prevent it.

Then again, looking back over the all science fiction I've read over the years, I'd hate to think that writers like Bixby and Dick were trying to predict the future or to prevent it with stories like "It's a *Good* Life" and *Ubik*. I found them entertaining, that's all.

John Brunner's *The Sheep Look Up* is probably the most realistic science fiction novel I've read. Of course, I could be wrong. It's hard to tell what exactly is going on behind Brunner's literary smokescreen.

There's no such cover-up in Tom Clancy's *Red Storm Rising*; both the language and the narrative free-climbed, naked, to the top of *The New York Times* bestsellers list. A near-future scenario in 1986, this novel of World War Three comes much closer than Brunner's *Sheep* to the falsifiability of a scientific claim. For example, Clancy was aware of stealth technology but he didn't know the details; he didn't have the clearance. So he speculated, he took some educated guesses, and—like a scientist—he put his hypotheses to the test. He put them in writing, and in a way that we can easily compare his speculations about stealth technology to the facts as we know them now.

But *Red Storm Rising* is not science fiction; it's a thriller.

Suppose Erwine's right. A lot has changed since the 1950s. What if everyone, not just the average science fiction fan, is more scientifically literate? Less naive, more worldly? Perhaps the "magic" of science fiction now has all the appeal of a cargo cult—or an inside joke.

Is this all that science fiction has to offer?

Hardly.

Can a Science Fiction Writer "Play Fair" With His Readers?

Dorothy Sayers defined the modern detective story according to "fair play." This means "the essential clues are all collected and set before the reader before the detective makes any deductions from them." (Sayers vii-viii) And "the writer might assume the reader to be acquainted with any established and recorded fact, however obscure or recently discovered." (Sayers xii)

If a victim was poisoned, the mystery reader wants to tell the poison from its symptoms. She wants to figure out who had access to both that poison and the victim. She's trying to solve the crime. She's trying to beat the detective at his own game. But if the poison and its symptoms are made up, or if the elderly culprit only had access by breaking down a door with his four-pronged aluminum cane—Foul! The author isn't playing fair. And if he isn't playing fair, it's no mystery.

In other words, the writer of detective stories can't just make things up as he goes along. He can't play God—or Philip K. Dick. And his characters can't have god-like powers.

In other words: No Magic.

What can anyone know about a killer's working time machine or actual powers of teleportation? Who has experience with these things? They run contrary to all established and recorded facts. Even as science fiction tropes, there are no facts; there are only precedents, which the writer is usually free and expected to disregard. Under these conditions, how can any reader make sense of the clues and solve the crime?

She can't.

Carter has a point.

Once he lets "magic" into his story, the bubble has burst. Anything has become logically possible and the writer can no longer "play fair" with his readers.

But if it's about a crime, it's a crime story. And Carter never said we can't have crime stories in science fiction. On the contrary…

If a time traveler commits murder, why not send a time traveling detective after him? That might be fun. But if it's a detective story just because it has a detective in it, then R. Austin Freeman's Dr. Thorndyke stories are science fiction because the hero uses science and the scientific method to solve crimes.

Anyway, there was no need to burst that bubble. What if a writer left the "magic" to Harry Potter, dismissed Clarke's Third Law as "not even wrong," and made his future as realistic as possible? He could write a future-detective story, then.

But would it be science fiction?

If a future-detective story is more like *Red Storm Rising* than *The Sheep Look Up* or *Time Out of Joint,* if there's "fair play," with a reliable narrative and no "magic," can it be science fiction? Who says? And does their opinion count?

To find out, let's do a thought experiment. Take one of today's detective stories…

The detective uses his cell phone and laptop during the course of a murder/terror investigation. He does an internet search. There's talk of hacking and identity theft. The suspect has left a cyber-trail. They track him down. There's a stake out. The cops use a thermal imaging camera to "see" through the walls of the suspect's house. Is this legal? How far do they go to avoid infringing on the suspect's Fifth Amendment rights? What special weapons and tactics do they use to break in and try to capture the suspect alive? Under what circumstances would they shoot to kill? The "science" of fingerprinting, blood-spatter, and bite-mark analysis has recently come under fire. Verdicts have been overturned by DNA tests. Spanish has become a second language in America. Civil rights and gender equality are virtually taken for granted. All of this might come into play.

Let's say this story just came out in *Ellery Queen's Mystery Magazine.* You like it so much that you type it up in standard MS format. You send it 60 years back in time and drop it in the slush at *Astounding*—or *Galaxy.*

Even from the POV of the 1950s, the present as we know it was far more likely than a trip back in time, or a killer stepping through a doorway in Topeka and into her victim's room in Damascus. Surely a writer in those days, if he had bothered to try, was far more likely to write a detective story like the one described above than he was to build a working time machine or teleporter. So our thought experiment is not as far-fetched as it might seem…

Finally, editor Campbell—or H.L. Gold—pulls the story out of his slush and takes a look at it. Does he call it science fiction? Is there any chance he'd publish the story in his magazine?

If so, Carter's wrong. We *can* have detective stories in science fiction.

And the question simply becomes:

Whodunit?

WORKS CITED

Houdek , D.A. and Rule, G.E. "Robert A. Heinlein: Murder Suspect." *Heinlein Society-Scholastic/Academic Articles.* (2007): n. page. Web. 12 Jan. 2013. <http://www.heinleinsociety.org/rah/works/articles/murdersuspect.html>.

Boucher, Anthony . *Rocket to the Morgue.* 3rd ed. New York: Pyramid Books, 1975. 76-7. Print.

Silverberg, Robert. *The Science Fiction Hall of Fame: The Greatest Science Fiction Stories of All Time vol. I.*

2nd ed. New York: Avon Books, 1971. ix. Print.

Gardner, Martin. *Fads & Fallacies In the Name of Science*. 2nd ed. New York: Dover, 1957. 240-1 and 347-8 . Print.

Baumgartner, Alison. "How Much Science Should Be in Science Fiction?" *ScienceFiction.com*. (30 Oct. 2013): n. page. Web. 17 Nov. 2013 http://sciencefiction.com/2013/10/29/much-science-science-fiction/

Sayers, Dorothy L. . *Great Tales of Detection*. Reprinted as an Everyman Classic. London and Melbourne: J.M. Dent & Sons, 1984. vii-viii and xii. Print.

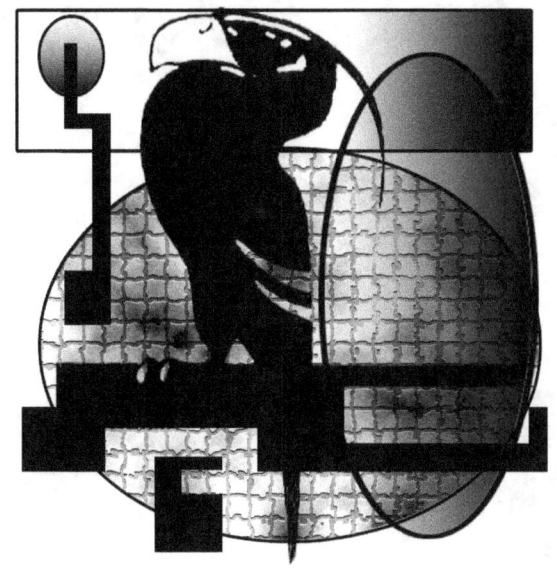

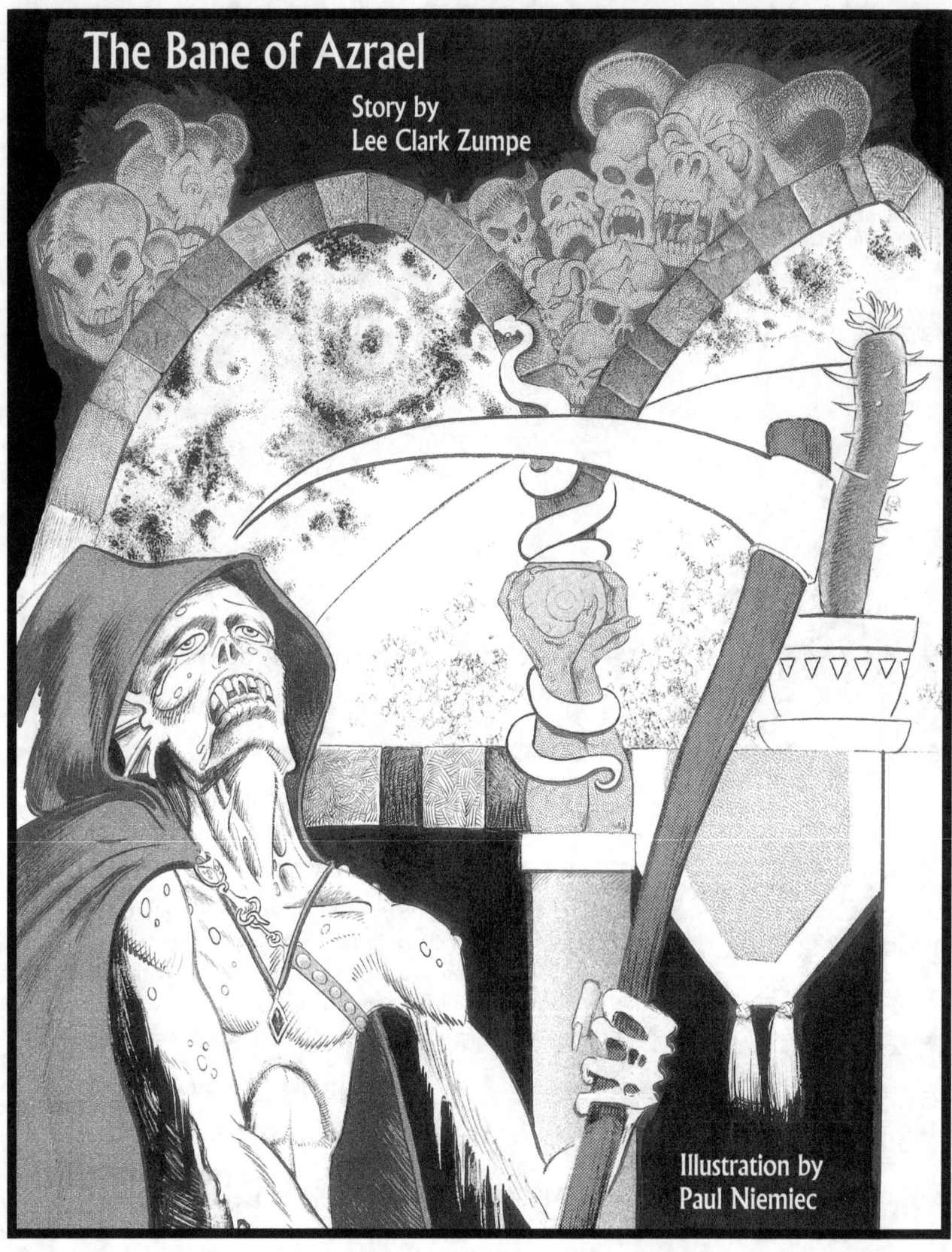

The Bane of Azrael

Story by
Lee Clark Zumpe

Illustration by
Paul Niemiec

"We'll need more psychopomps," Aztael says, his wispy pronouncement a mere whisper, though those within earshot grasp its grave significance without vacillation. Not since the dark days of the Black Death has the Grim Reaper looked so—well, grim. "Call for them," he commands, "call for them all."

It is my turn to sit with him, to tend to his wounds.

A modest attendant with limited perception and only a tinge of insight, I gather shards of wisdom from his sporadic ravings and the gibbering of his various avatars as they execute his strict mandate. Piecing together these random details, I gradually come to realize what has transpired. I shudder at the thought of it and at the permanent repercussions.

"Try to rest." Azrael reclines in his divan, slouched against plush, lavender pillows. Black silken sheets collect in crumpled knots around his legs and stretch across his midsection. With trembling hand I gently wipe each lesion with a moistened cloth, trying to ease his agony. Every moment, a dozen new sores blossom. "Try to remain still." He never listens.

"So many," he says in his soft, wretched voice. He scratches at the puss-filled abscesses until his nails are slick and smeared with the viscous toxins of arriving souls, the final moments of their earthbound agonies encapsulated in each emerging blister. His torment increases exponentially as the sudden spark of another heartless massacre shimmers in his midnight eyes. "No mercy have they."

"No mercy," Morrigu says, mimicking his master's words. The carrion crow darts through the open window and through a part in the heavy curtains, then flutters about the room momentarily before finally settling on his customary perch at the foot of the bed. 'No mercy at all."

"A scrap of cheerful news would be appreciated." Azrael shifts his weight and redirects his gaze, The bird squawks as he scrambles to orchestrate a credible lie. His bleak hesitation reveals the severity of circumstances. "They must choke on the very ashes of the dead."

"The dead are scattered over pastoral lands and city streets alike, rotting with no likelihood of burial or cremation." Morrígu nervously picks at his wings with his shiny, black beak. Souls spill from his overloaded feathers, sprinkling across the bedclothes. "There is no end in sight, no prospect for a reversal of fortune."

"No end?" Azrael winces, a hint of anger and disapproval twisting his face. "This deluge of death is inundating my empire, overburdening my emissaries and taxing both my patience and my generosity."

I lean back as Azrael brushes aside my hand. Below, the mortal world has become entangled in dark and devious designs, enslaved by the whims of the wicked and fouled by chronic apathy and intolerance. Its descent into madness has been a measured one to be sure, not entirely unexpected. Civilizations always collapse, traditionally terminating in some form of prolonged bloodbath. Such spikes in the morality rate are predictable, calculated and considered and absorbed. Allowances can be made.

Not this time. Technology changes the age-old equation.

"Another city has burned." Thanatos steps into the chamber unannounced. Encircled by a thick haze of fluttering black butterflies, he bows silently in token respect and admiration. His young face sags, the corners of his mouth droop with a combination solemnity and fatigue. "Leveled by another extremist—a suicide bomber with a nuclear device. Millions are dead or dying."

The butterflies coalesce into a syrupy shadow and descend upon Azrael

When we are alone again, he weeps silently and I resume my ministration. Few hear his muffled pleas for amnesty, his pitiful prayers soliciting the very condition for which he has become a symbol. His immortality has become his blight. Long ago he entered into a contract which established his dominion over all those drifting souls lacking destination. He is the gate through which all must pass on their final journey to be judged. His is the empire where those in limbo linger eternally. His very house is purgatory.

"Their suffering rivals only their malice in its repugnance." I nod in agreement, knowing it is not my place to comment. "A simple custodian, consigned to wash these accursed blisters endlessly—even you can see the hopelessness, can't you?"

The jackal-headed shadow-lurker Anpu bursts into the room, his sinister smile disclosing his fanaticism and self-satisfaction. Still, even the most enthusiastic and voracious harvester of death knows his limits. Drunk with power and overexertion, he trembles on the verge of exhaustion.

"Famine and pestilence, brothers of the apocalypse, send their regards. I bring you a bouquet of flowers from the twins." Again, souls fall victim to shameless science, to engineered viruses designed to target ethnicity and affect genocide. Bowing, he sets the blackened blooms beside Azrael. I watch as the delicate petals wilt, wither and fade into fine ash. "A varied ensemble, encompassing peasants and prime ministers, laborers and lords, soldiers and saints, and infants and elderly."

Azrael sighs, the skin of his lips cracking and seeping inky blood. He offers no word of gratitude or acknowledgment. As each new tenant passes through him, he bears their pain, their despair, their distress, displeasure and untimely defeat.

"Leave me be," he says, turning to me, muttering the words like a frail old man about to be sick. "Let me have a moment to compose myself." Though straightforward and seemingly unproblematic, his request comes as a shock. For the first time ever, Azrael has closed his door to visitors, forced his many incarnations to wait, to shoulder their burden a few minutes longer, to grant him a single respite. "I'll beckon you when I am ready."

I step outside for a breath of stale air. The twisted branches of leafless trees claw at the grim, gray skies. On the dirt path outside Azrael's castle, I chance upon Ankou. Wearing his fedora and a long, black coat, he sits in his rickety cart driven by a team of four bony horses. Behind him, two attendant skeletons prepare to harvest more souls.

Prudish and terminally punctual, Ankou materialized in the earliest days of Azrael's reign—a dark reflection of his dourness and indifference, obsessed with formalities and ritual. Each avatar epitomized some aspect of Azrael's character, including his wit, his charm, his zeal and his regret. Of them all, only Ankou had shown no tremors of disgruntlement in recent days, no trace of tiredness.

Of them all, I found him the most likely candidate with whom to conspire.

Summoning up my courage, I approach him.

"He's tired." I stare into his pallid, emaciated face. His gnarled fingers fidget on the reigns.

"We are all tired," he says tentatively, unaccustomed to addressing the humble servants of Azrael's house. His admission surprises me, underscores the gravity of the situation.

"He hasn't the strength." The suggestion shrivels in the stagnant air like some blasphemous argument spoken to a pious disciple.

"He hasn't the luxury of rest or retirement."

"Hasn't he?" Ankou's ashen face glows with a dark, invisible shimmer. Turning toward me, his eyes become swirling chasms concealing dead galaxies containing worlds I cannot fathom. With fast-fading audacity, I make one last appeal. "Your knuckles are bloody from all the doors you have rapped over the centuries. Have you ever thought to knock on his door?"

Having insinuated the unthinkable, I turn and leave Ankou to contemplate in silence. Only afterward as I trace the many roads leading to the castle do I find time to reassess the rebellion I have instigated and to ponder the ramifications. Should it be viewed as sacrilege, my exile would be guaranteed. Should it provide the seed to revolution, my services would no longer be needed.

Mictlanteculhtli, the blood-spattered skeleton king of Chicunauhmictlan, finds me brooding on the Edge of Despair, the ledge of a precipice overlooking the festering earth.

"Azrael will see you shortly," I assure him, thinking he has come to inquire about the anomalous delay. "He needed to rest."

"I know, little one." Mictlanteculhtli sits down on the cliff, dangling his bones precariously over the shelf. "That's not why I came looking for you."

"'What, then?" Immediately I assume that word of my radical incitement has reached Azrael and that I am to be banished.

"Did you know that you have always been his favorite, little one?"

"What do you mean?"

"He knows no other so selfless, none whose concern for him is as genuine and limitless as yours." Mictlanteculhtli gazed down at the earth through two cold, empty sockets. "They neither embrace nor fear him any longer. Their precious science has made them indifferent and coldhearted."

Science had inexorably altered the relationship between life and death. Discoveries and advances simultaneously provided methods to extend, destroy and create life. Where once war, famine and disease culled the herd, the constant cloning of soldiers on scattered breeding farms keeps the population from becoming even marginally depleted.

Azrael faces an endless parade of grisly, gory death. Extinction is an unlikely aspiration, abolished by technology.

"Azrael has served them well, He deserves to rest in peace."

"And so he shall." Mictlanteculhtli pats me on the shoulder, a token of his admiration. "So shall we all."

I join Azrael at his bedside. The room teeters on the brink of darkness as the vestiges of a candle flicker a few last sparks in the final throes of death. I place a cool, clean cloth on his forehead and Azrael smiles as its coolness curbs his fever.

"Thank you," he says as we hear a knock on the

chamber door. He tilts his head to the side, his momentary contentedness apparently ended, expecting to resume his duties. "Come in."

And as his weary soul lifts from its sickly shell, I know that from that moment on the dead shall walk the earth—and I feel no regret.

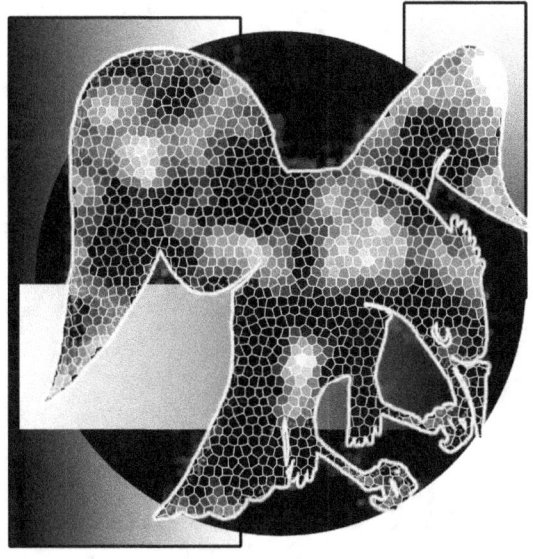

Misery of He Who is Older than All Men
for Martin Andersson

He who is older than all men suffers a misery deeper than the sum of man's wars and plagues. Left, for reasons known only to the gods, to ponder his existence amidst the cosmic fog outside space and time, to know only his purpose, his destiny, a task performed mindlessly and without pause.

As a consequence, many questions relative to his plight arise but are never answered. He bears no recollection of birth, no sense of an earlier time or even of time itself, save for hints gleaned from the ever-heightening awareness of mankind as it fumbles through its chaotic existence.

He cannot talk to men. There has never been kith or kin with which to converse. Yet now and again come flashes of having once been human: a cave strewn with ancient paintings, the dirty faces of woman and child, crude weapons in the hand, the fearful eyes of his prey and the grim stone idols of worship....

Adding to his misery is the probability that these flashes are merely residual energies from the endless stream of human souls passing through his boney fingers.

Was I truly once a man? he thinks. *How long must I endure this limbotic state? How long before I may again know the thrill of the hunt, the touch of a woman? Certainly there is another to replace me.*

And he cannot help but be convinced of a return to life, for all souls make their way back to Earth in one form or another—to this cycle he is first witness.

But he who is older than all men and whose core is a diamond of misery must endure his current destiny without fail, for always there is war and rampant disease, starvation, senseless murder, agedness....

For who knew, that he who first *personified* Death, *became* Death. That with a cave wall and crude ochres had released it from the intangible realm of nightmare.

— Jason Sturner

The Breath Thief
Story by Karissa B. Sluss
Illustration by Kathy Ferrell

Tabitha watched him suckle the lip of his mug, but the last of its contents disappeared down his throat a quarter of an hour ago, and she knew he lacked the funds to purchase a refill. He peered into his tankard as if he misplaced a pint of beer somewhere within its depths, but after a thorough search, he admitted defeat. His shoulders slumped, and he heaved a sigh.

"What a mournful sound," said Tabitha.

The man turned to find a small woman sitting beside him; one who looked like a fall leaf—brown and crinkled around the edges.

She gazed at him with knitted brows. "What's got you down?"

He tipped his empty mug towards her in reply.

"Oh, that's an easy problem to fix." Tabitha threw her hand up to catch the barman's attention; and as he switched empty mugs for full ones, Tabitha leaned closer and asked, "What's your name, friend?"

The stranger grunted. "Who says I'm your friend?"

"I just bought you a drink. That's got to make us acquaintances at least."

Tabitha watched the man's face turn from sullen to sunny as he came to the realization that a bit of cordiality on his part might result in more benevolence on hers. He stuck out his hand and smiled. "Name's Franklin Massey. S'nice to meetcha."

Tabitha thought if Franklin knew of the state of his dentition, he would hesitate to smile with such enthusiasm, but she would overlook his teeth, and his odiferous exterior, if he gave her what she wanted in return. She took his hand and squeezed it. "Tabitha Lowrie."

"I know lotsa Lowries, but I don't know you. You from around here?"

"My kin are from these parts, but I'm a bit of a loose end. Like to go where the wind takes me—you know?"

"Nah," said Franklin. "My momma birthed me in a cabin just up the road and I never found reason to travel more'n a couple counties away."

Franklin gripped his beer in anticipation as he waited for the last bit of foam to fizzle away. "If you don't mind my asking, what's brought you here?"

"I'm starting a business," said Tabitha.

Franklin choked on astonishment and Tabitha supposed he never encountered a woman with a professional trade that didn't involve lying on her back. She and Franklin drank a while longer in stilted silence, but at last the barman called for final orders.

"S'not safe for a woman to travel alone at night,"
said Franklin. "I'd be happy to escort you home."

Tabitha produced several coins from her coat pocket and deposited them on the bar next to their empties. "Don't have a home," she said.

Franklin steadied himself on his feet and then tugged his earlobe—a nervous tick, Tabitha guessed. "You planning to room here?"

"No, I don't plan to stay here."

"So, where you gonna go?"

"With you." She said it in such a matter-of-fact way that it likely never occurred to Franklin to contradict her. She laced her hand around his arm—never mind that he hadn't offered it—and led them out the door.

* * *

Though fouled by decay and the lingering residue of beer, the breath released from Franklin's lungs flew easily between them as they slept. Slipping from his mouth, it crept into Tabitha's, taking residence in her chest. Unaware, Franklin gave freely, but it was insufficient. She had learned to ration her larceny to keep the victim's body strong and his suspicions weak. She would require months of nights like this to gather her fill. By daybreak, Franklin's lips would be blue as if he spent the night lying in snow, and he would vaguely remember an autumnal woman buying rounds of drinks before following him back to his cabin.

At the first light of morning, Tabitha eased from Franklin's cabin and put him out of her thoughts as she trudged deep into the nearby cypress woods of the Ashepole Swamp. Eventually she located the thing that had compelled her journey. An old distillery hunkered expectantly on the bank of a small creek, its copper body gleaming in spots through a green patina. Tabitha rubbed the rough belly of the worm box where alcohol steam condensed into liquid. Water trickled throughout the contraption in a steady stream, urging her to put it to use.

The still had once belonged to her great aunt, but the ancient lady bequeathed it to Tabitha when her first disastrous attempt at romance revealed she had inherited the Lowerie family legacy. By her nature, Tabitha lived an evanescent life, and distilling moonshine proved a compatible means of support.

"Hello old friend," she said, giving the still another pat. "It's been a long time."

* * *

That night, Tabitha eased into bed next to Franklin, exhausted and blistered on her hands and feet from her day of labors—cleaning, gathering supplies, preparing the still for production. From the sour smell of him, she supposed Franklin spent the day in the same manner as he spent the one previous. He mumbled something, threw an arm over her, and took up snoring in her ear.

* * *

"I thought I dreamed you."

Tabitha pried one eye open to find Franklin awake and surprisingly sober and clear headed. "How do you know this isn't the same dream?"

He reached out and pinched her. "You feel real enough to me."

"Ouch!" she cried. "You're supposed to pinch yourself."

"Hurts less if I pinch you, though. What're you doing here anyway?"

"I told you. I don't have any place to go."

"What makes you think you can stay with me?"

"You never said I couldn't."

Franklin coughed to clear his throat and his cheeks lit with embarrassment. "It's been a while since I had anything to do with a woman. What exactly do you expect from me?"

The corner of Tabitha's lip curled up in a suggestive manner and she saw the pulse in Franklin's neck react accordingly. "Besides providing me with a roof and a bed?" she asked.

Franklin gulped and nodded.

"I'd like you to work for me."

He recoiled from her. "Work?"

Tabitha rearranged her position, sitting up to face him with more formality—if such a thing could be done between two people sharing a bed. "Yes, I'd like to offer you a job."

Franklin's hairy brows drew together into a scowl. "What kind of job?"

And so Tabitha explained her business proposition. She would run the still and bottle the whiskey. He would transport and sell the liquor for her thereby earning a commission—a risky endeavor, considering the government's outspoken aversion to the private commerce of alcohol.

"Why me?" he asked.

"I suspect you have valuable connections because of your regular patronage of the local drinking establishments."

"You mean I'm the resident drunk, so I must know all the other boozers in the county."

"If I had said that, it would have been undiplomatic of me."

Franklin's scowl deepened.

"It's a mutually beneficial relationship. What do you say?" Tabitha held her hand out for him to shake in agreement, but Franklin paused and seemed to ponder the proposal.

"Why moonshine?"

"Do you ask because I'm a woman, or because you have moral reservations?" Tabitha said the last bit with a snicker.

Franklin dropped his gaze, gave a contrite shrug, and waited for her answer.

"I happen to know where a still is—the tradition of moonshine has been passed through the women in my family for years. There aren't many other ways of making a living around here. Is that good enough for you?"

Franklin raised his chin and met Tabitha's eyes. "I was mostly curious." He took her hand and gave it a firm shake. "I guess you can count me in."

"Just promise you won't drink all the profits."

Franklin shot her a withering glance. "And you just worry about keeping the law off our backs."

* * *

They spent much time apart while they waited for the barley to malt and then the corn mixture to ferment and convert to ethanol. Tabitha tended the still while Franklin traveled the county, establishing a list of interested clients and studying the habits of tax inspectors and sheriff's deputies. Having a purpose seemed to agree with him. He took to bathing semi-regularly. He trimmed his hair and beard and even changed clothes from time to time. Tabitha barely noticed, often falling into bed hours after him, weary to the bone.

She persisted in the drudgery because she knew the caress of air coursing over her body would diminish all her aches and pains the moment she launched into the heavens. In the beginning, after losing her first love, after the fright of physical transformation and the nausea inducing sensation of flight, Tabitha judged her condition more an anathema than blessing. But in the course of forming an addiction, she overcame the terrible side effects and succumbed to the irresistible urge to fly, to the freedom of shedding responsibility and retreating from the world.

Franklin continued to give his breath to Tabitha and she felt a buoyancy filling her body that promised to eventually carry her away. If he noticed her thievery, he gave no indication. He kept his distance in the waking hours, but during the night, Tabitha often woke to find he had drawn her close. In those moments, unwelcome slivers of dread pricked her heart.

The weeks passed in this flurry of work and sleep, but one morning, during their usual breakfast of chicory coffee and hoe cakes, Tabitha made a long awaited announcement. "I think tomorrow is the day."

Franklin swallowed a gulp of coffee. "The day for what?"

"Bottling. It's ready."

Excitement washed over Franklin's features, but Tabitha noticed his good cheer did little to mask the effects of their parasitic relationship. The blue tinge of oxygen deprivation stained his lips for longer periods and dark circles permanently ringed his eyes. Tabitha took much from him in their short time together; soon she would drain the rest. Her conscience should have objected, but these days it merely whimpered in despair.

Franklin guzzled the remainder of his coffee and then pushed back from the table. "What do you need me to do?" His question drew a piteous smile from Tabitha, which he misinterpreted. "Whatever it is, I don't mind."

She made an effort to blank her face. "I need you to find us transportation."

"I already thought about that," he said, "and I have an idea."

Even though Franklin's father never saw fit to produce any other offspring, the Massey family feared no threat of extinction. Aunts, uncles, cousins, and in-laws littered the countryside. Franklin told Tabitha he knew a few who would happily trade the use of a mule and wagon for a jug or two of whiskey. "A sample of your finished product would be mighty convincing."

Tabitha agreed to meet Franklin later in the morning and bring him several bottles to share.

"Why can't I go to the still with you?" he asked.

"I don't like anyone to know where it is."

"You don't trust me?"

Tabitha winked at him. "I trust no one. Don't take it personally."

* * *

True to his word, Franklin persuaded a cousin to lend him a mule and wagon. Throughout the night and for numerous nights thereafter, Franklin met Tabitha on country roads at prearranged spots where she stashed her merchandise. They loaded the wagon fast and silent, covering the bottles with bales of hay to hush the rattles. They had no hopes of fooling law enforcement with the poor camouflage, only of selling out the contents of their hoard before igniting suspicion.

At the end of a week filled with surreptitious deliveries, Franklin halted the wagon at a designated bend in the road. Tabitha whispered to him as she appeared from her hiding spot in the nearby brush. "Tonight's the last night. After we get rid of this cache, I won't have anything left."

"Then what?"

Tabitha shrugged. "Then the wind will blow me on, I reckon."

"You won't stay?"

"For what purpose? If I keep shining, I'll eventually get caught. It's better for me to keep moving."

Franklin grunted a sound of displeasure. "What about me?"

"What *about* you?"

"What will I do next?"

"Go back to what you were doing before."

Franklin barked a harsh laugh. "Drinking myself to death?"

"You seemed fine with it when I met you."

They walked in silence for a while before Franklin worked up the courage to say what he felt. "That was before I knew what it was to be with you."

Tabitha stumbled, but Franklin's hand shot out and caught her before she fell. He held her even after she regained her footing and he used his leverage to pull her close. Never in all the years of stealing breath did she manage to leave without eliciting her victims' affections. It was an intrinsic hazard of her trade and it was the only thing she never learned to obviate.

After her first love had forfeited his life to placate her insatiable birthright, Tabitha swore against the change and denied her nature. It eventually left her comatose and close to death. Desperate to save her, Tabitha's great aunt—the same one who gave her the distillery—rented the attic in her barn to an itinerate preacher passing through on his way to a church in the next county. Auntie waited for him to fall asleep before heaving Tabitha into the loft, laying her niece's lifeless body close to the snoring clergyman. Tabitha's deprived and ravenous appetite plundered the preacher's essence and ripped it from him, raw and pulsing. In the morning Auntie buried the dead man and set out a plate of dried corn and sunflower seeds for her absent niece. This time the change hooked Tabitha and she made peace with taking her victims' lives, but vowed never again to accept their affections.

Tabitha tugged her arm from Franklin's grasp, but his touch lingered, icy on her skin. "I told you I was a drifter."

Franklin's shadow bobbed its head. "You did. But

maybe you never had someone to change your mind."

He was right. No one ever changed her mind and Tabitha lacked the courage to tell him he never would. Instead she used the coward's tactic and changed the subject. "I've got somewhere special to take this batch. Have you got further commitments for any of it?"

"No," said Franklin. "I already told you I filled all the standing orders."

Tabitha patted his shoulder. "You've been a big help to me."

"Then why don't you stay with me? We're good together and it doesn't have to end."

Tabitha sighed and drew to a stop. "It's nothing personal. It's just the way it has to be."

"Why?"

"None of your business."

"I'm your partner, so it is my business."

"After tonight we're done. You can take your earnings now, if you like, and go home. I'll finish this last delivery on my own."

Franklin drew up tall and straight, crossed his arms over his chest and stepped close to loom over her. Tabitha held her breath, wondering what he would decide. Finally he exhaled and let his shoulder's droop. "I keep my bargains. Partners to the end."

"Fine," she said, and turned on her heel and strode away.

Franklin swatted the mule's rump and the wagon started with a clatter. "Where're we going anyway?"

"Gotta pay my tithe."

Franklin's eyebrows arched in surprise. "You gonna deliver this to a church?"

"Not hardly. You'll see soon enough."

They walked through the night to a section of the county into which Franklin rarely strayed. Outsiders, even ones from a few miles up the road, rarely received welcome in these parts.

"You sure you know where you're going?"

Tabitha chuckled. "If you're having second thoughts, you're welcome to tuck tail and run."

"I just never knew the people around here to take kindly to strangers."

"Good thing I'm no stranger."

Franklin grumbled something inaudible before he said, "You won't explain what you mean by that, will you?"

He took her silence as her answer.

They turned off the main path onto a rutted road. Even with the straw packed between them, the bottles rattled and gave away their contents. Tabitha could tell by his silence and the tight way held his shoulders

that Franklin's nerves were rattled as well. Eventually they drew up to a ramshackle cabin hidden by thick swaths of Spanish moss and tall pines and cypress that blocked the moonlight. If not for the reflection of their lantern light on the windows and her ingrained knowledge of its location, Tabitha could have easily missed it in the darkness.

Tabitha approached the front of the cabin with quiet steps. When she reached the door, she knocked softly and waited. A lantern flared to life somewhere inside and floorboards creaked as the cabin's occupant shuffled across them. "Is that you, my little Brown Bird?"

"Yes, Auntie," said Tabitha. "I've brought my tribute."

The door swung open and revealed a hunched and withered figure. The lantern light held near her chin limned the valleys and peaks of her haggard face; long gray hair swaddled her head and shoulders. Franklin uttered a choked cry of alarm and hissed something about a witch.

"Well bring it in, bring it in," said the little old woman.

"I have someone to help me, if that's all right," said Tabitha.

"Who is it?"

"He is my breath."

"Oh?" Auntie held her lantern higher and peered into the dark. "Tell him to come here. Let me look at him."

Tabitha motioned to Franklin's shadow. He hesitated, obviously thinking about running away, but the old lady's compulsion held sway. Franklin stumbled to the porch.

The old woman *tsk tsked*. "Not much left, is there?"

Franklin looked at Tabitha for a clue, but she avoided his gaze, finding something inside the cabin on which to focus her attention. Anuntie gave Tabitha her lantern. "Well, bring it on inside. It's either too late or too early, but either way, this ain't the time for an old woman to be out of her bed."

Tabitha and Franklin set to work, toting quart after quart of the wagon's illicit cargo into the cabin while Auntie set about lighting candles and clearing space on her pantry shelf.

"Do you think this will be enough to hold you?" Tabitha said as she waited for Auntie to shove aside several jars of peaches.

The old woman shrugged. "Depends on how long you plan to be gone this time. You been staying away longer and longer."

Tabitha sighed. "I've been trying to make it last as long as possible."

When they stowed away the final jar, Franklin brushed his hands on his pants and started towards the door, anxious to make his escape. Tabitha stopped him with a hand on his shoulder. "What's your hurry?"

"I'm eager for home, for my bed."

"Auntie offered to let us stay here for the night."

Franklin turned to face the old woman and forced his lips into a smile. "I thank you, ma'am. But, it's been a long, hard week and I look forward to getting home." He turned to Tabitha. "I'd be happy to come back tomorrow and pick you up, but I don't think I'll stay."

"You're sure? It's a long way back."

Franklin stepped closer to the door. "Oh, I'm sure."

Tabitha nodded and turned towards the old woman. "Thank you, Auntie, for your offer, but I guess we'll decline."

Auntie smacked her gums. "When will I see you again?"

Tabitha took Auntie's hand and squeezed. "I'll drop by very soon. I promise."

* * *

"What's an old woman do with all that liquor?" Franklin asked as they made their way home.

Tabitha chuckled. "Well, she sure doesn't drink it."

"Does she sell it?"

"Sells it, trades for supplies. It's how she makes a living."

"Why is it up to you to take care of her?"

"I'm all she has, really. Auntie and I are pretty much each other's only family. We look out for each other."

"And you're going away, going to leave her all alone? She doesn't look like she's long for this world."

Tabitha sighed and dragged her heels through the dirt. Franklin pressed her for more information, but she ignored him or flat refused to answer. He gave up and trod beside her in silence made heavy by the weight of their shared frustration, but when they reached his home sometime late in the morning, he did not chase her away or forbid her entry. Instead they fell with exhaustion onto his worn mattress, and when he drew her into his arms, she came willingly.

They slept through the day, oblivious to the turnings of the world, but at the onset of twilight, Franklin came awake, gasping for breath. He coughed and gulped for air, but to no benefit. His body convulsed. The glow of life drained from his cheeks and left him pallid. Tabitha woke and put a hand to his forehead, trying to soothe him, but her touch only panicked him further.

"Hush … hush," Tabitha whispered. "You can't resist the inevitable."

Franklin's face screwed into something frightful. He opened his mouth to voice his helplessness, to ask for answers one more time, but he didn't have the strength. He gasped, fighting against that which he had no chance of defeating. Tabitha read the terror in his bulging eyes, but as he continued to choke, the fear turned into hopelessness and then, at last, to resignation.

Tabitha leaned over Franklin and placed her lips on his. She knew she was supposed to mourn the sacrifice of his life, but hers were ephemeral emotions. The best she could do was honor his memory by keeping it trapped in her chest until the dreaded day came when her feet touched the earth again.

"You give me wings, Franklin—you fill me head to foot. The ground is now a thing far below. It reminds me, but it rules me no longer."

In his last moment of consciousness, a flash of beak and feathers reflected in Franklin's eye, but then his life faded away until all went dull and dark.

* * *

Auntie shuffled across her porch and down her front steps, clutching a pouch filled with a mixture of corn kernles, sunflower seeds, and millet. When she reached the clearing that qualified as her yard, she pursed her withered lips and whistled a twittering song. She whistled a second time and then a third. Finally a reply came from somewhere high in the canopy of the surrounding trees.

"There's my little Brown Bird." Auntie opened the pouch and scattered some of its contents around her feet. "Come see what I got for you."

The swamp sparrow fluttered to the ground and plucked a kernel of corn before turning a shiny black eye up to the old woman.

Auntie chuckled. "Hungry, ain't ya? The breath gives you wings, but it don't fill your gullet."

The sparrow swallowed the corn, bobbed her head, and then sang something short and sweet. Auntie crouched low and held out a palm full of feed. The brown bird hopped up to her fingers and pecked at the offering. "Enjoy your time, m'dear," she told the bird. "I predict it'll be your last. You ain't no spring chicken, anymore."

The sparrow chirped in a questioning way.

"Oh, yes. You'll soon take my place, and when the next Thief of Breath finds her wings, you'll keep her safe and take her tithe in return—same as I done for you."

The brown bird stretched her neck and flapped her wings with agitation. Auntie cackled. "That's the way it is and you know it. Since the first of our kind crawled up outta this swamp."

A gust of wind blew through the trees and lifted Auntie's silver hair into a gossamer web around her head. The brown bird danced in Auntie's palm and rustled her feathers with obvious anticipation. Auntie sighed. "You're eager to get on your way. I remember them days. But don't forget to come back before the last breath is gone. It's your job to carry my spirit home."

The sparrow tweeted and unfurled her wings. Like a shot, she hurtled into the sky. A warm current caught her and spiraled her higher into the blue. Deep in her chest, held fiercely between two lungs, Franklin's breath carried her, and together they flew.

Persephone's Dream

I live with my father in a house of many rooms
(In my father's house are many mansions).
Each day a handsome blade pays court to me
(With golden hair and violet eyes and the sweetest
    smile).
I think I love him; probably we will marry.
He's very respectful to Father, who stands behind
My chair (a highly ornate and cushioned affair
Faintly redolent of dust and incense)—
A pose like those in Victorian family portraits.
The young man brings me gifts and kneels before
    me;
His little golden moustache tickles slightly
When he presses my hand with reverence to his
    lips.
He speaks to Father of his love and of his prospects;
And Father nods and smiles, offers cigars.
Later my lover takes his leave with a smile
That bathes me in a beatific light.
I feel that I will burst with happiness.

But when night falls and Father and I retire,
He to a room many echoing chambers from mine,
A cloud of vast uneasiness descends,
Foreboding what I know will happen soon:
At the window the night marauder will appear
And try to destroy me. I have no defense;
I am as vulnerable as an opened oyster;
He can scoop me up and devour me
With a lewd smacking of lips, and I will be nothing.
Suddenly there he is, as I foresaw,
His head and shoulders framed by the window
    casing.
He is changed: the mild violet eyes
Are turned to pitiless purple, the moustache
Is stained with blood, the sensual underlip
Is overhung with hideous fangs. I know
There is not a drop of mercy in his being,
Only voracious lust to drink my blood

Till I am pale as an ivory figurine,
And then to carry me to his underground lair
Where he will cut me into seven portions
For seven ritual meals with subtle music.
He doesn't speak, but I know what he is thinking.

The shoulders stir, preparing for a leap;
He sucks his underlip beneath his fangs
And expels his breath with terrifying hiss.
Dissolved with fear, I try to rise from bed,
But my legs refuse to move. He suddenly bounds
Into the room, and—I don't know how—
I am flying, flying, flapping my feathered arms
And trailing my useless legs behind me. I flit
Through many rooms just out of reach of the demon,
While he pursues with intermittent leaps.
My mouth forms soundless words: "O Father, save
    me!"
Then I am kneeling in my father's room
Beside the bed and sobbing out my fear;
The beast, I know, will not come through this door.

Drowsy and grumpy, Father rouses up.
"Go back to bed; it's only a foolish dream."
"I can't go back to my room alone," I whimper.
"The fiend is waiting right outside the door!"
But Father doesn't understand the horror;
To him it's only a silly girlish fear,
And he wants his sleep. I plead with him,
For if I can stay with him till morning comes
Or till the dream is over (I vaguely sense
That I am dreaming), I know I will be safe.
He finally lets me curl up in a chair,
Where I doze securely (almost) till the dawn.
But a time will come when Father will send me out
Into the night marauder's arms; and from
That dream of death, can I awake to love?

— Delbert R. Gardner

Clean Ricky

Story by
Steve Mitchell

Illustration by
Larua Givens

I.

This was exactly the type of job that Enrico hated. The targets really were just targets, gagged and tied back to back in a rough cross pattern in the middle of the floor. He was only here because his boss, Joseph "Smiling Joe" Modesky, owed these people a favor, although how a man like Modesky could possibly owe these two anything was beyond comprehension.

The fat, bald guy turned and looked over his shoulder, and Enrico had to swallow the urge to slap the smirk off of his face. He was wearing a purple robe that made him look like a flabby drag queen; the hem was dragging on the floor and collecting dust. The woman was taller and thinner, with dyed blonde hair and too much makeup, wearing a black robe and standing at the sort of podium that belonged in a rundown Elk's lodge. She was muttering under her breath and flipping through a leather book that was so old that Enrico could smell it from where he stood; every once in a while the fat guy would lift his hands in the air like he was checking for rain. Lit candles of various shapes and sizes were scattered around the room; they provided the only light, except for the faint glimmer from the streetlight that crept into their open fifth floor window.

"We're almost ready," said the fat guy. His jowls quivered when he spoke.

Enrico did not try to hide his disgust. It was not the killing that bothered him; he had been killing people since his first week in Afghanistan. And it had nothing to do with the wigged-out ritual either; he once hunted down a couple of cartel boys who wound up in shackles at a seriously bizarre Santeria ceremony. He even played a part, standing there until he got the signal, and then slitting their jugular veins and bleeding them into a copper basin like they were oversized chickens. The Santeria thing was different though. The cartel boys were players, stone-cold, with dozens of kills to their credit. They did not even blink when they saw the knife.

These targets were not players, they did not even look like junkies; they looked like college kids. The oldest target, who had hair the color of a peeled carrot, was probably the only one who could buy his own booze. He and the girl next to him were trembling and staring at him with eyes the size of golf balls; the other two were gray skinned and sunken, like they had spent a few days without much food or water. Killing was one thing; starving people to death was another.

"What did they do?" said Enrico.

"Don't interrupt," said the woman without looking up.

She flipped the page in her rotted book and the man turned and gave Enrico another of his thick lipped, oily smiles. Enrico stepped forward and pulled the rag out of the redhead's mouth.

"Why are you here?"

"I don't know, please," said the kid. His voice was quaking so badly that Enrico could barely understand him.

"Get away from him!' said the woman. This time she turned around, but Enrico crouched down in front of the boy.

"I know how to spot a liar. That's what I do. Tell me what happened. If you change a single detail, I'll know it. You understand?" The kid nodded.

"My car broke down, I swear to God. I thought they were stopping to help."

"You're telling me these two got the best of you?"

"I felt a jab in my neck. I woke up here."

Enrico pulled down the kid's collar; he could still see the welt from the needle stick. The girl next to him was nodding her head desperately. Enrico pulled the rag out of her mouth and she started to sob and cough.

"I said get away from them." The woman took a step forward.

Enrico had two pistols with him. The .32 caliber in his coat pocket was loaded with solid slugs; it was for the targets: once through the head and once through the heart, quick, clean, and efficient. The .45 in his shoulder holster was loaded with hollow points; it had a different purpose. He stood up, pulled out the .45, and jacked a round into the chamber. The woman stopped moving.

"You have no idea what you're toying with," she said, but Enrico was already turning away.

"You with him?" he said to the girl. She shook her head.

"I was on my way to work, at the bus stop. I didn't even see what happened. God help me. Please, God help me." She was hyperventilating, and her eyes were bright and pleading.

Enrico walked around to the other two and got rid of their gags as well. Their swollen tongues looked wooden. There might still be a water fountain working in one of the other offices, but this was not the time to leave the room. He did not bother to ask the kids how they came to be here.

This was an idiot job, a wino could pull it off, but Smiling Joe had made a point of pulling Enrico out of the middle of a complicated setup and sending him here. The boss had acted funny too, standing in his office with his eyes on the floor. He never did that; he always looked you straight in the eye, with a cold grin, like he was just about to smash in your face.

"Clean Ricky," he said, and he looked up like he was really saying something else. Modesky had never called him that before; it was Enrico's nick-name in the Army, when he was with the snipers. One round, one kill, no collateral damage; clean. He did not use that name anymore; it belonged to a different time and place. He did not know that Modesky was even aware of it. But one thing that he did know, for sure, was that Smiling Joe never did anything without a reason.

The bastards that Enrico took out in Afghanistan had it coming, and so did the bottom feeders that he dealt with for Modesky, but that did not include families or bystanders, and it sure as hell did not include four kids who were just minding their own damn business and trying to make it through the day.

He pulled out his Spartan knife; the blade snapping open in the silent room sounded like an RPG hitting a tank. The redhead caught his breath, but Enrico reached behind him and cut the plastic tie that was binding his hands. Rivulets of blood flowed from his wrists from where the sharp edges had dug into the skin.

"Cut everybody loose and get out of here," said Enrico.

The kid started to work right away, but the two freaks came running up like tweekers whose last gram was going down the drain. Enrico cocked the .45 and pointed it at the fat guy's forehead.

"One more step," he said.

"It doesn't matter," said the woman triumphantly. "It's too late."

She was looking over his shoulder, and the poison in her expression made him turn around in a hurry.

There were two of them, just inside the open window, and they were not human. Their skin was metallic but fleshy, scaled in shades of red and green like giant reptiles, and their backs were covered with so many wings that he could not sort them out, like the clustered wings of dragonflies. The claws on their hands and feet curved like talons, but the worst part was their eyes. They had multiple pairs, and the eyes moved back and forth independently, like radar beacons. Some of those beacons were always focused on Enrico.

It was more than he could comprehend; it was more than anyone could comprehend, and his mind began the slow shut-down, circuit by circuit. Time no

longer seemed to matter, and he stood like a statue, unable to move, or react, or even think. He could have died that way, but sniper school was a funny thing. The sergeants preached one essential message, and it had been pounded into his head so many times that it was automatic, like breathing. A sniper never froze. The entire world could be blowing up around you, but that did not matter; as long as you were alive, you completed your mission. Enrico had a new mission. He raised the .45.

The bullets did not ricochet; they disappeared, like he was firing into quicksand. He could not even see a ripple where the rounds stuck home. He ejected the spent clip and was reaching for the spare when the first creature began to move. It glanced at him as it walked by, and its wings swept over him.

Enrico remembered stealing taffy from the grocery store when he was seven, and lying to his parents about the beer in his room when he was twelve, and pooling money with his two best friends to buy time with the hooker at the corner of 17th and Harper before he was old enough to drive. The memories roared back at him in a torrent and he stepped backwards and almost stumbled over the redhead, who was crouched on the floor with the knife clutched forgotten in his hand.

The fat guy was babbling in a squeaky-high voice about how great all of this was and how faithful a servant he would be, but the thing just stood in front of him and stared with all of its eyes; its wings began to flap ever so slightly. The guy finally faltered to a stop, but it still stood there, cocking its head like a curious dog. Enrico did not see it lift its hand, but he saw it casually slip its claws in just below the man's double chin. He choked and gagged, but not for long, because the creature flipped its wrist and the guy's bald head hit the floor with a surprised expression on its face. It happened so fast that the body remained standing for a few seconds, shooting arterial blood against the wall before it slumped toward the woman.

She started to scream and held the mildewed book in front of her like a shield, but the thing slipped its talons straight through the book and into her thin chest cavity. The scream became a gurgle, and she sagged down. The weight of her own body tore the razor-sharp claws up through her rib-cage and out of the top of her left shoulder. She fell to the ground and twitched spasmodically.

The thing next to the window began to walk toward the kids, staring down at them like they were the next hors d'oeuvres. Enrico could not allow that to happen. He dropped the empty .45, leapt forward, and emptied the .32 point-blank into the second creature's face. It barely glanced at him, with only two of its eyes, before it wrapped the pistol in a massive paw and threw it into the far corner, like it was depriving a child of an annoying toy. Enrico felt something directly behind him and slowly turned around. The first thing stood inches away, with its wings spread wide and all of its eyes fixed forward, like they were sucking the marrow out of his bones.

"Hello Clean Ricky," it said.

The world went black.

II.

Enrico was having a good morning. He barely noticed the trembling, and the dreams of the night before had been manageable; he only woke up twice, and he was not screaming either time. He even had company for breakfast.

"There are multiple references, in both the Old and New Testaments," said the man seated across from him. "Our Lord Himself interacted with them many times."

Father Taylor was from the old neighborhood. Enrico had not seen him for over a decade, but the old guy was holding up pretty well, a lot better than the battered book that lay opened on his lap. That was a good sign; you should never trust a priest with a spotless Bible.

He was a little surprised that Taylor actually showed. He knew all about Enrico's line of work, but some clerics take all that talk about forgiveness seriously. Enrico had invited him with a letter so poorly written that it would have embarrassed a first-grader, but the staff here dealt with that sort of thing all the time. An aide had typed it up for him, word for word, although she stopped and gave him a long look a few times during the process. Maybe she just wanted to make sure that Taylor had a full case history.

They were sitting in the lobby of the "Abriendo Extended Care" nursing facility. Enrico had never stayed in a hotel this nice. He had been here for months and would be here for the foreseeable future; his stroke had nearly killed him. Smiling Joe was paying for everything, and he had even visited a few times, but he would never breathe a word about what had happened in that abandoned office building. That was where the old priest came in. He knew how to dig.

"Wooo." Enrico stopped, concentrated, and tried again. "Who?" he said.

It was not much, but he was pleased to be speaking at all. Taylor looked annoyed at the interruption.

"The victims?" he said. Enrico shook his head.

"The Satanists. We still don't know their names. Your boss sent a couple of his thugs to the building when you didn't turn up, but all that they found was you and a lot of blood that wasn't yours."

Enrico knew the men who found him, and they were actually stand-up guys, but there was no way to argue the point. He focused for a few seconds, and then very clearly said: "Debt?" He even got the intonation right.

Taylor shrugged. "A man like Modesky is going to owe a lot of favors to the wrong people. It looks like this was one debt he didn't want to pay. That's why he sent you."

Not that it did much good. Everybody was just as dead as if he had pulled the trigger himself. At least the fat guy and the woman got theirs, and he was not awake to watch those things tear the kids apart. He still did not understand why they had not killed him while they were at it. One more of the thousands of questions he would love to ask, if he could only spit them out.

He rolled his hands forward in an attempt to keep the priest talking. Taylor seemed to get the point.

"The rite was probably a summoning. That usually means a sacrifice, but they either didn't have the stomach for it, or they had to keep their hands clean. That's where you came in. Thank God it didn't work."

Enrico shook his head in frustration. The old man had clearly not read the letter all the way through; the damn thing worked like a charm, and there was a body count to prove it, if only anyone could find the bodies. He rapped the table twice, hard, while he marshaled his words.

"Dead."

"The Satanists?"

"No, no, no! Everybody."

"That's obviously not true."

Was Taylor getting senile? Or was he just playing games? Yes, it was true that Enrico was not dead, be he was not exactly the picture of health either, and there were six other people involved. He took a few deep breaths and tried again.

"Kids."

"They're still in therapy. They'll probably be in therapy for the rest of their lives."

Enrico could only stare, and Taylor stared right back for a few seconds, before something seemed to dawn on him.

"You don't know."

Enrico shrugged.

"The kids turned up in the middle of the food court at the shopping center. They had no idea how they got there. A couple of them spent significant time in the hospital, but they're fine now. Physically, at least."

"Alive?"

It was not possible. Enrico could still picture the creatures, with their metallic scales glinting in the candlelight. He had described them in the letter, right down to the blood on their claws. He emptied everything he had at them, but it did not make a damn bit of difference.

"Demons," he said, with all of the conviction that he could muster, but now the light really seemed to go on in the old priest's face; he actually laughed.

"They weren't demons, Enrico. You should have let me finish. The Satanists never completed the ritual. It's right here in the Old Testament, my friend: Ezekiel, chapter one, verses one through fifteen. What did you think angels looked like?"

Indefensible

Ground is being broken
for the champion's grave.
The gravediggers forget crucial
implements. An improbable vista gives
the impression of having been created
under coercion—something about
the frightened trees, the fanged turtles.
Never mind benevolence; but reckless
endangerment is well-established,
with a history handmade from rocks
and rotting leaves to which we were briefly
attached. Then our attention is drawn
to a noise of cracking branches in another
part of the forest, rapidly moving away,
and we know it is something that needs
to be hunted to its death. Sometimes,
that's where you find yourself.
The victorious challenger said as much
in his ghost-written eulogy.

— F.J. Bergmann

The Catacombs

Story by
Derek Muk

Illustration by
Paul Niemiec

When Anson reached the bend in the dark, dank underground passageway he stopped and leaned against the brick wall, catching his breath. Peering around the corner he saw nothing but pitch blackness. Heck, he might as well have been staring into a bottle of black ink! The feeble light of his flashlight was like a dying firefly, only going so far. He'd been running all night. Running from what? *My imagination?* he mused. No, he saw something out there all right, he just wasn't sure what the hell it was … the shadows of the night combined with his slightly intoxicated state of mind were playing tricks with him. Was this his just reward for swiping that bottle from the liquor store? *Aw, c'mon, I just needed to quench my thirst. That was it, man.* No other malicious intent besides that.

Just when he was about to turn away, resolved that nothing was pursuing him anymore, he heard someone licking their lips in the quiet darkness of the tunnel. Only it didn't sound *completely* human. Was it a dog or a coyote?

"Who's there?" Anson asked calmly, parting back his sweaty, matted blonde hair. Whoever it was licked their lips again. "C'mon, stop playing games. This isn't funny. If this is about that bottle I took I'm sorry about that."

The eerie silence that followed sent a chill up his spine. He pointed the weak beam of his flashlight out there, expecting something to jump out of the black void. After waiting a few minutes he gauged that it was safe to move on. So he spun on his heel and started running, not seeing the brick on the ground. His foot hit it, sending him flying headlong into the darkness, his face landing on the dirt floor with a hard smack.

Clutching his bloody nose in pain, Anson tried to get up, but began to notice that someone or something had pinned him down to the ground. Whatever it was, it had what felt like claws. Or was he imagining things? He stared up at the blackest eyes he had ever witnessed. By God, there was no feeling or emotion at all in those eyes. Nothing, it seemed, except pure evil.

Before Anson could plead for his life the thing on top of him quickly slashed his throat.

* * *

Albert Taylor looked through the peephole of the hotel room door after the second knock. After opening the door he stood face-to-face with a forty-something white man with curly brown hair, resembling an old character actor named Alan Feinstein. Dressed casually in a brown leather jacket, khaki slacks, and loafers.

Yup, he looks like a lawyer, all right, Taylor thought.

Do we need another lawyer in this world? Maybe not. But since the man is one of the 'good lawyers' and is going to pay me for a job it doesn't matter much.

Taylor suppressed a yawn. "Good morning. Are you Kip Peterson?"

The man smiled. "The one and only. You must be Professor Albert Taylor."

He returned a friendly grin. "In the flesh. Sorry, I overslept. The hotel was supposed to give me a wake-up call but they never did."

"No worries. It happens to the best of us."

Taylor, feeling totally embarrassed standing there in his pajamas, said: "Please, come in."

"Thanks." Peterson stepped into the hotel room. "Nice accommodations."

"The Holiday Inn always has nice rooms, at least the ones I've stayed in. Uhhh, lemme quickly get dressed." Taylor grabbed some clothes and went into the bathroom.

Peterson maintained his smile. "Take your time. No rush." He sat down in a chair before the television, turning it on. "I'll just occupy myself with the news for a bit."

Taylor came out moments later, shrugging into his brown corduroy blazer. "Thanks for waiting." He sat down in a chair across a table from Peterson. "So, tell me about these murders in Old Sacramento."

Peterson turned off the TV. "Well, a third victim was discovered in the catacombs yesterday. A homeless man. A lot of the homeless and runaway kids often sneak down there to crash for the night or, in the case of the kids, go in there to party and get stoned. All the victims were male, had their throats cut, and had their hearts torn out."

"Satanic sacrifices?" Taylor offered. "There's been a rise in cult crimes like that."

"That's what the police speculate. So far, their investigation has yielded no solid leads or suspects. No witnesses. So that's when I stumbled across your name when I was at a metaphysical bookshop here in Sacramento. You did a reading and book signing there several months back and luckily the owner still had some of your business cards handy. You come highly recommended."

Taylor smirked. "So all my hard work at networking, marketing, and self-promotion paid off, after all."

Peterson chuckled. "That and the fact that the police department owes me a couple of favors. The chief's also a friend of mine, and after some gentle persuasion, he agreed to let me find some outside talent to assist with their unproductive investigation.

They've hired psychics before to help solve crimes so this isn't anything new."

"I see. But you also mentioned on the phone that you have a deeper investment in all this."

Peterson nodded, quiet for a moment. "All three victims were my clients."

* * *

At ten that night Peterson led Taylor down a deserted cobble-stoned street in Old Sacramento. Most of the tourists were safely tucked back in their hotel rooms now. A black and white police cruiser stopped in front of a bar where a bunch of Harleys were parked, and where two stocky men were engaged in a vicious brawl.

They turned into an alleyway where the street level dipped considerably. "I don't know how well versed you are with Sacramento history, but some of these old buildings were raised during the great floods of 1861 and 1862," Peterson explained. "Sac was virtually an ocean back then, people traveled by boats to get from point to point."

"Yes, I know about that," Taylor replied, looking up when they arrived at a barn-style door. He noticed one side of a brick building was mostly devoid of windows, a remnant of the flood era.

Peterson looked around him before he took out a key and unlocked the barn door. They turned on their flashlights and went in, the musty, damp smell of earth enveloping them instantly. The distinct smell of cellars and basements.

They strode along a wooden plank walkway, the yellow cone from Peterson's flashlight shining on a shattered ceramic bowl that was off the walkway on the dirt. Upon closer inspection, Taylor noticed an engraving on the bottom of the bowl that read: 'Sacramento, 1849.' Further down the walkway he saw an old, grimy toy doll, with one of its arms missing, wearing a Victorian dress. A tag on the doll said: 'Handcrafted by Burke and Sons, San Francisco, 1852.'

"The most recent victim, Anson Gibson, was found two blocks from here," Peterson whispered. "This underground tunnel eventually leads to the area where he was murdered, but of course, the police have sealed off the crime scene."

Taylor nodded. "How extensive are these tunnels?"

"Legend has it that they're pretty vast, and archaeologists uncover new passageways from time to time." He pointed his light ahead, at an arched brick doorway, looking like a portal into another dimension. "Back in the day, these tunnels were used by mer-chants to transport goods into their respective cellars."

"I heard they were used to smuggle in slaves and illegal substances, too," Taylor whispered.

"Yes."

They proceeded through the arched brick doorway. Except for their flashlights the pair was engulfed in complete darkness. Taylor swept some dust and cobwebs out of his way with his hand. He whipped out his electromagnetic field meter, waving it around.

"What's that?" Peterson asked.

"It picks up energy readings from ghosts." He frowned when the device failed to capture anything. "Did your clients have enemies? Could anyone like that have killed them?"

"Well, they were all homeless. Living on the streets toughened them, and sure, they ran across people they didn't like."

"Can you drop specific names?"

Peterson thought for a moment, shaking his head. "I don't think these people would've slit their throats and ripped out their hearts like that."

"You never know. Anger can make you do pretty extreme things sometimes."

"I hear ya. But, no, if I'm a betting man, I'm wagering that it was something supernatural that committed these murders." Peterson shot him an intrigued look. "And you know what else is interesting? There's rumors that these ancient subterranean tunnels are haunted. There are eyewitness reports of an Old West gunfighter's ghost who still roams these catacombs, supposedly searching for the men who killed him."

"What's his name?"

"Frank Goff."

* * *

Back at the hotel room Taylor brushed up on Sacramento history by surfing a few websites. He learned that Frank Goff was gunned down on these very same streets way back in 1857, just a few years shy of the big floods. Goff was a respectable businessman before he turned to the dark side, robbing banks, stagecoaches, and trains. Taylor scrolled down the page using his mouse and continued reading. His outlaw lifestyle didn't bode well with his wife, a schoolteacher, and they went separate ways. The exact nature of why he was slain remained a mystery and his killers were never found.

Some speculated that Goff was simply at the wrong place at the wrong time when he got struck with bullets. *I don't buy that for a second*, Taylor thought. Others think that he was murdered for a bank job gone awry. Another theory posed was that after robbing a stagecoach he split with all the money instead of sharing it, as he had promised, with his fellow conspirators. Some hunched that he was killed by a former jealous lover, a Madame Dorian, who ran a thriving bordello in the heart of the city. The conjecture surrounding Frank Goff's murky death could fill a book, quite frankly, and suddenly gave birth to an idea for a feature story for Taylor's magazine. He quickly jotted down some notes on a pad.

Taylor then clicked on another site that detailed where geographically Goff was shot down. He printed out the page, studying it further.

* * *

Taylor showed the printed page to Peterson the following late afternoon. "Can you take me there?"

"Sure."

"How was work today?" Taylor asked, as he fell in line next to him, both strolling down the wooden plank sidewalk in Old Sacramento, where most of the walkways were fashioned the same way. The buildings here retained that 19th century saloon-style and 'general store' appearance, reminiscent of the Old West. Nowadays, the area was a bustling tourist trap that pumped money into the city's economy. Taylor lost track of how many souvenir stores there were that sold tacky gifts and T-shirts. Across the street a gun fight reenactment was in progress, where eager suburbanite families thronged around to watch. Prop guns were fired and the whole shebang.

"Productive," Peterson answered.

Minutes later, they stood before a modern day parking structure. Taylor looked at Peterson, a puzzled expression on his face.

"This *was* where Goff was killed before they erected this ugly old parking lot," Peterson remarked. "Hey, a lot has happened over the one hundred plus years, my friend."

"Progress?" Taylor asked philosophically, staring up at the cement monolith.

Peterson chuckled. "Hardly."

"Still, what I proposed to do at this location might not be vain, after all." Taylor took out his EMF detector and walked into the parking garage, waving the object around. Nothing registered on the screen, however. They went to another level. Still no readings. Undeterred, Taylor hiked up to the next level. This time, the small, hand-held detector emitted a faint, weak pulse.

Peterson looked around. "So are ghosts gonna magically appear out of nowhere now?"

"Possibly. Sometimes it's not as simple as that, I'm afraid." As he approached a rail overlooking the street below the signal grew stronger. He scanned the area carefully. Suddenly, out of the corner of his eye he saw someone in black, really just a dark speck it seemed. When he turned to see who it actually was the person was gone.

Peterson looked at him. "You look like you just saw a ghost!"

"I think I did."

"Whoa! What? Where?"

"It's gone now. Sometimes spirits make brief appearances and then vanish just as fast. It may be that they're afraid of humans and don't want a confrontation, especially if they're running away from something. One thing's for sure: spirits don't like crowds."

"Really? I thought they would like the attention. You know, being in the spotlight and all that."

Taylor shook his head. "That's a common misperception." He checked his EMF meter again. Nothing.

* * *

Robby was exhausted. He'd been on his feet all day, walkin' all day, pushin' his cart and going all over the place. That Sacramento heat wasn't makin' things easier, either, that's for sure. He needed to rest his weary bones. He had been searchin' all night for a spot to crash but it seemed every joint was taken. What's up with that? Was there a big convention in town for homeless people? He laughed at the thought. Nice to be able to make fun of something like that.

Robby pushed his cart along a stretch of road in the Midtown section of the city, headin' towards downtown. If he was lucky, there might be some places near the mall. He grew impatient waiting at an intersection, at looking at the 'Do Not Cross' symbol, and decided to cross the street. Halfway across, a Mustang almost rammed into him.

"Get off the road, you stinky bum!" the driver yelled.

Robby kept walking. He was a man on a mission. And that mission was to reach the downtown mall. His poor, aching feet refused to give up. C'mon, man, you can do it! More than thirty minutes had passed when he reached the edge of the mall area. He scoped out some of his old haunts but others had beaten him in setting up camp. *Shoot!* So he decided to head through the pedestrian tunnel that connected the mall to Old Sacramento. Might be some free spots there. When he came out on the Old Sac side he received a lot of stares from the tourists that thronged the thoroughfare.

Don't worry, I ain't gonna bite cha! he thought.

Suddenly, he had an idea. He'd heard of the old catacombs beneath the city. Like everyone else, he figured it was just an urban legend, a myth, rumors, etc. Some said there were even alligators in those catacombs. Hah! And as it just so happened, Robby knew how to gain access into that underground world.

He turned his overloaded cart down a quiet alleyway and kept walking until he saw the flimsy door with the chipped brown paint. He approached it and was able to pick the padlock securing the door. He quickly pushed his cart inside and shut the door. Robby switched on his flashlight and continued pushing his cart down a grade until he got to a lower level. His nose wrinkled at the musty, damp odor.

As he inched closer towards an arched brick doorway someone abruptly shoved him from behind. "Hey!" he said, startled. Spinning around he saw no one! "What the?!" His eyes widened. "Who's there?"

Silence was his only response. He didn't like this at all. Livin' on the street, he'd been mugged, robbed, and attacked many a time. So he was no stranger to the ugly shades of humanity. He wasn't lookin' for any trouble. He just wanted to crash for the night and rest his tired soul.

Seconds later, someone grabbed a hold of his afro and started pulling hard. "Ouch!" They kept pulling. "Stop that!"

Going through the arched brick doorway he was shoved again by the unseen force. Before he had an opportunity to turn around and defend himself, Robby's neck was slashed and he collapsed to the ground.

His flashlight rolled next to him on the floor, illuminating the whites of his wide open eyes.

* * *

Kip Peterson's law office was located smack dab in the center of Old Sacramento. He couldn't complain at all about the prime real estate, where self-walk in pedestrian traffic was half of his clientele.

"Believe it or not, tourists represent a quarter of my client base," he smiled proudly.

"Good for you," Taylor replied. "They need legal assistance just like the rest of us."

"And, being a member of the Old Sacramento community watchdog group, I help keep an eye out on other businesses. Membership has its privileges: each member of the watchdog group has a key to the catacombs."

Taylor turned away from Peterson's second story window overlooking a busy street. It was going to be another hot day from the looks of it. He hoped Peterson wouldn't chew his ears off with more stories glorifying his law firm. The guy was a bit of a braggart.

"So that everyone can contribute in keeping the underground safe, correct?" Taylor asked.

Peterson nodded, leaning back in his black leather office chair. "The catacombs are a historical landmark. We don't want reckless kids defacing or vandalizing it."

Taylor nodded.

The phone on Peterson's desk rang, and he picked it up and answered it. When he replaced the receiver minutes later there was a frown on his face.

"What was that about?" Taylor inquired.

"Another homeless man was found murdered in the catacombs."

"Oh, no! Client of yours?"

Peterson shook his head. "C'mon, let's go."

* * *

"Same M.O. as the other victims," Kip Peterson said. "Who is this sicko? And why does he take these guys' hearts? What does he do with them?"

"Definitely seems like the work of a Satanic cult given the ritualistic style of the killings," Taylor replied. "Let's take a look here." He punched in some words on his laptop for Satanic cults in the Sacramento area, yielding a generous number of results.

Peterson was sitting next to him, looking at the screen, shaking his head. "Jeez, don't people have better things to do with their free time than indulge in crap like that? What happened to *real* hobbies and interests? When I was young I had tons of safe, normal hobbies. I'm telling you, Albert, the Internet and cell phones are to blame for our youth going downhill, dabbling with the dark side."

"You of all people should know better. There's this thing called *freedom of religion*. Some people think Christianity is a cult."

Peterson put his hands up in the air. "Hey, I'm not taking any sides! The last thing I wanna do is argue religion with you." He chuckled to lighten the mood.

Taylor scanned some articles, reading one aloud. "'Last April, a group known as Baphomet's Circle, performed a series of rituals on the site of a former cathedral in Citrus Heights. These rites included sacrificing dead animals and extracting their hearts. The group was arrested and charged with animal cruelty, animal neglect, killing animals, and for trespassing.' Couldn't be these guys. They're still in the slammer." He clicked on another article. "'Members of a Satanic cult calling themselves Legion, after a William Peter Blatty novel, have been apprehended and arrested for stealing neighborhood cats and using them in Satanic ceremonies. The hearts of all the cats were removed. The sect is still serving out their sentences.'" Taylor turned away from the laptop. "I propose going back to the catacombs tonight."

"Sure. Just as long as you don't tell any lawyer jokes."

Taylor smiled. "Wouldn't dream of it. That would be totally disrespectful on my part."

* * *

Taylor looked down at his EMF meter in the darkness of the catacombs. The readings were getting stronger and the little screen flashed wildly with different colors. Peterson glanced at him nervously, sweating more than usual. He felt his forehead. It was unusually warm for some reason. And it was cool down here in the underground.

Taylor scanned the environment with his flashlight. They were standing on one of the wooden plank walkways, near a dirt ditch. In the ditch were more objects from the past: a cracked tea pot, a rusty harmonica, and a Chinese fan. Seconds later, a beefy man dressed in black cowboy attire from the 19th century, appeared before them, gazing at them with sinister, dark eyes. Those eyes didn't have whites! The man's face was obscured by a large black cowboy hat.

"Are you Frank Goff?" Taylor asked calmly. But he knew he was, based on photos he had seen.

The beefy man remained silent, regarding them like they were sheer filth. His right hand moved down to his holster, withdrawing a gun. He pointed it at them.

Peterson backed away. "Uhhh, I think we'd better split!" he whispered.

"Frank Goff, my name is Albert Taylor. We come in peace. We mean you no harm."

The beefy man did not lower his weapon.

"Your spirit is trapped in torment here," Taylor continued. "Let me assist your soul in moving on."

Goff did not respond. Taylor repeated his offer, but to deaf ears. Suddenly, Goff returned his gun to his holster, and took out a sharp razor from his coat pocket.

"Okay, I think we really need to leave now!" Peterson whispered.

But Taylor's feet remained firmly planted on the ground. It was in situations like these that his teaching assistant, Jan, would play Peterson's part, urging them to flee for their lives, but Taylor, stubborn old dinosaur that he was, always decided to remain committed to the cause and to fight their foes. Here was another classic example.

Goff lunged at him, trying to slash his throat. The blade missed his neckline by mere inches. Before giving Goff a chance to try again, Taylor whipped out his gun and fired two rounds of rock salt at him, sending Goff flying backwards and slamming into a brick wall. He landed on the ground with a thud.

"I knew he wasn't a ghost!" Taylor remarked, mostly to himself.

"What?" Peterson asked.

Goff stood up and went after Taylor again with the sharp razor, arcing through the air with a loud swish. That one was close too! The Old West gunfighter delivered another jab that was met by Taylor's foot, a vicious kick that knocked the razor out of his hand.

Goff glared at him with those pure black eyes, devoid of whites, hissing. Taylor shot him in the face and he was hurled backwards once again, smashing into a brick wall. Taylor aimed and was ready to shoot again but the gunfighter's body vanished into thin air.

Peterson looked at the empty spot where his body was, staring in disbelief. "What did you mean when you said you knew he wasn't a ghost?"

"Ghosts don't have black eyes like that. He's a demon."

* * *

"So how are you going to stop this guy?" Peterson asked, spearing another big meatball with his fork. He took a bite out of it.

"Well, demons have an aversion to fire and heat," Taylor replied. "And they can be exorcised."

"I see. You can always depend on the good old church to get rid of 'em."

They were sitting inside an Italian restaurant near the Arden Fair Mall in Sacramento, at a table with a red and white checkered tablecloth, being served by a waiter named Mario. A couple of rotund gents were playing violins in one corner for the patrons. Real Italian ambiance here.

"But, before we go back to fight Goff, we have to be satiated. One rule of thumb from the monster hunter bible: never fight on an empty stomach."

Peterson laughed.

Taylor finished his pasta. "I'm serious." He gestured at the restaurant. "Great recommendation, by the way."

"Thanks. Knew you'd like it. When you wanted Italian, this immediately came to my mind. I helped represent a waitress from here once, and we won." He smiled proudly at the memory. "It was a sexual harassment case. A customer kept asking her out, even stalked her. And she politely declined the guy each time."

"You're doing good work, Kip. Helping the homeless and other oppressed groups. Keep it up." He looked at his watch. "We'd better get going."

Later that night, when all the souvenir shops and restaurants had closed up, they returned to Old Sacramento and entered that subterranean world of the catacombs once more. After flicking on their flashlights, they headed down a grade into the cellar level. Taylor's light shined on a rat scurrying across the dirt. He checked his EMF meter. No signal yet.

"Okay, where are you, gunslinger?" he asked.

"Your patience wearing thin, buddy?" Peterson smiled.

"Another rule of thumb from the monster hunter bible: always practice patience and always be aware of your surroundings."

"Noted."

"Then how come you don't see Mr. Goff standing behind you then?"

"What?!" Peterson asked, spinning around to face the black clad gunfighter. His face turned white.

Goff grabbed him and threw him hard against a brick wall. He picked him up and pummeled him in the chest. Taylor jumped Goff from behind, riding piggy back on the beefy guy, smashing his head with the butt of his gun until Goff collapsed to the ground.

Goff's face was a wet, pulpy mess. But soon he sprang back up like a reanimated spider, deft and nimble. He deflected Taylor's next blow, ducked his kick, and sidestepped the bullets he fired. Goff knocked the weapon out of Taylor's hand.

Gripping the razor, the Goff demon then pounced on him, the blade making a loud swishing sound as it tried to slice open his neck. It almost succeeded were it not for Taylor's quick reflexes. He dodged the blow, backpedaling, which gave him enough time to whip out the mini flamethrower he had rigged up in his hotel room.

Before Goff could attempt another rip through

the air, Taylor squeezed the trigger and Goff was scorched toast. An inhuman, bloodcurdling shriek echoed throughout the underground tunnels as the demon paced around in circles, his entire body soon engulfed in flames as Taylor kept spraying him. The demon kept walking around aimlessly, as if pondering its very existence, perhaps also wondering how to overcome the wild orange flames but it was too late now to do anything.

Moments later, it crumbled to the floor, the fire having completely devoured the body. Taylor and Peterson watched silently.

* * *

Before Taylor left Sacramento he came across an old, yellowed newspaper article at the public library. He was in the archives department. And being an old article, some of the words had long since faded and he had to fill in the omissions using his own intellect as he read.

There was one section, in particular, that captured his interest. It was something that had to do with hearts … it went something like this, as best as he could piece together: "Mr. Goff, respectable businessman turned outlaw gunfighter, was discovered crouching on all fours, like some vicious, wild animal, ravenously chewing on a human heart ripped from the chest of the deceased, a Miss Francine Barney. According to Sheriff Robert Kinley, who looked in the eyes of Mr. Goff, he had this to say about what he witnessed: 'It was like looking in the eyes of the devil himself.'

"Thus, authorities have labeled Mr. Goff as 'the cannibal gunfighter.'"

Die Alone, the Demon Said

Do I have to die?
I'm very small. I won't
Eat anything at all.

Alone's all right, if you'll come too.
Let's crunch some bones. I'm ready to.
Or let's read Poe till lights grow dim—chill
Nights we let the raven in.
Enter terror, dusk, and dark.

The bed is cold. I don't miss Marc.
He chose to leave. I couldn't hold—
Evil loves no heart of gold.

Demons chew my entrails tart—
Eventually I'll love this part.
My anguish grows, a separate beast—
One for the head, and one to feast—
No saints without the torment first—

So come and help me! Do your worst!
At least I'll know I was your first—
Is death not love—my Self to kill?
Delicious demon, do your will.

       — Adele Gardner

Thornway Hollow

Story by
Simon Bleaken

Illustration by
Jag Lall

For Matt, Mario and Gino

Two men stepped into the silent stillness, torch beams lancing the darkness and playing across narrow hallways covered with flaking paint and over a floor strewn with litter and rubble—discarded fragments of tile, wood and broken glass. Dust motes hung thickly in the air, and the brooding silence was broken only by the breathing of the men, and the occasional creak and groan from somewhere deep within the heart of the old building.

"Here, take this." The first man handed his torch to his colleague as he slipped the rucksack from his shoulders and carefully removed a small video camera.

"Figured they'd have tightened security by now." The second man glanced out through the open door at the starless dark of the night and the stretch of overgrown uneven lawn they had just darted across. "Lucky they never fixed that break in the fence."

"Come on, Tony," his colleague laughed as he switched on the camera and activated the light at the front of it, "there's nothing here worth taking."

"True," he passed the torch back. "So where first, Mark?"

"The morgue and the chapel, and then we'll work out from there. I want to try and get over into the south wing as well if we can. I think there might be a way through the underground tunnels."

"What's in the south wing?" Tony frowned, fishing a small rectangular device from his pack and switching it on. On the tiny screen a temperature and EMF reading flickered into life.

"There was a big fire there, right around the time this place was shut. A few nurses and patients died in it. If we want to find ghosts, well, traumatic deaths tend to leave traces."

Together they moved down the long hallway, passing boarded up exterior windows and pushing through creaking interior doors with shattered glass panels, footsteps scrunching and crunching noisily on the debris underfoot as their lights danced across broken glass and illuminated the black recesses of side rooms.

Around them the once-venerable corridors and steep crumbling stairwells of Thornway Hollow Sanatorium stretched out in eerie emptiness, wearing a grimy and desolate shroud of decay and neglect that the long years of closure and abandonment had gifted with abundance. The sanatorium itself was actually a series of five large buildings linked by a network of underground passageways and set amidst an overgrown chaos of trees, bushes and tall grasses that were once gentle lawns and landscaped gardens. And like all such institutions, especially those that had been derelict for some time, legends of ghosts and strange activity abounded. The security huts at the two main gates, and the many prominent "beware of the dogs" signs posted there were meant to deter the curious or those who had come to steal and vandalise, but in truth had little effect on those who were truly determined to get inside, as the state of the buildings testified.

"Wonder what this place was like before," Tony mused, pulling a flap of flaking paint off the wall. "Do you think the spirits can see this? Or do they just see it as it was?"

"Depends if the haunting is residual, an echo caught in time—or intelligent, an actual aware presence," Mark explained. "Even then, I believe there are some that aren't even aware they are dead. Then you have those spirits that know exactly what they are, and see the world as it is, but are unable to rest for whatever reason."

"And those are the ones you try to help?"

"If they'll listen, and if they want to be helped. Too many people treat intelligent haunting sites like some kind of sideshow attraction. They forget that these are still living spirits that are trapped."

Tony let the peeling paint fall to the floor and turned his attention back to the readings he had been taking.

"How's it looking?" Mark cast a glance at Tony. With his dark clothing it almost appeared as if his head were moving without a body, but then he stepped around into the light at the front of the camera and moved a little way ahead.

"Steady so far. No significant temperature changes or cold spots. No EMF either."

"Watch out up ahead," Mark cautioned, his eye returning to the viewer of the video camera. "There's a big hole in the floor. Don't forget what happened last time."

"Hey, I saw it," Tony bristled, shooting an annoyed glance at the camera.

"You almost went straight in," Mark smiled. "Too busy staring at your readings, as I recall."

Tony waved a hand dismissively, but took great care to step around the hole as they came to it all the same. It was deep, and flooded with murky water and filled with floating debris, some clearly very old, and others—crushed and half submerged beer cans and bottles—less so. "Looks like somebody's been having a party here."

"Tell me about it," Mark gestured at a nearby wall that was covered with a scrawl of graffiti. "That wasn't here last time, either."

"We're in the wrong jobs," Tony laughed. "We should get hired as a guard here. They don't seem to actually do anything."

"Lucky for us," Mark reminded him.

They moved deeper in, past murky reception hatches festooned with cobwebs and narrow side rooms that were mostly missing their doors, with rotting beds and festering mattresses still in place within. In one they could see some kind of rusted surgical device beside one of the beds, but time had rendered it unidentifiable. In the next they saw a smashed toilet still fixed in place, and shattered shards of yellowing tile and flaked plaster covered the floor, along with fragments of an old porcelain sink. While from another a small brown bat shot suddenly out of the doorway as they shone their lights inside, causing them both to jump as it fluttered down the hallway.

"This place looks even worse than it did six months ago," Mark muttered, noting that there was now not a single window that hadn't been smashed, or an electrical box that hadn't been torn open and robbed for parts and wiring. He also noted more crushed beer cans and cigarette stubs littering the hallways and rooms, and a few cleaner mattresses in some of the rooms. "Squatters?" he suggested.

"Crack-heads more likely," Tony frowned, checking the floor warily for used needles. "Or kids getting high and screwing out here. I think the guards at the gate have stopped caring," Tony shrugged. "It's only that this place is supposed to be listed that keeps them from tearing it down."

"Who's got the cash to fix it up?" Mark sighed. "And who'd want to?"

They moved through another set of internal doors, the floor creaking and flexing unnervingly in places under their shoes, and the flaking walls streaked with moisture stains. In this part of the building the boards had been ripped away from the shattered outside windows, and the rain and the elements had left their mark clearly, as had the heaps of wind-blown leaves that littered the floor.

"Looks like this place has been under water," Mark muttered as he panned the camera across the walls and into the side rooms. Even the graffiti here

was wearing off as the paint crumbled under it. He could just make out a few random scrawls—parts of names, messages that somebody "woz ere", and the word "LEAVE" scrawled in some kind of black ink in large letters across one part of the wall. He turned the camera back onto the hallway, keeping his eyes peeled for any glimpses of shadow figures, or light anomalies that might indicate the presence of a spirit.

"Here's the chapel," Tony remarked as they approached a warped set of double wooden doors. The dusty glass panels set into them were unbroken and the faintest outline of a gold cross could be seen etched on each. "May as well start here then go down to the morgue?"

"Yeah, go for it," Mark nodded. "We didn't get much time in here last visit."

The doors opened with a groaning shriek as rusting hinges were forced to move once more, and torchlight flooded into a room that had not seen anything but shadows for a long time. The air was stale and stank of dampness, mould and mildew. The rows of disintegrating pews lining the room were thick with dust and cobwebs, and a leaning lectern still sat at the far end. The paint on the walls hung down in tattered strips, and the faint dripping of moisture echoed out from the back of the room.

"Get some stills," Mark suggested, as he finished sweeping the camera slowly around the room and then moved to respectfully straighten an old crucifix still mounted to the far wall. "See if we get anything."

"Stay over there so I can get you in too," Tony gestured at a spot near the lectern as he unhooked a small digital camera from his belt.

The flash whined and exploded with light, flooding the room with brightness in quick succession as Tony worked his way around it.

"Anything?" Mark asked, walking over to him.

He got half way when the doors to the chapel slammed shut.

The two men turned instantly, flashlights flaring through the gloom and picking out the doors.

"Could have been a draught?" Tony ventured, feeling his heart thumping.

"Would take a lot to slam those, and the air in here is still," Mark reasoned. He lifted the video camera up to his eye and started filming as he approached the doors warily. "If there is a spirit here with us," he said loudly, "we mean you no harm or disrespect. Please, show us that you are here. Move these doors for us again."

Nothing happened, and Tony checked the readings

on the temperature in the room.

He shook his head. "No change."

"If anyone is with us, please, let us know you are here. Show us you are here."

After a few minutes of silence Mark reached out and opened the doors himself, the hinges shrieking once again as they swung open. "It was just the breeze coming in from outside. A broken window or something."

"Maybe." Tony nodded, but he didn't sound convinced.

"This place has been abandoned for close to ten years. It's full of holes."

"Yeah, but I'm not feeling a breeze here."

"Let's move on anyway," Mark suggested. "We've a lot more ground to cover, and I think we'll get more activity downstairs."

Tony held up his digital voice recorder. "What about trying to catch some EVPs?"

"Not here," Mark shook his head, and Tony detected the tiniest trace of irritation in his voice. "I really want to get down to the morgue."

"What is it with you and morgues?" Tony sighed. "You know, this is not a healthy obsession."

Mark shot him a look of weary amusement. "I don't have an obsession. We both know they're usually hotspots of activity, and last time we never even got down there, because of Jenny."

"I already said sorry about bringing her," Tony explained as they moved out into the hall. "I didn't know she was going to scream at every single little thing."

"You know she went and set her own group up?" Mark scowled. "With that friend of hers—Ian, the one who thinks he's a medium. Medium intelligence, more like."

"I'd say even that's pushing it. He needs a manual just to figure out how to wipe his ass. It was funny though, when she accused you of being a Zak Bagans wannabe," Tony chuckled, then fell swiftly silent when he caught Mark's glare.

"Moving on," Mark muttered softly, gesturing ahead with the torch.

They descended a narrow staircase, shoulders and elbows rubbing flaking paint off the walls as they moved and the steps groaning faintly under them. The door at the bottom was different from the rest they had seen—sturdier and made of white-painted metal. But someone had scrawled the word "LEAVE" across it in what looked like dried mud.

"Encouraging sign," Tony smiled. "Do we leave?"

Mark gave him a sideways glance and grinned as he pulled the door open. "Yes, because we came all this way to run at a message left by some kids."

"That's what I thought."

The hallway they emerged into was wider than the last, with heavy windowless walls and a solid concrete floor. The rotting metal skeleton of an old hospital bed loomed out of the gloom in the middle of the passageway as their torches beat back the shadows, and they squeezed past it. Mark again with his eye glued to the video camera and Tony checking the temperature.

"It's colder down here," he remarked.

"Could just be that we've gone below ground level," Mark cautioned. "Let's see what happens as we get deeper in."

"This place stinks," Tony wrinkled his nose as they walked on, his eyes watching the temperature reading as it steadily dropped. "Guess there's no supply of fresh air getting in here."

"At least we can rule out draughts."

"I just hope we don't stumble onto a body or anything down here. That would freak me out more than any ghost. Imagine if we came across some dead homeless—"

"Hold it!" Mark stopped so abruptly that Tony had to turn and double-back.

"What?"

He held up the video camera. "Battery just went dead."

"I thought you charged it yesterday?"

"I did."

Somewhere in the deep darkness ahead of them a door slammed loudly.

Both men felt their hearts quicken.

"Where did that come from?"

"The morgue, I think," Mark said, a faint smile crossing his face.

Tony rolled his eyes.

They made their way silently forward as their torches glinted on pools of stagnant water that had gathered in the recesses of the corridor and shone on droplets dripping from the ceiling. Their hearts were hammering fast and despite the growing chill, Tony felt hot and uncomfortable. But the adrenaline was surging too, and the sense of fear he felt was coupled with a nervous excitement—but he forced himself to keep a calm head. It would be too easy to let his imagination get the better of him. Too easy to let himself see what he wanted to see, instead of staying rational and considering the possible mundane explanations for things first. But it was hard not to. Unlike Mark, he had only been ghost-hunting for just over four months, though he had harboured a fascination for most of his life, and had only caught a few tantalising glimpses that hinted at the existence of spirits walking unseen amongst the living. Mark had been at this game for a couple of years, and had stories that could chill the blood about things he had witnessed—shadow figures flitting down hallways, disembodied voices calling his name, doors opening and closing by themselves, poltergeist activity hurling pots and cups furiously around a kitchen, and strange glowing wisps caught moving in darkened rooms on night vision cameras while EMF meters spiked and surged.

"The smell's getting worse. And the temperature's really dropping too," Tony whispered as they turned a corner and found themselves staring down another hallway, the few feet of torchlight revealing a concrete floor strewn with old pipes, years of dust and grit, an old ladder—and then darkness ahead and darkness behind, leaving them all alone in a tiny oasis of light. He could feel his heart pounding and felt the hairs on the back of his neck and arms prickle, and cast a sideways glance at Mark. But if his colleague felt the same sense of nervous fear, it didn't show. Tony wasn't sure if he was just better at hiding it, or if he genuinely was a tough nut to crack, but he envied him either way.

"EMF?"

"None."

"Okay, it should be just down here on the right," Mark whispered, gesturing with the torch. As the light flashed over the wall, they both saw the word "Morgue" picked out in silver reflective writing on a small sign fastened to a heavy metal door. "There."

"Yeah, but—hang on," Tony directed his own torch at it. "Look at that."

Beneath the sign on the door they could just make out a second word—it looked like it has been scratched into the paint on the metal: LEAVE.

"Are you sure that's kids doing that?"

"You saw the graffiti and beer cans upstairs. It's just people messing about."

The door to the morgue opened with surprisingly little effort, and surprisingly little noise. They followed the guiding light of their torches down a grimy tile-clad passageway and emerged into a larger open space that was so icy their breath frosted on the air as it left their lips. Against one wall there was a huge row of silver cold chambers, but all but two of the doors were missing.

"Should have brought the night-vision camera," Mark cursed softly.

"Yeah, why didn't you?"

"I put it on charge last night and forgot it wasn't packed," Mark sighed. "Must be getting o—"

From deep in the darkness somewhere further down the hallway another door slammed.

"Shit," Tony craned his neck to look back, but saw only shadows. Suddenly his bladder was starting to feel uncomfortably full. In the back of his mind a little voice was wondering what they would do if the batteries went in the torches as well. He didn't like the thought of blundering around blindly in this pitch-black maze.

"Okay, get some stills in here, and keep an eye on the EMF readings," Mark suggested, crouching down and rooting around in the rucksack. "I'm going to see if I can find that spare battery."

Tony moved cautiously through the darkness as he explored the other end of the long room, his feet scraping and clattering against the debris underfoot as he lifted the camera and pressed the button. Darkness turned to light for a second as he captured an image of the room, then had to wait as his eyes adjusted back after the sudden flare. When his vision returned he checked the image, disappointed not to see any orbs or spectral figures, but intrigued to notice a small doorway in the corner that the shadows had concealed before.

"There's another room back here."

"Be right there," Mark called back, still foraging for the spare battery.

Tony fumbled as he searched for the door handle while trying to juggle a camera and a torch, and finally succeeded in pulling it open. Like the main door to the morgue it opened unusually easily and without a sound, and he found himself stepping into the unknown darkness of a smaller adjoining room. The air in here stank, something sweet and rotten, far worse than any of the mould and mildew from the building above, and he recoiled as something spidery brushed and tickled against the side of his face. He breathed a sigh of relief when it saw it was just an old dead wire hanging down from the ceiling. As he unhooked the torch from his belt and shone the light cautiously around him, he realised this must be some kind of office. A long row of battered filing cabinets stood against one wall, and close to it a murky water cooler and an old desk that looked buried beneath a pile of debris, dozens of dead flies and accumulated rubbish.

That was when his foot landed in something soft and moist, and the sweet rotten smell suddenly grew in strength, becoming overwhelming.

With a cry of revulsion he directed his torch down at the floor. His stomach churned as his torch beam revealed the grisly remains of countless small animals—cats, dogs, bats and squirrels, littering the floor like some kind of nightmarish carpet. Most were festering, in various stages of decomposition, crawling with maggots and barely recognisable. But the few that were fresher bore clear signs of having been gnawed upon—flesh stripped from bones, and bones snapped to get at the marrow inside. They also appeared to be missing their eyes.

His torch began to flicker as the new batteries started to fail and a surge of panic rushed through him. As his lunch from earlier that day made a poor attempt at reincarnation, he turned, blundering almost blindly for the door in his panic. His shaking fingers made four attempts before he finally pulled it open. He was just hurrying through, pulse racing and his mind screaming at him to get out, when from out of the corner of his eye he half saw and half sensed movement, and glanced back…

…only to crumple to the floor as something heavy struck the side of his head.

His camera hit the tiled floor with a crack, scattering parts across the floor, as did his torch—the light finally fizzling out as it rolled against the wall.

In the middle of the morgue Mark heard the sound and glanced up.

"You okay?" he called, standing slowly and directing his torch at the darkened corner of the room where he knew Tony had been headed. "You trip over something?"

When there was no reply he took a step forward, the light from his torch sweeping across the room. His foot came down on an old light bulb and it shattered like a small gunshot going off. He drew in a sharp intake of breath as he felt his heart leap.

"Shit! Tony?"

The air ahead reeked of decay and rot, and he cupped his hand over his mouth and nose as he drew closer, trying not to gag. He could see something up ahead now. A dark shape, unmoving, sprawled out on the filthy floor half out of an open doorway.

Another step and he was close enough to recognise it as Tony.

He hurried to his side, hardly feeling the sharp shards of broken tile that now bit into his knees as he knelt.

"Tony? Can you hear me?"

He gently shook his friend and felt a flood of relief as the sprawled form gave a soft moan and began to stir. Tony was still clutching his EMF metre in his hand like it was some kind of protective charm, but the screen was dead and lifeless now, totally drained of power.

"What happen—"

But the rest of that sentence was lost underneath the squeaking and crashing as the two remaining doors of the morgue's cold chambers began slamming furiously open and shut behind him as though by some unseen hand.

Reaching into his pocket Mark pulled out the digital voice recorder he carried with him and activated it. As he did the doors froze, one almost shut and the other wide open, and the room fell silent again.

"Can you hear me?" he asked uneasily. "Can you tell me your name?" He paused, and then: "Did you do this to my friend?"

He waited a few seconds, then pressed 'play' and held the speaker close to his ear, hearing his own words echoing back to him.

"Can you hear me? Can you tell me your name? Did you do this to my friend?"

Silence, and then a female voice—so faint Mark had to strain to hear it—hissed:

"Leave … not … safe!"

"What isn't safe?" Mark asked, pressing 'record' again. "Please, we mean you no harm. We only want to speak with you. To help you."

That was when he heard movement behind him, unknown feet crunching and scraping as they moved across the floor.

He started to turn—but before he could fully react two hands seized the front of his jacket, hauling him up and back. In the torchlight he caught a glimpse of a man's face, dirty and wild-eyed, staring back at him, flaking lips curled back to reveal blackened teeth gritted in a silent snarl.

Then the wall slammed into his back with such force the torch almost fell from his grip. The face was inches away from his now, staring into his eyes with a crazed fury.

Mark gasped, struggling against the hands now pinning him against the wall. He could feel the body heat from the figure before him, and knew this was no spirit.

"What   what do you want?" he asked, his voice shaking.

The face that was watching him began to laugh,

a maddened and terrifying sound as spittle foamed from those peeling lips and long fingers with splintered nails tightened their grip painfully. Mark maintained eye contact with his attacker's demented gaze hoping to keep the man distracted while he got a better grip on the torch, brandishing it like a weapon. If he could move fast enough, he reasoned, he might be able to catch his attacker off guard.

"Unn-gee!" the man cackled, a thick string of drool running from his lip.

"Hungry?" Mark repeated, his whole body trembling, he tried to recoil from the man's rank breath, but with the wall against his back there was nowhere to go. "We can bring you food—let us go."

The man released his grip and took a step back, and Mark readied himself, planning to rush at his attacker. But then he saw the man was drawing a long stainless steel kitchen knife from his belt with his right hand, and pulling some strange tarnished metal tags out of the tattered remnants of his soiled clothing with his left. Mark recognised them instantly as pet tags from collars.

"UNN-GEE!" the man declared again as he waved the pet tags in the air, his tone getting angrier and more aggressive, the knife twisting in his hand as the torchlight glinted on it.

A numbing dread washed over Mark then as he suddenly and vividly recalled the scandal years ago that had forced the closure of the sanatorium—the fire that had consumed part of the kitchens in the south wing, where the most disturbed and dangerous of the patients had been housed. Dozens of nurses and patients had been trapped and killed, and the fire had been so intense they had found only fragments of some of them, at least three patients had never been accounted for. The whole place had been closed down soon after, but ever since the closure, houses in the vicinity of the sanatorium always seemed to be putting up posters for missing cats and dogs. As it all suddenly fell into place, he felt his blood run cold.

Over on the floor he heard Tony starting to stir, and saw him lift one hand sluggishly up to the back of his head with a faint groan.

The man squealed in eager anticipation at that, his eyes gleaming wildly in the torchlight as he span around, lifting the knife—a high-pitched squeal of excited laughter bursting from his mouth.

"Tony!" Mark screamed out a warning as he rushed forward, driving his shoulder into their crazed assailant's back and sending them both crashing to the floor. As they landed, Mark heard the knife clatter across the floor, and then his head was driven sideways as the man's elbow connected savagely with the side of his face. Reeling, Mark tried frantically to snatch at the knife that lay just out of reach, but with a high-pitched shriek that sounded more like a wounded pig than a human, the man seized his head. Sharp broken nails slashed skin as the man tried to claw at Mark's eyes.

Mark fought back as best he could, blindly driving blow after blow into his attacker's body with as much force as he could muster, but nothing seemed to have any effect. He could feel blood running down his stinging face and dripping onto the floor, and twisted his head to the side—anything to keep those splintered nails from tearing into his eyes.

And then suddenly the weight that had been pinning him was gone as his attacker lunged for the knife. Mark staggered desperately to his feet, blinking his own blood from his eyes as his vision started to blur. He felt the wall next to him and almost crashed into it as he stumbled.

Got to find a weapon—something…

Then he heard movement behind him and glanced back. His heart turned to ice as he saw the man rushing at him. There was a burning, demented hunger filling the man's face, and the knife glinted in the torchlight as it lifted, ready to begin flashing down in a lethal arc.

And then the man staggered as a length of wood from the floor suddenly impacted against the side of his head, as though thrown by an invisible force. The look of hunger changed to a pained confusion, and he dropped to the floor as his legs buckled under him, clutching his head with a howl of agony, the knife clattering away across the tiles.

Mark blinked, trying to understand what had happened. The room seemed to be swaying—or was it him?

"Mark?" a hoarse voice called. Tony was sitting up, his face pale and stark with fear. He had a hand cupped over his forehead and there was a deep cut on his cheek where he had hit the floor.

"Tony!" Mark hurried over to him. "We've got to—"

But Tony wasn't looking at him. He was staring at something behind Mark, and his eyes had gone so wide his pupils seemed lost in an expanse of white.

Mark followed his gaze—and there, in the shaking light of the torch that was still clutched in his trembling hands, he saw a length of old rope rise up into the air as though held by invisible hands. It turned slowly, once, and then shot forward like an arrow, coiling around the dirt-encrusted limbs of the filthy madman on the floor. They watched in silent shock as he writhed and thrashed, flopping on the tiled floor like a fish out of water as his eyes bulged and frothing spittle foamed from his lips. Then the man fell still, like a rag doll cast aside by a child, glaring furiously at them, with only the rise and fall of his chest to show he still lived.

"Did you see—?" Tony's voice was barely even a whisper.

A woman emerged slowly from out of the shadows. She was middle-aged and wearing a nurse's uniform. Her lined face was grave and concerned as she looked from the grimy body lying restrained on the floor to the pale and bloodless faces of the men before her. As she moved closer, it took Mark's dazed mind a second to register that she must have stepped into the room through the wall itself. He could feel the air growing colder as she drew nearer, her feet making no sound on the floor and stirring up none of the debris. His torch flickered as she reached him and the hairs on his arms and the nape of his neck rose up as his skin prickled into gooseflesh.

"You should have listened," she said softly, her voice echoing through his mind, as though it had bypassed his ears altogether.

"What?" Mark stared at the nurse, who now shook her head and pointed at the door.

"Leave," she said, placing her other hand on his shoulder. He felt a tingle run through his flesh like pins and needles. "This place is not safe."

Tony rose to his feet, shaky and unstable, and staggered for the door—his EMF metre falling to the floor as he scrabbled crazily for the handle. He disappeared out into the hallway, the morgue door slamming behind him, but Mark could hear him crashing about in the dark as he hurried blindly away.

"Go after him," she gestured to the door, "before he hurts himself."

"But—you're what we came looking for," Mark said, his wounded face forgotten as his eyes widened in wonder.

"Go!" she ordered, her eyes narrowing. Against the far wall the two remaining doors to the cold chambers began to slam once more, and fragments of broken tile lifted from the floor and hurled themselves against the wall with savage fury, sending razor-sharp shards flying as they shattered. "Leave now!"

"But…"

"LEAVE!" she roared, the cold chamber doors slamming so hard that they buckled while tile shards flew like shrapnel through the air and the subdued patient on the floor gave a wild howl. Overhead the light fixtures flicked as though a final surge of power had been forced into them, and then exploded in a shower of glass and sparks.

Without another word Mark turned and raced after Tony, weaving his way back through the underground tunnel without so much as a backward glance.

The spirit of the middle-aged nurse stood in the doorway watching him go, her arms folded. Already her body was starting to fade away as the temperature steadily rose again.

"People," she smiled to herself as the single frantically-wavering torch-beam turned a corner and vanished from sight. She stepped back into the morgue, the door slamming loudly behind her as she returned to tend to her subdued patient. It was, after all, time to feed him. But first she picked up the drained EMF metre from where it had fallen and walked over to a small cabinet in the far corner. She opened it silently and placed it inside next to several other similar devices—cracked K-IIs and shattered trifield metres—and a whole collection of broken torches, lifeless EM pumps and dusty cameras. "Why do they never listen when you're trying to help them?"

abandoned nursing home
the mahjong tiles
still move

— Greg Schwartz

SHERMAN - I'VE GOT A PRESENT FOR YOUR BIG MELON!
OH BOY! OH BOY! OH BOY! WHAT IS IT?
IT'S A VIKING HELMET TO PROTECT THAT FLAT NOGGIN' OF YOURS. I JUST GOT IT STRETCHED OUT
SAY GRAMPA DO YOU GET THE FEELING WE'RE BEING WATCHED?
LAST TIME I GOT THIS FEELIN' - VILLAGERS SHOWED UP WITH TORCHES! I AIN'T FIRE-PROOF YA KNOW.
HA HA HA HA HA HA HA
LAFF TRACK
MIIIIIIIILLY!
SOME MEANIE IS AFTER MY SKULL! IT JUST GOT BROKEN IN - AND I'M KINDA FOND OF IT!
SHERMAN - DON'T BE SUCH A BIG BABY. NOW YOU MARCH RIGHT OVER THERE AND TELL THE NICE MAN YOU'RE STILL USING IT!
HOME HAUNTED HOME
LOLLIPOP CELLAR

Book Review

About Those Breath Mints...
Douglas Empringham
Self published
Approx. 118 pages
eBook: $6.99

Arthur Caery is a fifteen-year-old albino with a serious attitude problem even though, or perhaps because, he inherited a fortune from his great grandparents. As the novella opens, he stumbles on a mystery. His eyesight has improved, his hair and eyes have changed color, and he's gained a positive outlook on life. All of this happens after he ate a sample pack of breath mints he received at the mall. As the day proceeds, he and a stranger meet and feel compelled to aim their empty breath mint tubes at each other. Arthur soon discovers that the tubes work as lethal laser weapons that contain precisely one shot before disintegrating. As a result of the encounter, he realizes he's entered a deadly game designed to eliminate all but the best player. Arthur must navigate the game and find clues to its origins while keeping the health benefits of the breath mints and the game itself a secret from his guardians: a grandmother who used to be a flower child and a conspiracy theorist uncle.

About Those Breath Mints... is a quirky, multi-faceted tale that defies easy classification, reminiscent of Empringham's stories that have appeared in *Tales of the Talisman*. Although I enjoyed the story, I felt it would have benefited from better copyediting. What's more, Empringham packs a lot of plot into 118 pages along with a rather complex situation for a teenager. While he does a great job exploring Arthur's reactions to his improved health, I would have liked more insight into Arthur's perceptions of the game itself. Why isn't he more frightened? Does he feel remorse for those he has to kill? Why or why not? Despite these issues, *About Those Breath Mints...* offers a fun story, memorable characters and an engaging mystery. If you enjoy Douglas Empringham's stories in this magazine, you should definitely look up his novel on line and support his latest effort.

— David Lee Summers

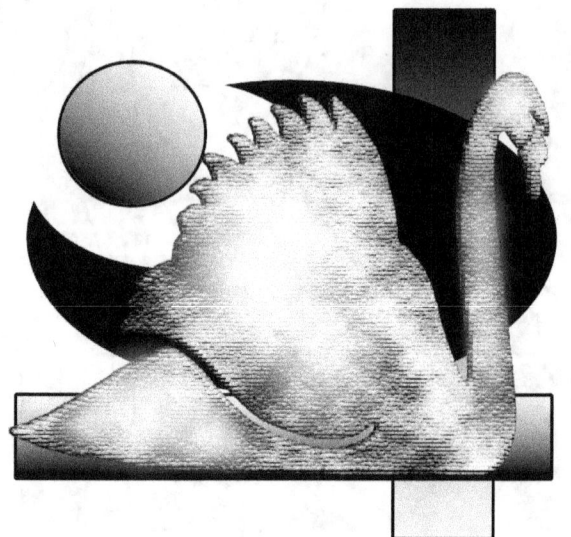

This spring, have a ball with *Tales of the Talisman!*

Jeff Samson takes us behind the scenes with the Greek soldiers who invaded Troy aboard a wooden horse.

M.E. Brines introduces us to a young gentleman who has just been assigned to one of the Royal Navy's best airships and now must prove his worth.

Ken Goldman takes us back stage at a comedy club and reminds us that hair restoration is no laughing matter, especially when your doctor is drop-dead gorgeous.

Melinda Moore shows us the dangers of learning about your true loves through the tarot deck.

These and other thrilling tales await in the spring issue of *Tales of the Talisman!*

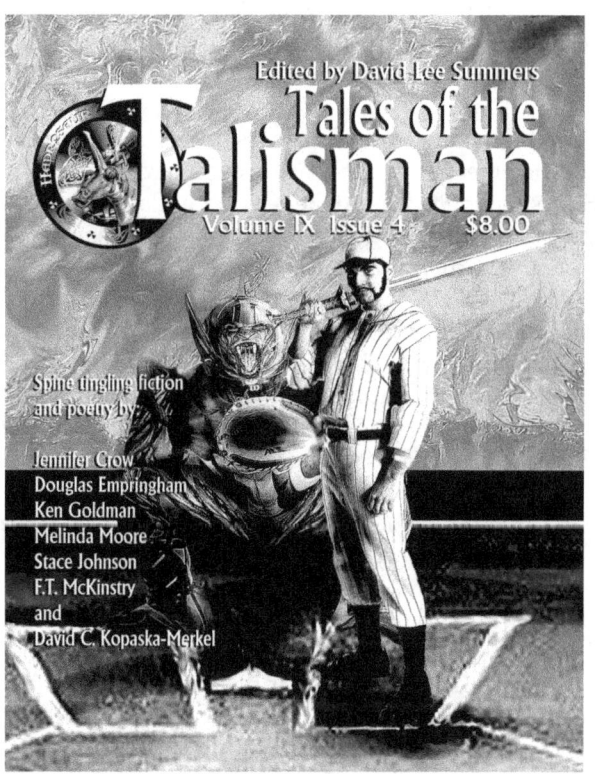

Don't miss a single issue, subscribe to *Tales of the Talisman* at www.talesofthetalisman.com today!

One year $24.00 (That's 25% off the cover price)

While you're there, check out the other great books and audio available from Hadrosaur Productions

Subscriptions also available by mail at:

Hadrosaur Productions, P.O. Box 2194, Mesilla Park, NM 88047-2194

About the Contributors

Megan Arkenberg lives and writes in Wisconsin. Her work has appeared in *Asimov's, Strange Horizons, Lightspeed,* and dozens of other places. In 2012, her poem "The Curator Speaks in the Department of Dead Languages" won the Rhysling Award in the long form category. Megan procrastinates by editing the fantasy e-zine *Mirror Dance.*

F.J. Bergmann regrets that she is no longer able to eke out her meager livelihood via commercial lactation. She is willing to undertake reckless endangerment—preferably, that of others—for sufficient remuneration. For further iniquities, visit fibitz.com.

Simon Bleaken is a long-time fan of the Sci-fi, fantasy and horror genres. His fiction has appeared in several magazines and chapbooks, including: *Lovecraft's Disciples, Strange Sorcery, Night Land, Beneath the Moons of Zandor, Weird World of Zandor* as well as in previous issues of *Tales of the Talisman.* He has also appeared in the anthologies: *Eldritch Horrors: Dark Tales* and *Space Horrors: Full-Throttle Space Tales #4.* He was also the winner of the first-ever short story competition held by the Museum of Witchcraft in Boscastle, Cornwall. He is a supporter of Greenpeace, the World Wildlife Fund and the Stonewall charity, as well as a member of OBOD and British Mensa. He lives near Bristol, England.

Alicia Cole, a writer and educator, lives in Lawrenceville, GA, with her photographer husband, their cat Hatshepsut, and two schools of fish. Her poetry can be found in *Asimov's, Strange Horizons, Goblin Fruit, Ideomancer,* and *Mythic Delirium.* She muses on writing and life at three-magpies.livejournal.com.

John C. Conway is a complex-litigation attorney and he writes science-fiction, romance and fantasy stories. He's a member of the World Science Fiction Society (Chicon 7 and LoneStarCon 3) and Romance Writers of America. Conway's recent stories have been published in *Battlespace Anthology* (Volume 1), *Mystic Signals* (Issue 16) (both available on Amazon); *Untied Shoelaces of the Mind* (Issue 7); NewMyths.com; *Romance Flash* and *Residential Aliens,* among others. Links to these and other works are at his website: www.jcconway.com

As a child, **Kathy Ferrell** refused to share her crayons, preferring to eat them all herself. Today she is an artist and writer working from her decidedly sinister 19th century home, nestled deep in the backwoods of Appalachia. When not creating, she can be found wrapped in a shawl, drinking tea and wondering what on earth could be making that incessant creaking on the stair. She also uses the internet, in spite of being warned.
  Paintings: cuposwank.carbonmade.com
  Words: cuposwank.wordpress.com

Karin L. Frank's poems have been published or are forthcoming in *Asimov's, Dark Matter Journal, Dreams and Nightmares* and in previous issues of *Tales of the Talisman.* In April 2012, her first book of poems entitled *A Meeting of Minds* was released. Except for the illustrations, it is entirely a work of speculative poetry.

M.E. Garber, who blogs at megarber.wordpress.com, revels in stories of 'otherness' in all its many facets, making speculative fiction her natural home.

Adele Gardner's poetry collection, *Dreaming of Days in Astophel*, is available from Sam's Dot Publishing. Her stories and poems have appeared in *Daily Science Fiction, Legends of the Pendragon, The Doom of Camelot, Penumbra, Scheherazade's Façade, Strange Horizons, Mythic Delirium, Goblin Fruit,* and *New Myths,* among others. In 2012, she chaired the Rhysling Awards for the Science Fiction Poetry Association. Currently cataloging librarian for a public library, she's also literary executor for her father, Delbert R. Gardner. Please visit www.gardnercastle.com.

A veteran of World War II, **Dr. Delbert R. Gardner** taught English literature and creative writing for Keuka College. Recent SF/F publications include poetry in *Star*Line, Goblin Fruit,* and the 2010 and 2009 Rhysling Award anthologies. Over forty of Dr. Gardner's poems and stories have appeared in publications such as *The Literary Review, Poetry Digest, American Poetry Magazine, Provincetown Review,* and *Christian Science Monitor,* among others. His nonfiction credits include the book *An "Idle Singer" and His Audience: A Study of William Morris's Poetic Reputation in England, 1858-1900.* Learn more at www.gardnercastle.com.

Morland Gonsoulin is a traditionally trained artist and avid science fiction fan living in Colorado Springs,

Colorado. He has done artwork for various publications before, including *Tales of the Talisman* Magazine.

Laura Givens is a Denver Based author and artist. Her art has graced the covers of numerous publishers' books and magazines. She has provided illustrations for Orson *Scott Card's Intergalactic Medicine Show, Jim Baen's Universe, Talebones, Science Fiction Trails* and *Tales of the Talisman*. Her work may be viewed at www.lauragivens-artist.com. In 2010 she naively decided she could probably write stories as good as many she had illustrated. She has sold works ranging from zombie stories to space operas. She was co-editor and contributor to *Six-Guns Straight From Hell*, a weird western anthology, and is art director for *Tales of the Talisman* magazine.

K.S. Hardy has had his poetry in *Talebones, Weird Tales, Mythic Delirium, Dreams and Nightmares,* and many others. His short stories have appeared in *Tales of the Talisman, Beyond Centauri,* and *Lore* where Brian Lumley took notice, and others now obscure. He has received numerous honorable mentions in the *Best Fantasy and Horror* anthologies and was nominated for a Rhysling Award.

John Hayes sculpts. He acts and directs in Community Theater. He appeared as a scurvy looking corpse on *Homicide* and has also appeared on *WIRE*. Now he gives poetry readings. Seven of his one-act plays have been produced.
   Hungur, Space and Time, Flesh and Blood, Aoife's Kiss, Liquid Imagination, BareBone, Modern Haiku, Tales of the Talisman, Cover of Darkness, Writers Journal, Dark Metre, Premonitions, and *NFG* are some of the many magazines that have published John's work.

Shoshana Holl has been drawing ever since she was old enough to hold a crayon, and has never looked back. A true child of the corn, she moved from Nebraska to Iowa five years ago and spends most of her time writing, drawing, reading and trying to keep her creaky old Victorian home from falling down around her.

Tom Kelly received a degree in Graphic Design from Lycoming College and holds a master's degree in Sequential Art from the Savannah College of Art and Design. Tom has worked for several years producing graphic design and illustration for numerous design and production companies. As a freelance artist, Tom has produced illustrations and cartoons using a wide variety of classical and electronic techniques. Tom focuses on creating dynamic visuals by fusing together a wide variety of elements into one thought-provoking illustration. Tom's sequential work focuses on the power of bold black and white elements as well as the power of graphic design to relate a narrative.

Jag Lall works in both the comic book industry and book illustration field producing bold, atmospheric artwork. The former is his lifeblood and he is currently working on a project to raise awareness of different cultures.

Sarah M. Lewis has a B. A. in Art History and a M. A. in History from Ole Miss. Her stories and poems have appeared in *Thema, Aoife's Kiss, Shelter of Daylight* and *Illumen*.

Faith, nature, molecular biology (a former researcher) and membership in the SFPA help to inspire **Lauren McBride's** stories and poems, which have appeared in various science fiction, fantasy, horror, nature and children's publications including *Tales of the Talisman, Scifaikuest* (featured poet, August 2010) and *The Drabbler* (second place, issue 21). She shares a love of laughter, science and the ocean with her husband and two children.

Lyn McConchie has just seen her 29th book published and has recently completed a standalone disaster novel. Her website and blog are at www.lynmcconchie.com. Lyn says that her imagination leads a far more exciting life than she does, but that's okay because she doesn't have the time to do everything she'd like to do in her reality.

Edward J. McFadden III juggles a full-time career as a university administrator and teacher, with his writing aspirations. His first novel, a mysterious-dark-thriller called *The Black Death of Babylon*, is now available from Post Mortem Press. His steampunk fantasy novelette, *Starwisps*, was recently published in the anthology *Fantastic Stories of the Imagination*, and his novella *Anywhere But Here* was published in 2013 by Padwolf Publishing. He is the author/editor of six published books: *Jigsaw Nation, Deconstructing Tolkien: A Fundamental Analysis of The Lord of the Rings* (to be re-released in eBook format Fall 2012), *Time Capsule, The Second Coming, Thoughts of Christmas*, and *The Best of Pirate Writings*. He has had more than 50 short stories published in places like

Fantastic Futures 13, From Beyond the Grave, Apocalypse 13, Hear Them Roar, CrimeSpree Magazine,Terminal Fright, Cyber-Psycho's AOD, The And, and *The Arizona Literary Review.* Over the last seven years he has written six novels, all of which are at various stages of rewriting and submission for publication. He lives on Long Island with his wife Dawn, their daughter Samantha, and their mutt Oli. See EdwardMcfadden.com for all things Ed.

Steve Mitchell lives in Pueblo, Colorado, with his wife, Kathy, who is endlessly patient with his collection of supernatural fiction, which he relentlessly leaves strewn around the house. He has been writing since he read "Kaleidoscope" by Ray Bradbury when he was a boy. All of the credit, but none of the blame, for Steve's stories should be laid at Mr. Bradbury's doorstep.

Derek Muk is a writer and social worker from California. His short stories have appeared in various online and small press magazines, including *The Trigger Reflex: Legends of the Monster Hunter II* (anthology), *Suffer the Little Children* (anthology), *Splatter: An Anthology of Horror, Death Rattle, Dark Things II* (Anthology), *Anthology of Ichor: Hearts of Darkness, Twisted Tongue Magazine, Static Movement, Sex and Murder Magazine, Sinister Tales, Night to Dawn, M-Brane SF, Sonar4 E-Zine, The Ethereal Gazette, 7ᵗʰ Dimension Magazine, Switchblade Magazine, ESC! Magazine, Scorched Wings Magazine, Hardboiled, Masque Noir, Detective Mystery Stories, Dawnsky, The Pinehurst Journal, Mystery Forum Magazine, The Green Queen, Kracked Mirror Mysteries, Golden Visions Magazine, Crossroads Magic, The Street Corner Magazine, Calliope Magazine, Unspoken Water, Space and Time Magazine, Infernal Ink Magazine, Tales of the Talisman Magazine,* and *Parabnormal Digest.*

He has three chapbooks published: *Three Parts, The Sacrifice and Other Stories,* and *Sin after Sin.* In addition to writing, he enjoys reading, traveling, museums, art, dining out, and meeting new people. He has a bachelor's and master's degree in social work.

The Occult Files of Albert Taylor is his first full length collection of short stories. His website address is: http://theoccultfilesofalberttaylor.wordpress.com/

Paul Niemiec plays guitar in a swing band—atomic pablo. Check it out at myspace.com. Paul's first job in high school was an art job doing safety filmstrips for hard-rock miners. After that, the office situation—smooth jazz radio, and chain-smoking co-workers—really put him off commercial art.

After a long hiatus, he got back into drawing. Paul was trying to figure out which way a camel's front legs bent, and he decided to go to the zoo to draw camels. Later, he met some of the Squid Works guys at a figure drawing class.

Robert E. Porter has spent the last 15 years in the margins of SF. His credits include articles, interviews, poems, short stories, and illustrations.

Robert Redwine has been killing player characters since 1982. Now he works in a sweatshop to support his writing habit. This is his first publication beyond trolling online message boards.

David B. Riley is a Colorado author and editor. He has written four novels and over 100 stories and is an active member of the Horror Writer's Association. He is the editor of six anthologies as well as *Science Fiction Trails,* an annual fiction magazine. When not involved in literary endeavors, he works in the hotel business.

Nicolo Santilli is a philosopher, poet, and fiction writer, currently residing in Berkeley, California.

Greg Schwartz fixes copiers and printers for a living while he tries to get rich. Some of his poems have appeared in *Illumen, Horror Carousel, Tales of the Talisman,* and *Star*Line.* He has been nominated for both the Rhysling and Dwarf Stars Awards, but sadly hasn't won either.

Jerry Shipee is a cartoonist-illustrator with eclectic interests. Everything, from asteroids to zoo animals, is potential subject matter for him. This attribute served him well as a print cartoonist for the Journal Register Company, and continues to be a contributing factor in his work as a caricaturist. Jerry holds an AFA in fine arts, and has apprenticed with the internationally syndicated cartoonist—Guy Gilchrist.

He works as a caricaturist with About Faces, and Goofy Faces. He is also a cartooning teacher with the Community College of Rhode Island, as well as being a contributor to Annex Comix.It is Jerry's focus to amuse, entertain, and sometimes educate by combining his art with good storytelling. His mantra: Cartoon the World!

Frances Silversmith grew up in Germany, where she lives with her husband, three guinea pigs, and an Icelandic horse. She works as a software developer and splits her free time between writing, reading every book she can get her hands on, and riding and teaching circus tricks to her pony.

Find out more about her at:
http://FrancesSilversmith.com
Or contact her on Facebook:
http://www.facebook.com/FrancesSilversmith.

Marge Simon's works appear in publications such as *Strange Horizons, Niteblade, DailySF Magazine, Pedestal,* and *Dreams & Nightmares*. A former Rhysling winner, she also won the SFPA Dwarf Stars Award in 2012. She edits a column for the HWA Newsletter, "Blood & Spades: Poets of the Dark Side," and serves as Chair of the Board of Trustees. She won the *Strange Horizons* Readers Choice Award for poetry, 2010. Bram Stoker Award™ for Superior Work in Poetry with Charlie Jacob, *Vectors: A Week in the Death of a Planet,* Dark Regions Press, 2008, and another this year for *Vampires, Zombies & Wanton Souls,* Elektrik Milk Bath Press, 2012. Her poetry placed in the winner's circle of the Balticon Poetry Contest this year, for the fourth time in recent years. Member HWA, SFWA, SFPA. www.margesimon.com

While holding down a nine to five job in a public legal arena, **Karissa B. Sluss** also maintains a household of wayward boys and dogs and cooks part-time on the weekends in a commercial kitchen for a captive audience. She blogs at "Songs in Squee Minor" which she co-authors with similarly squee! minded fan-girls (er, women). Her fiction appears in the *Return of the Dead Men (and Women) Walking* anthology and in a forthcoming volume of *Stupefying Stories*.

David Lee Summers is the author of seven novels and over sixty published short stories. His writing spans a wide range of the imaginative from science fiction to fantasy to horror. David's novels include the wild west/steampunk adventure *Owl Dance* and *Vampires of the Scarlet Order*, which tells the story of a band of vampire mercenaries who fight evil. His short stories and poems have appeared in such magazines and anthologies as *Realms of Fantasy, Human Tales, Cemetery Dance,* and *Apocalypse 13*. In 2010, he was nominated for the Science Fiction Poetry Association's Rhysling Award. In addition to writing and editing this magazine, David has edited three science fiction anthologies, *Space Pirates, Space Horrors* and *A Kepler's Dozen*. When not working with the written word, David operates telescopes at Kitt Peak National Observatory. Learn more about David at davidleesummers.com.

With over a million words in print **Patrick Thomas** keeps busy writing the fantasy humor series *Murphy's Lore* (*Tales From Bulfinche's Pub, Fools' Day, Through the Drinking Glass, Shadow of the Wolf, Redemption Road, Bartender of the Gods, Nightcaps* and *Empty Graves*) as well as the *After Hours* spin offs *Fairy With A Gun, Fairy Rides the Lightning, Dead To Rites, Rites of Passage,* and *Lore & Dysorder*. His Mystic Investigators paranormal mystery series has grown to include *Bullets & Brimstone* and *From The Shadows*—both with John L. French; and *Once More Upon A Time* and the upcoming *Partners In Crime*—both with Diane Raetz. He co-edited *New Blood* and *Hear Them Roar*. Patrick's syndicated humorous advice column Dear Cthulhu has been collected in *Have A Dark Day, Good Advice For Bad People,* and *Cthulhu Knows Best*. A number of his books are part of the set and props department at the CSI television show and have been spotted on the show. His urban fantasy *Fairy With A Gun* has been optioned by Laurence Fishburne's Cinema Gypsy Productions for film and TV. Drop by www.patthomas.net to learn more or find out about The Patrick Thomas Show mockumentary

Originating from the UK but now residing in the Canary Islands, **Teresa Tunaley** finds more time to devote to her love of art and writing. For more than 30 years she has been doodling traditionally with pencils and dabbling with watercolors.

Along with published stories and poetry, she can be credited with award winning cover art and illustrations for author stories. Her work can be seen online and in print across the UK, US, Canada and Europe.

"I like to think that I am very versatile in my choice of subject matter—my new surroundings provide the inspiration for me to paint on a daily basis and the fact that others may enjoy my work gives me the confidence to continue."

Deborah Walker grew up in the most English town in the country, but she soon high-tailed it down to London, where she now lives with her partner, Chris, and her two young children. Find Deborah in the British Museum trawling the past for future inspiration or on her blog:

http://deborahwalkersbibliography.blogspot.com

Her poems have appeared in *Dreams & Nightmares, Star*Line* and *Enchanted Conversation*.

Sarah Wright lives in Missouri, works in learning support on the college level, and writes lots of lyric poetry.

Alessio Zanelli, Italian, writes poetry in English and has published widely in literary magazines around the world, including: *Acumen, California Quarterly, Italian Americana, New Contrast, Poetry News, Poetry New Zealand, Vallum* and *World Literature Today*. His fourth collection, *Over Misty Plains*, was published in 2012 by Indigo Dreams. He is the poetry editor of *Private Photo Review* and the Italian Stanza Representative for the Poetry Society of London.

Lee Clark Zumpe has been writing and publishing horror, dark fantasy and speculative fiction since the late 1990s. His short stories and poetry have appeared in a variety of publications such as *Weird Tales, Space and Time* and *Dark Wisdom;* and in anthologies such as *Horrors Beyond, Corpse Blossoms, Best New Zombie Tales Vol. 3, Cthulhu Unbound Vol. 1 and Future Lovecraft*. His work has earned several honorable mentions in *The Year's Best Fantasy and Horror* collections.

An entertainment columnist with Tampa Bay Newspapers, Lee has penned hundreds of film, theater and book reviews and has interviewed novelists as well as music industry icons such as Paddy Moloney of The Chieftains and Alan Parsons. His work for TBN has been recognized repeatedly by the Florida Press Association, including a first place award for criticism in the 2007 Better Weekly Newspaper Contest.

Lee lives on the west coast of Florida with his wife and daughter. Visit www.leeclarkzumpe.com.

www.ingramcontent.com/pod-product-compliance
Lightning Source LLC
Chambersburg PA
CBHW080752120626
46557CB00005B/1234